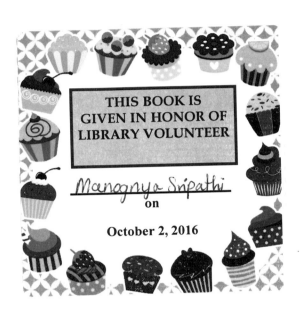

THIS BOOK IS
GIVEN IN HONOR OF
LIBRARY VOLUNTEER

Manognya Sripathi
on

October 2, 2016

The
Possibility
of Somewhere

The
Possibility
of Somewhere

◆

JULIA DAY

St. Martin's Griffin
New York

THE POSSIBILITY OF SOMEWHERE. Copyright © 2016 by Elizabeth Langston. All rights reserved. Printed in the United States of America. For information, address St. Martin's Press, 175 Fifth Avenue, New York, N.Y. 10010.

www.stmartins.com

The Library of Congress Cataloging-in-Publication Data is available upon request.

ISBN 978-1-250-09735-4 (hardcover)
ISBN 978-1-250-09736-1 (e-book)

Our books may be purchased in bulk for promotional, educational, or business use. Please contact your local bookseller or the Macmillan Corporate and Premium Sales Department at 1-800-221-7945, extension 5442, or by e-mail at MacmillanSpecial Markets@macmillan.com.

First Edition: September 2016

10 9 8 7 6 5 4 3 2 1

To those who are judged for reasons beyond their control:

Disregard the noise and stay true to your dreams.

Acknowledgments

✦

Writing these acknowledgments has been a pleasure. It's impossible to create a good story alone, and I'm happy for the opportunity to highlight the people who contributed. I'd like to thank beta readers Matt Sproul, Anna Rodriguez, Jan O'Neal, and Patricia Nelson for your fabulous feedback. To Anjali, Pranav, and many others who answered my questions about Indian American culture, I'm grateful for your patience and candor. For all things football, I knew I could count on Jaime to keep me straight. Thanks to Molly M. for her insights; to the Rubies, Capital Eyes, and Retreaters for all the ways you support authors; and to Cynthia, for understanding. For Laura Ownbey, I can't imagine the writing process without you.

Thanks to the team at St. Martin's for everything—the beautiful cover and interior and collaboration . . . Like I said, everything! To my talented editor, Eileen, it's been a joy to work with you. To my amazing agent, Kevan Lyon, I'm grateful for all that you are.

Finally, my love and gratitude go to my daughters for their extreme persistence in keeping me honest and to my husband for his unwavering belief in this dream.

The
Possibility
of Somewhere

An Exercise in Probabilities

My normal dress code was designed to keep me invisible, but today I made an exception. I wore a teal shirt (stolen from my dad) over jeans that had only been owned by me. I finished off with my best sneakers, freshly bleached.

After yanking my hair into a ponytail, I grabbed my backpack, charged out of my bedroom, and screeched to a halt in the den. The trailer smelled like toast and bacon. Why?

I crossed to the table and stared down at the plate of food waiting there.

My stepmom came out of the kitchen, holding two mugs of coffee. She offered one to me.

I took it as my backpack slid to the floor with a thud. "You made me breakfast?"

She laughed. "I've done this before."

"When I was nine, maybe." The bacon looked like it had been fried to crispy perfection. I parked my butt on the chair and snagged a slice. "What's the occasion?"

Her smile wobbled. "It's the first day of your last year of high school."

Oh, damn. She was going to get emotional on me. This day must remind her that I'd be gone in a few months. It wouldn't be a good idea to act all happy about escaping town soon. Better change the mood fast. "Breakfast is amazing. You can repeat it whenever you want."

"I'll keep that in mind." She set her mug on the table and pointed at my ponytail. "Can I do something special with your hair?"

Clearly she wanted to, so sure. "That'd be great."

While I finished my toast, she twisted my hair into a thick French braid. It took only a couple of minutes before she pressed a kiss to the top of my head. "There you are, sweetie. Now go on, or you'll miss the bus."

"Okay." I stood, gave her a quick hug, and slung my backpack over one shoulder. "Thanks, Marnie. For everything."

The bus dropped us off fifteen minutes early, something that would never happen again. I went straight to my first-period class. AP English Lit with my favorite teacher.

"Morning, Ms. Barrie," I said.

She didn't look up from her computer. "Hello, Eden."

I slipped into a desk in the back row and watched as my classmates trickled in.

My next class would be statistics, although it had been a recent change. I'd realized in middle school that college was my best route out of Heron, and I wouldn't get to college without serious scholarships. So I'd mapped out my high school curriculum in seventh grade, picking each course to maximize my GPA. Everything had gone according to plan until three weeks ago, when I'd switched to a different math class and elective. The decision had seemed bold at the time. Now, it felt crazy.

After English, I dropped by my locker and arrived late for second period. With nervous anticipation, I smiled at my statistics teacher and turned toward the back.

"Wait, Eden. Sit there." Mrs. Menzies gestured at an empty seat on the front row.

I paused, looking from the desk to her. She eyed me steadily, a challenge in her expression.

Did she expect me to argue with her? I certainly wanted to.

Swallowing hard, I took my seat.

"All right, everyone. I'm glad that you've chosen to take Advanced Placement Statistics . . ."

I tuned out what she said, too annoyed to listen to whatever welcoming remarks she had for us. They would be on her syllabus anyway. I was consumed with shrugging off how much it bothered me to sit in the front with a dozen pairs of eyes behind me. Were they watching me? Probably not, but I didn't like that it was a possibility.

Even deep breaths betrayed me, because they filled my head with the soapy-clean, spicy-cologne scent of Ash Gupta. Why did Mrs. Menzies have me sitting next to him?

". . . you'll have one group project and one individual assignment due each week . . ."

I glanced at her. Group projects already? Was that why we had assigned seats?

". . . that's it for now. Form into your teams. I'll hand out your first project."

The sounds of dragging chairs and laughing voices filled the room. I checked around. Was I the only one who didn't know what to do?

Ash was looking at me, pained resignation on his face. "You're with us, Eden."

I dragged my desk into the circle beside him. There were five of us in the group. Upala and Dev were Ash's friends. A built-in alliance. They would vote as a bloc even if I could get the last guy on my side.

The next few minutes blurred into the rhythms of a project team pretending to become cohesive. I didn't join in, listening instead to Ash control the discussion and watching as Mrs. Menzies went from group to group, dropping off a large bag of M&Ms, several paper bowls, and the project sheet. When she finally arrived at our circle, she described what she wanted and then gave me a hard stare.

"I want collaboration from everyone."

Message received—although it was unnecessary. I participated when it mattered. Reaching for the M&M bag, I filled a bowl and began separating the candies by color. An exercise in probabilities.

"Before we go any further," Ash was saying, "we should pick a leader for the team. How do we want to choose?"

"Might as well cut the bullshit, Ash," I said without looking up. "You want the job. No one's going to fight you. Just take it by acclamation."

Silence greeted my speech. I glanced at him. His gaze held mine for a second before he frowned at his notebook, picked up a pen, and began drawing tiny perfect squares, one after the other. I looked at the rest of the team. Upala and Dev glared at me but didn't disagree with my suggestion. Probably hated that it had come from me, though.

The final guy shrugged.

I resumed separating the candies. "See. Done."

All seniors had lunch immediately following second period. I stopped briefly at my locker before heading toward the cafeteria. Ash fell into step beside me, his entourage of Indian friends trailing behind.

"Eden? Can I ask you something?"

I halted, shocked that he wanted to speak with me outside of a classroom. "Sure."

His dark eyes bored into mine. "It's the first day of school. Did you have to take me on already?"

"Take you on?" Was he talking about our exchange in statistics? It had been pretty tame. I was mildly insulted. "If I'd wanted to come after you, I would've done a better job than that."

"Then what was the point?"

"You were wasting my time on fake modesty. And while I don't care what you think, I would like to make a good grade in statistics."

His jaw flexed, but he remained silent. I could almost read his thoughts, like captions scrolling across his face. I was the girl he couldn't explain, the girl who looked like she was one bad day away from living in a homeless shelter. Yet I had a perfect GPA. His gaze swept slowly down me, taking in the golden braid, the lack of makeup, the mouth that cussed, the thrift-store clothes.

"Ash? Are you done?"

Faint color rose up his neck as his gaze returned to mine. "If you don't mind, I'd like us to call a truce."

"Why? We're not at war."

"It feels like it. You fight me every chance you get."

His accusation baffled me. In three years of high school, we'd only talked to each other when an assignment required it. And although it was true that I could get stubborn about ideas, it was only because I believed I was right. It had never been anything personal against him. "I don't fight you."

His eyebrow arched skeptically.

Okay, I was curious now. "Like when?"

"You rewrote every one of our lab reports in freshman biology."

"You had just moved here and didn't know how to impress Mr. Tuttle. I did."

"On our project team in US history, you vetoed every suggestion I made."

An exaggeration. Mostly. "We were capable of more. You never took chances."

He flinched and cut a glance at his friends. They hovered nearby, staring with open animosity. He shifted a step closer to me, his body blocking them from view, and lowered his voice. "You propose insane ideas just to stir things up."

"Not the point at all." He must be determined to misread me. The obvious motives were actually the correct ones. "An idea has to be insane to make an A-plus."

"*Insane* is more likely to crash and burn."

"Students like us do not crash and burn, Ash. You play it too safe."

"Easy for you to say. You've got valedictorian in the bag."

What?

It stunned me that he would allude to such a thing. Did being valedictorian matter to him? It never really had to me. As long as colleges threw buckets of money at me, they could call me anything they wanted. "I don't care about being valedictorian. Do you?"

"My parents—" His lips clamped shut.

Whoa. His parents must be harassing him about being ranked number two, especially behind someone like Eden Moore. Pity stirred within me, laced with a decent amount of envy. My parents didn't have a clue about what I did at school. And if my dad could have his way, my grades would suck so that I would never leave home.

I looked around us. The hallway had grown quiet. My precious break was ticking away while I wondered how to respond to Ash. I would *not* call a truce. That would be confessing to something I hadn't done, but I also didn't want him to think I fought him for no reason. "Why is this so important to you?"

"I'm not sure. Why did you punt control of the project to me?"

"You were the best person for the job." I held his gaze, oddly anxious for him to believe me.

"Wow. That was not what I expected you to say." His expression softened from pissed to puzzled. "Thanks. I think."

I smiled, which was more like a happy twitching of the mouth. He must've recognized it, though, because his lips twitched, too.

With a relieved nod, I brushed past him and continued to the cafeteria. Although I hadn't enjoyed that little confrontation, the way it ended gave me hope that this year might be bearable.

· 2 ·

The Tackle or the Save

When I got off the bus on Wednesday, I saw my stepmom—still in her work uniform—standing with my dad in our carport. His truck was parked there. Her car was missing. Not a good sign.

As I walked up the driveway, I could hear them arguing. At the crunch of my shoes on the gravel, they stopped abruptly and faced me.

"What's going on?" I asked.

Marnie chewed on a ragged thumbnail. "My car had a flat."

"Where?"

"On the highway, not far from the nursing home."

"Can you use the spare?"

"I was driving on the spare." She looked like she was about to cry.

My parents couldn't afford whatever it would take to replace a tire. The three drivers in our family were down to Dad's truck. That was bad on many levels. "I'll pay for it."

She squeezed her eyes shut.

Dad shook his head. "It gets worse."

"How?"

"A sheriff's deputy pulled over to help her. He noticed that the car wasn't registered."

I groaned. "What did he do?"

"Gave her a warning, and told her not to let him see the car on the road again until that was taken care of."

I got a sick feeling in the pit of my stomach. "Why did you let the registration lapse?"

Her eyes fluttered open. "The car can't pass inspection."

"What's wrong with it?"

"The main problem is the tires. They don't have enough tread left."

Marnie was driving on bald tires? *"All of them?"*

She nodded, her face a mask of anguish.

I made a worst-case calculation in my head and . . . holy shit.

Dad cleared his throat. "Eden—"

"No, Byron. Stop," Marnie hissed.

He shrugged and looked away.

Here was the part where I should offer to cover all costs, but the thought of it made me dizzy. My savings account was the closest thing I had to a college fund. I'd worked my ass off for every penny. I had big plans for that account. A road trip or two to visit college campuses. Food and textbooks next year. If I fixed my stepmom's car, the balance would drop by a third or more.

That option was likely what they had been arguing about earlier. Dad would take my money. Marnie wouldn't. "Is your car still parked on the highway?"

"Yes." She sounded defeated.

I couldn't let this slide. I met my dad's gaze and nodded.

"Are you babysitting the Fremonts tonight?" he asked.

"Yeah."

"I'll drive, if you want."

Choking on a sob, Marnie spun around and ran up the front porch steps and into the house.

I was tired of bailing my parents out, but what choice did I have? I couldn't let her drive like that, and Dad didn't have a solution. He hadn't been steadily employed since he was laid off from the power plant two years ago. He'd scrounged up a job as the caretaker of this mobile-home community, although it had never been clear to me how they paid him. Our trailer appeared to be rent-free, but there never seemed to be anything in the way of actual cash. We'd be on food stamps without Marnie's job, and she couldn't hold onto it without a dependable car.

Why was I even bothering to debate this? I had no choice. "Let's leave soon, Dad. We have to make a stop at the bank."

He gave me a quick, one-armed hug. "Thanks, baby girl."

My arrangement with the Fremonts was different from most babysitting jobs. I slept over in their guest room several nights each week, taking care of two little kids while their mom worked a shift at a hospital down the Carolina coast in Wilmington.

This evening's bedtime routine was not going well.

Kurt was in a particularly bad mood after his third day as a first-grader, and he was taking it out on me. Everything got to him. He complained about washing his hair. Loudly. Then I put too much toothpaste on his toothbrush. He splashed water on his pajamas—not much, but enough that he wouldn't go to bed in them. Since they were his favorite pajamas this week, he wasn't sleeping in anything else.

Into the dryer went the Spider-Man pajamas. After they cooled down to room temperature, he put them on, slid into bed, and dropped off within three minutes.

My teachers had loaded me down with homework tonight, so it sucked that I lost a half hour trying to get Kurt in bed. But I knew he hadn't done it on purpose. Sometimes, bad days happened.

While I was reviewing my chemistry notes, small feet padded across the den and stopped at the entrance to the kitchen. I could practically feel eyes focusing on my head.

I shifted in my chair. Marta stared at me, her face solemn, her thin body enveloped from neck to knees in a Carolina Panthers football jersey.

"Hey, Marta. What's up?"

"I'm ready for bed."

"Did you have a good day at school?"

"Yes."

"Do you have any homework?"

"I won't have any this week."

"Great," I said with a smile. "I guess I'll see you in the morning, then."

She didn't move.

It was hard to tell what went on behind those big dark eyes, but it did seem like she was waiting on me. I nodded with encouragement. "Is there something else?"

"Can we talk?"

Not now pressed against my lips, but I swallowed the words. "Sure."

She slipped her hand into mine and tugged. "We should check on Kurt."

"Okay." This was interesting. There was no need to check on

him. He always fell into a dead sleep once his head touched the pillow. "Your brother was a little poopy tonight."

"He was a lot poopy tonight."

We pushed open his bedroom door, sending a narrow beam of light cutting through the darkness. Kurt was motionless, his lips pursed in a little rosebud.

She snuggled against my side, warm and smelling of Dove soap and citrus toothpaste. "Will he ever get better?"

A shudder rippled through me. She looked up, eyes narrowing with concern. I slid an arm around her bony shoulders and hugged her close.

Why had she picked today to ask me about Kurt's disabilities?

Okay, why *not* today?

I'd dreaded this question from the moment I was hired. I'd often wondered when it might show up and hoped it was something she would only ask her mom, because there was no safe answer. It was hard to predict what would happen to a kid like Kurt. I had no idea what to say—no one did—but *I don't know* wasn't good enough.

What did I want the answer to be? "I think Kurt will surprise us all."

Her mouth wanted to smile but was afraid to. "You think so?"

"I do." I nudged her the two steps to her bedroom.

She ran in, took a flying leap, and landed in the middle of her purple comforter. "My friend Missy says he won't graduate from high school. Is that true, Eden?"

Her friend Missy needed to butt out. "I think he absolutely will."

"What about college?"

"Kurt is smart. He'll go to college if he wants to." I snapped out the lights and stepped into the hall.

"Will I always have to take care of him?"

The question whispered down my spine, stopping me in my tracks. What a thing to wonder about at age ten. I ached to be optimistic, but who knew what might happen? "It's what sisters do."

"Yeah." She gave me a small smile before rolling to her side, her back to me.

I closed her door and wandered to the kitchen, but I couldn't concentrate on chemistry, my mind turning over Marta's questions. How long had they bothered her? And if I knew Marta, she wasn't through. There would be more questions, and I ought to have better answers.

In the months since I'd been working for the Fremonts, I'd made it a habit to search the Internet for *high-functioning autism*. It had only been a couple of weeks since my last try, but maybe it wouldn't hurt to look again tonight and add the string *college*.

There were hundreds of hits, and I had homework waiting on me. I shouldn't be sitting here clicking on links, but I was hooked.

When I'd agreed to babysit Kurt and Marta, it had been for two reasons. They had high-speed Internet (while my house had none) and the money was great. I had to sleep anyway. I might as well be paid to do it.

So, yes, I'd accepted the job since it was a good deal, and anyway, how hard could it be? All I had to do was get two kids to take a bath, brush their teeth, and climb into bed.

It hadn't worked out the way I expected. I'd become a member of the family. I adored Marta—my big, brave fifth-grader who was too busy worrying about her brother to be a little girl. I admired Mrs. Fremont, working twelve-hour shifts at a hospital, catching a long nap in the morning, and being the best mom she could be on adrenaline and coffee—all because her jerk of an ex-husband freaked out when his son failed to live up to his standards of perfection.

And finally, there was Kurt. Funny, sweet, tough, magical Kurt. I'd witnessed the intelligence shimmering behind his eyes, the confusion when his words didn't communicate, and the frustration when autism caged him in.

I wanted to learn all I could about unlocking that cage.

For years, I'd been so set on escaping Heron that it hadn't mattered what college major I pursued. I'd figured I could pick something related to computers. Writing software was fun, and I could make good money at it.

Then I met Kurt Fremont. He filled me with purpose. His issues had pointed me in a completely different direction than I would've ever imagined. I would seek a major in special education, and I wouldn't have far to go. UNC–Chapel Hill had an internationally recognized program in autism research. Carolina had rocketed to the top of my college list, and I would bust my butt to get there.

I ran all the way from the carpool lane to my locker, later than I liked since it was Mrs. Fremont driving me to school today. As I rounded the corner onto the senior hallway, I skidded to avoid several members of the football team who were playing a pickup game with a Nerf ball. Not that I minded. Our team had their first game tomorrow night and, with them, it could never hurt to practice. It just would've been safer for everyone if they'd taken it outside.

Maneuvering to my locker, I unzipped my backpack, which promptly intercepted a pass. This struck me as awesome until the intended receiver failed to stop. Two hundred pounds of hairy muscle tripped over my feet, sending us both to the concrete floor.

"Sorry. Didn't see you," he said.

"No shit." His body lay half over me, my nose awkwardly lodged in the sweaty cave of his armpit. I drank in a shallow breath and then wished I hadn't. "You can get up now."

"Oh, right." He jumped gracefully to his feet, probably because he was used to untangling from piles of people. Since I didn't get tackled all that often, remaining motionless seemed like the next best option.

I made some interesting discoveries while lying there in a crumpled heap. Like how cold the floor was against my skin where my cami and shirt had ridden up. Or how much unmentionable debris had accumulated beneath the lockers. Or how shortsighted it had been to leave the zippers open on my backpack.

Everything ached. My head. My hip. My dignity.

A new pair of Nikes squeaked to a stop a few inches from my face. Someone held out a hand—a guy's hand, with a light crescent-shaped scar marring an otherwise smooth, brown thumb.

"Here, Eden. Let me help you up."

Ash? That made the second time this week he'd acknowledged me outside of a classroom. This had to be a record.

I closed my fingers around his.

He pulled me gently to my feet, but the movement left my head spinning anyway. When I wavered, his other hand dropped to my waist to steady me, his fingertips brushing the exposed skin below my cami.

I jerked away from his touch, my gaze locking with his. Something odd flashed in his eyes, hot and aware.

No, wait. I knew that couldn't be right.

"Ash?" one of his friends called.

"Just a second." Dragging his gaze from mine, he knelt to scoop my stuff into the backpack. Then he rose and handed it over.

"Thanks," I said, looking away. Gratitude made me uncomfortable.

"No problem." He nodded at his circle of friends and took off down the hall. They fell into step behind him.

Whoa. Not sure which bothered me more, the tackle or the save. I turned and fumbled with my locker. As I reached for an old paperback copy of *Pride and Prejudice*, another wave of dizziness hit me. I leaned my forehead against the cool metal door to catch my breath.

"Are you all right?" a girl asked from beside me, her tone soft with concern.

"I'm fine."

"You don't look fine." The locker next to mine clanged open. Objects thudded into it rhythmically. "I'll stick around until you're okay."

I refocused my scattered thoughts on this new puzzle. Beside me stood a girl whose voice I didn't recognize. She was shoving her belongings into a formerly empty locker. Those clues would suggest a new student. I shifted to see her better.

Wherever she came from, it couldn't be coastal North Carolina. Her skin was too pale to have spent any time at the beach this summer, and her clothes looked like they would fit in better in a big city. Her white dress could've been a retro nurse's uniform, sleeveless and hemmed at the knees, and she wore white flats covered in sunflowers, hand-painted by a budding Van Gogh.

She faced me. "Maybe you should sit down."

Damn, she could be a cover model for *Teen Vogue*. "Thanks, but I'll make it to class."

"Fair enough." She searched my face with blatant curiosity. "I'm Mundy Cruz."

"Eden Moore."

"I'm new here."

As if we wouldn't notice. "I'm not." A smile tugged at my lips.

"We're being stared at."

I stopped fighting the smile. New *and* oblivious. "*You* are being stared at."

"You don't get many transfers here?"

"No." She would be the only one since Heron High got six new students my freshman year. The other seventy kids in our graduating class had been together since elementary school. There wasn't enough happening in this part of the world to make anyone else want to move here.

The bell rang.

"Well, good luck today. Do you know where your first class is?"

"Room 123? English with Ms. Barrie?"

I blinked with surprise. Mundy was taking an AP course from the hardest teacher in the school, and she'd missed three days of the semester. That was impressive. "Follow me."

As I led the way, my smile widened. I would've expected a transfer student to be hesitant and nervous. The new girl was none of those things. She walked beside me, asking questions, eager and confident. It would be a lot of fun to see how the senior class reacted to Mundy Cruz.

· 3 ·

Pain to Pain

When my statistics teacher ended Friday's lecture, there were fifteen minutes left in the period. Maybe she'd let us get started on our homework.

"All right, class, find your project teams."

Or maybe not.

The classroom exploded with noise as students burst into conversation and chairs smacked the floor.

I flipped my notebook shut, dropped my pen in my bag, and shifted my desk into the circle already being formed by the other members of my team.

"Any ideas?" Ash asked.

I waited, curious to see if the others had come up with something worthwhile. It was a respectable project. Our teacher wanted us to collect some real data to use with the statistics we were learning, but she'd included an extra challenge. The data had to be related somehow to North Carolina, and the team with the most intriguing set would have three bonus points added to their semester grades. I was determined that our team would win.

Upala hitched forward and said in her sweet voice, "I thought we could use high-school graduation rates for each county . . ."

She expanded on the suggestion. The others jumped in and debated it. I listened but didn't share my opinion. Her idea was too predictable to be the best in the class, and I was hoping another team member would point that out. Upala didn't like me much.

When she stopped talking, Dev tossed in another proposal on tax revenue from tourism.

I rolled my eyes. This was an AP class. Couldn't we brainstorm better ideas than the most obvious data around?

"Eden?" Ash asked.

I looked up to find the team members staring at me. Had I zoned out? "Yeah?"

"Did you want to add anything before we vote?"

"We're voting now?"

"The project's due next Wednesday. We'd like to start collecting the data over the weekend."

"If we pick well, downloading data is the easiest part." I shook my head. "We're not ready to vote."

The others sagged. Ash reclined against his seat, stretched his long legs before him, and watched me through narrowed eyes. "Do you have a suggestion that you haven't bothered to share yet?"

Sure did. "A lot of movies are made in North Carolina. *The Hunger Games.* Stuff by Nicholas Sparks. It might be fun to focus on the film industry."

Upala frowned. "What type of data?"

"Box-office receipts. Film budgets. Number of extras hired per county."

Her gaze skittered to Ash.

He straightened in his chair, interest warming in the depths of his eyes. "We could map the data over the locations where the movies were made. Maybe we could see if they affect high school graduation rates or tax revenue."

Was I the only one who noticed how smoothly he'd circled back to Upala's and Dev's suggestions? Had he done it because he thought their proposals were good or because he was such a perfect leader?

Whatever. It wasn't half bad to include that data, too. "Damn, Ash. Those ideas are just insane enough to get my vote."

He laughed. I smiled.

Upala and Dev stared at us with surprise, although I couldn't tell if it was over Ash's reaction or mine.

"Does everyone agree to using movies?" He checked each team member's response, ending with me. "Thanks, Eden. That was great."

I nodded, pleased by his praise. We weren't likely to sustain this level of cooperation, but it had been nice for once.

During lunch break, I claimed my usual cafeteria table, the one isolated in a corner under a broken overhead light. This location gave me a half hour of peace. I had a complete view of the dining area, which made it easy to see Mundy Cruz enter, spot me, and approach.

"Hi. Can I sit here?" She slipped onto the opposite seat without waiting for an answer.

I stiffened. Nobody ever sat with me, which was their choice and mine. Mundy's interruption was too unexpected and sudden for me to process. "Be my guest."

With a happy sigh, she emptied the contents of a large lunch pack onto the table. Several reusable containers spilled out.

While she arranged them in a neat line, I considered how I felt about her company. There were pros and cons. I'd wait a bit longer before deciding.

She unzipped an insulated pouch and drew out a gooey slice of pepperoni pizza. "I've been asking around about you."

That was creepy. Was she joking? I studied her expression, but no, she was waiting on me. "Why?"

"I'd like to understand what happened in the hall yesterday."

She just went there. Impressive. "What about it?"

"A football player tackled you and left you lying on the ground. A dozen people walked past, and no one stopped. When someone finally did help, you weren't expecting it. The whole scene seemed strange to me."

"It won't after you've been here a few more days." I preferred being left alone, and people respected that. She'd get used to it.

"Want to explain?" Mundy took a bite of pizza.

"No."

"Okay."

It got quiet while she attacked her lunch. I clamped my lips together as I considered the so-called Italian casserole oozing on my lunch tray. With my head bowed, I couldn't see her, but I knew she was over there, shoveling in her food.

Was she this candid with everyone?

Much as I hated to admit it, I had to know what the others had told her. Curiosity was stronger than my need for privacy. "What did you learn about me?"

"You're the smartest girl in the senior class."

"As long as I don't screw up, I'll be the valedictorian."

"Not Ash Gupta?"

"They award it here to the highest unweighted GPA. I have a 4.0."

"What happened to him?"

"He got a B in PE his freshman year." I'd heard that he was grounded for a week after receiving his physical education grade, but that could also be an urban legend.

She popped the top on a yogurt carton. "You have a reputation for not speaking with anyone unless you have to."

"I'm talking to you."

"I haven't given you much choice."

That surprised a laugh out of me. "True."

"You live in a trailer park."

Really? Anger tightened my jaw. Why had my home made it into the top three? "Who told you that?"

"Wow." The spoon stirring her yogurt paused. "You're okay with your classmates treating you like crap. You don't care that they think you're a rude witch. But you're pissed off that I know where you live?"

"We live in a vacation community." Most of the homeowners worked in Raleigh and came here on the weekends. As the caretaker, Dad had a deluxe unit with three bedrooms and a multi-level deck. I hated that someone had mentioned it. "Our *mobile home* overlooks Heron's Bay."

"Got it." Mundy grabbed a celery stick and crunched it to a nub before waving a hand toward the rest of the room. "Do students always segregate like this?"

Why did she switch from my home to segregation?

Okay, didn't matter. She'd used a word that couldn't be ignored. I shook my head with the resignation all Southerners felt when an outsider hinted at racism. "Don't get started on us."

"It's not an accusation. I'm from California. I'm expecting stereotypes. Just wondering if I got them."

That wasn't entirely unreasonable. "People are sitting in their cliques."

"The Latinos sit to my left. Next to them are the blacks. In the center, near the Asians, are the Arab Americans." She inclined her head toward the windows. "The whites take up the perimeter as well as the patio."

Whoa. She had her back to the room and still knew where everyone sat. "The emos and the geeks eat on the patio."

"Uh-huh. Does everyone stay in their cliques when they hang out after school?"

"Pretty much."

"So they're *ethnic* cliques."

I gave that some thought. Prejudice had to be as much a problem in California as it was here. The only differences were the *who* and the *how*. I picked up an apple from my lunch tray and peeled off the little grocery-store sticker. "Where we sit may be more about religion than anything else. Hindus, Buddhists, and Muslims are in the center. Atheists are on the patio. Christians sit around the perimeter."

"Black Christians don't sit with white ones."

Yeah, it was one of those things I knew without thinking about, and I really didn't want to think about it now. "Christians segregate according to money. Doesn't matter what your religion is, you're going to sit with people who dress like you."

Her gaze dropped to her lunch, her thoughts nearly audible. When she looked up again, she was smiling. "Your answer doesn't totally suck."

"Thanks."

She crushed her empty yogurt carton. "How well do you know Ash Gupta?"

A conversation with Mundy took too much effort for the lunch period. "Do you always jump around like this?"

"Yes. Do you need a break?"

"Nah, I'm good." I hid my smile behind a forkful of mushy green beans.

"So . . . you and Ash?"

"We take a lot of the same classes."

"I noticed a little *thing* between the two of you yesterday morning."

"A little *thing*?" I eyed her warily.

"Yeah. Sort of sweet, but sad too. I thought you might be exes."

"We've never dated." She was getting too personal, and yet I kept answering. Time to go. I started piling trash on my tray.

"People are wrong, you know."

"About what?"

"You've been friendly to me."

My smile returned. "You haven't given me much choice."

"Why don't the others know this?"

She swung from topic to topic—and pain to pain—so quickly that it was hard to create defenses. "I guess they're confusing wary with antisocial."

"Like they might confuse candid with kind."

Whoa. Was she trying to warn me off?

We watched each other for a long, silent moment, the shadows of our smiles still in place.

"Here." She held up her last container. Two bite-size chocolate cupcakes sat inside. "Want one?"

Was this a bribe?

I considered her expression. It was *kind.*

Okay, bribes were good, especially when they included choco-late. "Hand it over."

I had Webmaster's Club after school on Friday. When I left around five, Marnie was waiting for me at the curb in her beat-up Honda. With its new tires.

"It's registered again, Eden. Thanks." She held herself stiffly and didn't look at me.

"Hey. Don't worry about it."

"I will. It shouldn't be your responsibility to clean up our mess. I feel guilty for taking your money." She put the car in gear.

"I wanted the car fixed as badly as you did. We're fine, Marnie."

"No, we're not. I owe you too much." One lone tear slipped from the corner of her eye and made a shiny trail down her cheek. "What did it do to your college fund?"

"Doesn't matter."

She turned onto the main street, drove around the town square, and headed for home, not speaking again until we were on the highway. "I'm paying you back."

I looked at her uneasily. "How will you do that?"

"Don't know."

"*Marnie.*" She had her fierce, determined, hard-ass face on. That meant trouble. "Are you going to look for a second job?"

"Not sure."

I felt a pinprick of fear. Marnie's "resume" had nothing more than a high-school diploma and years of dead-end jobs. The places that would hire her were bad news. "Please don't."

"Done with this topic." With a slice of her hand, she shut me down. "Did you see Tiffany today?"

That conversation wasn't over, but I'd follow Marnie's lead for now. "Yes, I did." It was impossible to miss Tiffany Barber at school. She made sure she was seen by everybody.

"Did you talk to her?"

"Never had the chance." Tiffany was Marnie's cousin. Tiffany and I got along well enough at family events, but mostly ignored each other at school.

"We've switched the Barber family reunion to Granny's house. I thought Tiffany might've told you."

"Nope. She's been practicing like crazy with the dance team. They're performing at the football game tonight."

"Oh. Are you going?"

"No."

Marnie sighed as she pulled into the carport. "Eden, this is your final year of high school. You should find someone to hang out with."

My stepmom had become obsessed with my social life since my friend Jordan had dropped out of school at sixteen and moved to the Outer Banks. Although I hadn't minded being alone since, it upset Marnie. I was about to make her day. "I ate lunch with someone today. A new girl in the senior class."

"A new girl? What's her name?"

"Mundy Cruz." I got out of the car and jogged up the front steps.

Marnie was right behind me. "Her name is Monday?"

"No. Mun. Dee." I unlocked the door and turned straight into my bedroom. I had homework in every subject over the Labor Day weekend. Might as well get started.

Marnie leaned against the doorframe, her sad mood replaced with excitement. "What's Mundy like?"

"She's bold."

"Is she pretty?"

You would think that once women reached their forties, they would stop caring about someone's looks and ask instead "Is she smart?" or "Is she nice?" But no. "*Pretty* doesn't do Mundy justice."

"Then what does?"

"Perfect." If I were a guy, I would've gone with *hot*, but the word was so overused it didn't seem fair to use it here. Mundy was in a league all her own. "She has perfect skin. Perfect hair, too—naturally black and cut real short." I dumped the contents of my backpack onto my bed and began to line up the books neatly. "Her eyes are a spooky shade of blue. More of a Duke blue than a Carolina blue, which is unfortunate but forgivable."

"Oh. Well." Marnie smiled. "You could be friends."

There might be a chance but, realistically, I kind of doubted it. Once Mundy discovered that she could be friends with either me or everybody else, she was likely to choose everybody else. But I wouldn't ruin it for my stepmom, not when she was looking hopeful. "Maybe."

"Invite Mundy over sometime."

The suggestion buzzed in my head. Invite her to our trailer? I grunted noncommittally. Not going to happen. Ever.

· 4 ·

Fake Delight

Dad burst through the front door around noon on Labor Day, long after he'd promised to return from repairing a bathroom in one of the trailers. Marnie was pissed. He was pumped.

"That was fun." He stomped into the kitchen and struck a bodybuilder pose. *"Yes."*

"Why are you late?" She stood with arms crossed and eyes blazing.

He winked at her. "There's a simple explanation, doll."

"I'm waiting."

"Okay, so I needed to get a part for the toilet, and I went to Cooper's Hardware Store. When I got to the plumbing section, there was two Mexicans standing there. They needed something, but the clerk couldn't figure out what it was. They don't speak English too good."

"Neither do you," I muttered.

"What?"

"Nothing."

Dad shot me a suspicious look before giving Marnie a lazy smile. "So I asked what was happening. And one of them pulled out his phone and showed me a photo of his shower head dripping. Then I handed them exactly what they needed." He grunted with satisfaction. "After they left, old Mr. Cooper walked over and offered me a job."

Dad's announcement fell into a stunned silence.

Really? He was employed? "Yay, Dad."

The smile on Marnie's face was tentative. "Minimum wage?"

"Yeah."

"When do you start?"

"Tomorrow. At first, it'll be twenty hours a week, but it could grow."

I was almost afraid to trust this news. In the two years since he'd been laid off, he'd wallowed in and out of misery, getting hired, only to leave the job when the boss was "too mean" or the work "too boring." Which actually meant that my father had lost his temper at the wrong person and been fired.

Marnie clasped her hands to her gut, as if she were also scared to hope. "This could be the one."

"Yeah." With a lightning-fast move, he yanked her into his arms.

"Gross," she said with a laugh. "You stink. Take a shower."

"I'll show you *stink*." He rubbed his stubbly chin against her cheek.

I looked away and tried to ignore the smacking sounds coming from their direction. Turning back to the huge pot of tea brewing on the stove, I poured in a second cup of sugar. Marnie had volunteered to bring the drinks to the reunion. Iced tea was cheap.

"Byron, let me go. I have to get ready." The words were stern, but her tone was happy. Once he released her, she disappeared down the hallway toward the master bedroom.

He leaned against the counter next to me, watching me stir the tea.

I flicked a glance at him. "Need something?"

"So you think this job might work out?"

"Yeah. It could be good."

"You don't sound too sure."

"Just being realistic. We know how things usually go. You get mad, and you blow it. If you'd just learn to walk away, maybe it will work out." I put the spoon down and gestured for him to leave. "Marnie was right. You need a shower."

He laughed. "Maybe I won't bother. Then she'll let me skip that crazy-ass pig-pickin'."

"I wouldn't push it, if I were you."

The last thing I wanted to do on Labor Day was attend the family reunion. My chemistry homework would be way more fun than the Barbers, but my stepmom wanted me to go. So here I was, sitting in the backseat of her car, waiting for Dad to emerge from the trailer.

Leaning my head against the window, I shut my eyes and tried to swallow my irritation. I'd learned long ago that the best way to survive Barber events was to look busy. If I had something to do, I wouldn't have to talk to anyone. When Marnie told me that I'd be stocking the drinks table, I was completely fine with the assignment.

Five minutes passed and Dad still hadn't come.

The delay was annoying Marnie. She stomped to the front door and screamed, "Byron?"

He appeared. "Ready."

She slid back in the car and slammed her door as he jumped in the passenger side.

By the time we arrived, Granny's lawn looked like a dealership for used trucks. Marnie fumed as she banged a palm against the steering wheel. She hated to be late.

"Sorry, doll," he mumbled.

"No one'll care." I got out and lifted two jugs of tea.

"Yes, they will." She glared at Dad, which he carefully didn't notice.

Once I made it to the back lawn, a card table had been placed under a big pecan tree. It held several towers of plastic cups, and underneath were coolers with ice. But there were obviously no drinks. I dropped off the first load and headed back to the car for more. When I returned with more jugs, the first two had been emptied, and Marnie's brother was arguing with her.

I was wrong. They cared. Damn, it was hard to like these people. How had they ever produced someone as nice as my stepmom?

After delivering a third load, I slipped into the shadows of a nearby weeping willow, far enough away from the crowd that it was like watching a movie on mute.

"Hey, Eden."

"Hey, Tiffany." I glanced at her, taking in her sequined tank, short skirt, and heels. Overdressed, even for her.

She sighed dramatically. "Heard you got tackled in the hall on Thursday."

"Yes, I did."

"Were you hurt?"

"No."

"It was good luck for the team, 'cause we won our first game."
I gave her a *really?* look. "Is that supposed to comfort me?"
She giggled.

We grew silent as we watched the weird choreography of an
eastern North Carolina family reunion. My dad was standing by
the pig cooker, speaking with Tiffany's father and some of the
other men. They were admiring the pig, with its four legs spread,
its eyes staring glassily into eternity, and a pile of chopped pork
mounded where its back used to be.

Tiffany's mom bustled about the dessert table with her
sisters-in-law, sampling from the dozen or more desserts, exclaim-
ing in fake delight over each one, all the while remaining convinced that she was the best baker of the bunch.

The little kids wore bathing suits and were running in and
out of a sprinkler. It looked like fun. I envied them.

Tiffany stepped into my line of vision, eyeing me like she was
dying to know something but was irritated that the answer would
have to come from me.

"Anything else?" I asked.

"You ate lunch with the new girl."

"Yes, I did." Maybe Tiffany thought I had inside information.
With any luck, she'd be disappointed soon and go away.

"How many classes do you have with her?"

"Two." English and art.

"Do you know where she's from? She dresses like a freak."

Oh, right, like I would let that pass. Tiffany coordinated her
clothes with the other members of the dance team. They wore
something pink or glittery every day. It was painful. "Mundy
doesn't need fashion advice from someone who takes her style
cues from the Barbie aisle at the Walmart."

Tiffany's eyes narrowed to slits. "Why do you and Byron come to our parties? Nobody wants you here." She stormed off in a swirl of sparkles.

"She's mistaken, you know."

I turned, relieved to see Gina Barber, one of Heron High's best teachers and, unfortunately, Tiffany's aunt. "Thanks, but I don't think she's making that up."

"I'm glad you're here. Granny is, too."

"That makes two people besides Marnie." Gina and I shared a smile as we dropped the subject, knowing that Tiffany hadn't exaggerated much. There was a reason for her attitude. When my biological mom had been in high school, she'd slept with several of the Barber men, including Tiffany's father. It was hard for people to forget. I understood. Mostly.

Gina excused herself so that she could drift over to her husband again. I stayed where I was, watching as Marnie wandered from group to group, checking in with her favorite cousins before settling in a lawn chair beside her grandmother.

They didn't have anything to drink. I went to the card table and poured two plastic cups of tea.

A burst of laughter caught my attention. Coming around the side of the farmhouse were three members of our high school baseball team.

Bad, bad news.

I'd expected Billy Barber, and his friend Sawyer Atkinson had to be the explanation for why Tiffany was all dressed up. They weren't the guys who had me cringing. It was the other guest. Murray Fielder. While I didn't believe that he'd been invited specifically to torment me, Billy had to have known I wouldn't stay once I'd seen Murray.

Anxiety pulsed inside me, urging me to flee, but I didn't give in. This was my family's get-together. I had more right to be here than he did. I wasn't leaving. Yet.

Sucking in a breath, I tried to appear calm as I fought back the awful memories, but they washed over me anyway. Last spring, Murray had asked me out, over and over. I'd refused, over and over, but he kept on asking, slowly chipping away at my resistance. He'd been so persuasive. So sweet. I'd finally been naïve enough to accept, maybe because he was cute, maybe because I was desperate to feel normal for once.

It should have been my first date in high school.

After suffering through a horrific wrestling match with a huge guy who was determined to get things from me that I wasn't willing to give, I'd managed to neutralize Murray long enough to escape his truck and call Marnie to rescue me. But the horrors hadn't ended there. When I got to school the following Monday, more humiliation awaited me. Plenty of people were willing to tell me that the whole nasty mess had been a dare.

I scanned the crowd wildly, hoping for a friendly face, but nobody looked my way. Shivers cascaded over me as I leaned on the table for support. I could do this. I would get through it.

"Hey, Eden." Sawyer stood before me.

"Hey." I released a shaky breath, happy to see him. So so happy. "Would you like some tea?"

"Sure." He took the cup with a smile. "School going okay?"

"Yeah." Over his shoulder, I could see Tiffany glaring at us. She had to be pissed that he'd spoken to me first. "Everything going okay for you?"

He nodded as he took a sip. "Good, thanks."

I watched him walk toward the pig cooker, only to be intercepted halfway there by Tiffany.

"Eden," an egotistical voice spoke from above me. "Something to drink?"

Shit. For a second there, I'd forgotten about Murray. "Do I look like a waitress?" I forced myself to frown up at him, gratified that I'd worn shades.

His lips pursed suggestively, as if in a kiss.

What an asshole.

I was done.

Making straight for Marnie, I handed her and Granny their cups of tea.

"Thanks, sweetie." She studied my face, her smile faltering.

I held out my hand. "Keys."

"What—?"

"I'm leaving."

She searched the crowd behind me. I could tell the instant she spotted Murray. Her face hardened. "What's he doing here?"

I wiggled my fingers. "Call me when you want to be picked up."

She dug into her pocket, pulled out her key ring, and dropped it into my hand.

I turned away from her fierce frown and stalked to the car. Maybe next time, she wouldn't ask me to come.

· 5 ·

A Calculated Plan

It was five minutes 'til eight when Mrs. Fremont braked her SUV against the curb in front of the high school.

"I'm sorry, Eden," she said for the fiftieth time.

"It's okay," I responded for the fiftieth time. She didn't need to apologize. Her graveyard shifts at the hospital rarely ended on time. I'd understood the risk when I agreed to babysit her kids. This job meant arriving late to school sometimes. So what if I hadn't expected it to happen every Wednesday morning?

I unclipped my seat belt and smiled into the back. "Bye, Marta." I blew her a kiss.

She giggled. "Bye, Eden."

I looked at her brother. "Be sweet today, Kurt."

He turned away to stare out the window, but I didn't let it worry me. It was hard to know if he didn't want to say good-bye or if he was lost in his own world at the moment.

I ran into my first-period classroom as the tardy bell rang, pretended not to see the steely-eyed stare from Ms. Barrie, and slipped into my desk on the last row.

Mundy Cruz was sitting in the desk beside me. She poked me with a sharp fingernail. "What's your phone number?"

I fumbled around inside my bag, hunting for a pen. "I don't have one."

"You don't have a phone?"

I shook my head at her. My dad had a cheap mobile phone since Heron Estates paid for it. He didn't like for the rest of us to give out the number.

The teacher rapped on the podium. "All right, class, please get out *Pride and Prejudice* and turn to chapter fourteen."

Desks creaked and notebooks rustled. As usual, a couple of kids had forgotten to bring a copy and had to approach the teacher to beg.

Mundy whispered across the aisle, "What's a MIM?"

That got my attention. "Where did you hear about MIMs?"

"It's written on the whiteboard."

I didn't bother to stifle my groan. AP certification brought out the worst in our faculty, like they were in some bizarre competition to be the teacher with the most original assignments. But they weren't being clever. They were just giving us work. Lots and lots of work. "MIM stands for *Make It Modern.*"

"Which means . . . ?"

"Ms. Barrie will pick a scene from the book. Then she'll assign a few students to act it out, except we'll have to use today's language and situations."

"Ah." Mundy's eyes gleamed with excitement. "Sounds like fun."

"No, it doesn't."

Ms. Barrie was speaking. "For homework this weekend, read volume two. We'll do the first MIM on chapter eleven." She looked up, her gaze scouring the classroom.

The eyes of every student (except Mundy) focused on their desk.

"Eden, you're Elizabeth."

Crap. I didn't want to do this scene, and it wasn't because I minded being Elizabeth Bennet. If I had to do a MIM, she was as amazing as a character got.

No, the problem was chapter eleven. The marriage-proposal scene.

Why couldn't I have been assigned a scene with a sword fight? Not that *P&P* had many of those. But still. I couldn't imagine anything worse than fending off the fake romantic feelings from a guy in this English class.

"Ash, you're Darcy."

Holy. Shit.

I glanced toward his desk in the front row. He stared straight ahead, back rigid, finger gripping his pen hard. Ash seemed as happy about this as I was.

"He's perfect," Mundy said in her normal speaking voice.

"Really?" I spoke through gritted teeth. "Do you think you can repeat that louder? I don't think the people in the main office heard you."

"It's brilliant."

"It's obnoxious."

"Excuse me, Eden, Mundy . . ." Ms. Barrie said.

We looked up. All eyes in the classroom were on us. I glanced at Ash and found him watching me, his expression stony.

"Let me know when you're done with your conversation. The rest of us are ready to begin," the teacher said.

I flushed. Mundy nodded.

Ms. Barrie launched into her lecture. I hunched in my seat and tried to focus, but the MIM wouldn't leave me alone. This didn't make sense. Ms. Barrie knew that Ash and I didn't get along.

Why had she picked us?

Mundy plopped onto a seat across from me in the cafeteria and opened her lunch pack. That made twice that she'd decided to eat with me. It could be a trend. I struggled to hold back a smile. My reputation hadn't scared her off.

"Why did Ms. Barrie assign *Pride and Prejudice* as our first novel this semester?" Mundy asked as she unwrapped a shrimp quesadilla. "It's kind of cliché."

"Why would you think that?" I loved *P&P.*

"That book has hundreds of knockoffs. She should try something that students haven't read before."

It was adorable that Mundy thought Heron kids had read anything longer than a tweet, much less a centuries-old classic. "Ms. Barrie has to pick books that have been made into movies. Otherwise, hardly anyone would take her class."

"Ah." Mundy chewed for a moment, nodding as if in conversation with herself. "The MIM will be amazing. I wouldn't mind hearing Ash speak Darcy's lines to me." She switched to a decent British accent. *"You must allow me to tell you how ardently I admire and love you."*

"If he says that, I'll bust out laughing."

"No, you won't. You'll be immersed in your character, enthralled by his hotness, mesmerized by his sexy voice." She bobbed her head like my reaction was inevitable. "And you will melt. A puddle on the floor."

"Not likely." Although he did have a sexy voice. "Ash would choke on those words."

"He admires you. You admire him. It'll feel real to you both."

"Oh, yeah. I'd forgotten. You've detected a hidden *thing* that no one else knows about. Not even the two of us."

"It's because I'm new. I'm not cluttered by the past."

"It's because you're wrong."

"What have you got against Ash Gupta?"

"I'm okay with him. We're polite." I picked up a fork and stabbed a french fry on my tray. "It seems kind of random, though, that Ms. Barrie put the two of us on this project."

"It wasn't random." Mundy took a bite of her quesadilla.

I blinked at her. "What was it then?"

She reached into her lunch pack for the next item. "The faculty doesn't like that you and Ash fight when you're on project teams together. They think you're both natural leaders who could be amazing if you would learn how to get along."

"You're joking."

"Nope."

"Ms. Barrie is forcing me to learn from Ash?"

"She's forcing you to work *with* him. She wants the MIM to teach you how to negotiate and teach him how to stand up for his ideas." Mundy nodded solemnly. "Mrs. Menzies wants the same thing."

"How can you possibly know this?"

"My dad is on the faculty. He overheard them in the teachers' lounge."

The information was flying too fast for me to process well. I lost interest in my lunch, my attention completely absorbed by what she was saying. "Wait. Who is your dad?"

"Campbell Holt."

Whoa. Dr. Campbell Holt had arrived this semester to substitute for our regular art teacher while she was on maternity leave. He'd created a sensation from the very first day, not only because he was unbelievably good at getting ordinary, untalented students to try things, but also because he was movie-star, underwear-model hot. "Dr. Holt doesn't look old enough to be your dad."

"Actually, Cam is my stepfather. He's younger than my mom."

"How have you kept this a secret?"

"It's not a secret. The teachers know. We asked them not to share it until I'd been here a couple of weeks. I didn't want kids treating me differently." She smiled. "I'm ready now. You're the first person I've told."

"Is that why you started three days late?"

"Yeah. I've been homeschooled all of my life, so I wasn't sure if I wanted to go to a regular high school. We let Cam scope it out to make sure it made sense."

"Apparently he thinks so."

"Yeah. I'm having a lot of new experiences, but I like it."

"Homeschool, huh?" That explained so much. "How did that work? Did you take classes online? Were you involved in home-school groups?"

"Both." She licked the lid of the yogurt container. "I belonged to an orchestra, a softball team, and a drama club."

"So what new experience are you getting by eating lunch with me?"

She looked up, her expression guarded. "You live in a trailer park."

Her response stunned me. Had she really just admitted I was the token poor person? I bowed my head and willed myself not to care.

"Eden, I'm sorry if that sounded harsh, but I didn't want to hide it from you. We have to be honest." When she extended her hand toward me, I jerked away. "Please listen. It was one of the reasons I came over here the first time, but I've come back because I like you."

"Excuse me, but can you give me a moment while I take this in? I've been around people who avoid me because of where I live. I've never had to think about the reverse." I shook my head slowly. My legs were jumping, as if this news were terrifying. Maybe it was. I enjoyed having her join me at lunch. I didn't want to end it, but I had to now. Right? "I suppose I should be proud to serve as a specimen in your poverty experiment. Maybe you can explain, though, what I'll gain."

"The same thing as me. A friend." She sighed. "I'm sorry I had to tell you this way, but I wanted that detail behind us. You know the worst of it now."

"Can't wait to hear the best of it."

"That would be Cam's opinion of you." When I looked up, she was watching me anxiously. "When I told him about the people I was interested in hanging out with, he was thrilled that I included you. He thinks you're exceptional."

"Thanks. I guess." Her voice held the ring of truth. I let it ease into me and wondered if it could heal the shock. I admired her stepfather. I was beginning to look forward to her company.

Had this been a calculated plan?

Investigate the options.

Monitor for a week.

Narrow the list.

I'd made the cut. Mundy had barfed out her confession. And now I was left to deal with whether it was too much. I picked at my meal and thought about Dr. Holt. And Mundy. And me.

Several minutes passed before she spoke again. "Are we still friends?"

"Were we ever?"

"Yes."

I'd have liked to hop to my feet and storm away in self-righteous outrage. But the reality was, Mundy was correct. It had felt like we were on our way to friendship, and that would be kind of nice to have.

"Are we okay again, Eden?"

"Maybe."

"Great, 'cause I have something to ask." She leaned on the table, propping her chin on her hand. "Can we play truth or dare—without the dare?"

Whoa. Already? "Depends on the question."

"I've heard a rumor about your family, and I want to know if it's true."

Did she bulldoze over everyone like this? I was still reeling. My defenses were down, which, now that I thought about it, was an interesting strategy. And successful in this instance, since I couldn't resist finding out if the rumor was about, well, Heather. "What have you heard?"

"What do you want to tell me?"

Damn, she was good. "You've been told about my biological mother."

"Yes."

Of course she had. My bio mom was a specter that never went away. I frowned at my food and tried to imagine what Heather might look like now. Plastic surgery was one of her favorite hobbies, which her last two husbands had been happy to indulge. "Heather got pregnant her senior year of high school and went into labor during commencement. My brother was born the next day." My lunch tray, with its soggy toasted cheese sandwich and canned peaches, blurred into a swirl of glistening yellow. "Dad had planned to go to a school to become a licensed plumber, but he had to abandon that idea to get a job. He married Heather when Boone was three months old."

"When did they divorce?"

"I was four." I slumped down until my head rested against the seat back, and allowed my eyelids to half close. It would be easy to drowse into a stupor. This was one history test whose answers I had memorized.

"How often do you see Heather?"

"Not at all since I was thirteen. We both went to her sister's funeral, although we didn't have much to say to each other. I'm not sure where Heather lives now." I lowered my chin until Mundy came into view. "It turned out well. Dad remarried, and Marnie is amazing."

"Heather did you a favor."

"Yeah." I hated what she'd done to us. I hated that she was likely living in luxury while I'd eaten too many meals bought with food stamps. Yet there was a tiny part of me that had grudging respect for Heather. She'd lived hard, partied hard, dressed the way she wanted, and hadn't worried about what anybody thought. I could never forgive her, but I couldn't blame her for wanting to get out of here.

Mundy whipped out a banana and held it out to me. "Hungry?"

"Thanks." I couldn't believe her reaction was so mild. She looked bored. Now I understood her earlier point. It *was* a relief to get past the ugliest part of the truth.

Mundy was cramming trash and containers into her lunch pack. "Why did your parents choose the names Boone and Eden?"

Another sore subject. "Heather named us after towns in North Carolina. How about yours?"

"It's short for Rosamund, which is the heroine's name in one of my mom's favorite books."

I added the banana peel to her trash pile. "Why did you move to Heron?"

"My grandfather has cancer. He'll move into a hospice house soon. We're here to be with him."

"I'm sorry."

"It's been hard on Cam. He doesn't want to believe Grampa is ready to die." She picked up her stuff and nodded toward my essentially untouched tray. "Do you want to bring in some food Friday? We could potluck."

"Sure, but why Friday?"

"I've got plans for tomorrow. Potluck, then?"

Raiding the pantry at home wouldn't be practical, but maybe I could check out Granny's cookie jar. "I could bring cookies," I said, hoping that the heat creeping up my neck wasn't obvious.

"Sounds good." She smiled. "See you Friday."

· 6 ·

A Scuzzy Place

After school let out, I headed straight to the computer lab. My dad was picking me up today after his shift at the hardware store. I would use the time for research. My in-state list of potential colleges and scholarships was in good shape. The out-of-state list had room to grow.

Ash and his friends were loitering in the hall near the lab. They stopped talking as I approached. Without making eye contact, I went around them and slipped inside. It was dim and quiet. Just as I liked it.

"Hey, Eden. Do you have a minute to talk about the MIM?"

I looked behind me. Ash had followed me in. "Sure." I dropped onto a chair in front of the closest desktop computer but kept my hands in my lap. No way would I get started until he left.

He sat next to me and set his iPad on the table while I tried to think about something besides how good he smelled.

His fingers tapped. "Did you know that Ms. Barrie gave us the proposal scene?"

"I did."

"Have you come up with anything yet? Because I have a few ideas."

"Already?" Less than seven hours had passed since we received the assignment, and we'd been in class for six of them.

"It's a major grade, and since it's due Monday, we don't have that much time."

"Understood." Was Ash already trying to take over? Where were his famous negotiation skills? Maybe I should channel Elizabeth Bennet right now and act the way she did in the proposal scene. Confrontational and prejudiced.

"Do you ever watch old TV shows—"

"Stop, Ash."

"—like *The Twilight Zone?*"

"*Stop.*" I reached over and flipped the cover across his iPad. "It's my project, too."

He didn't twitch a single muscle, except his hands—and they had fisted. "Okay. What have you got?"

"Nothing yet, but I will when I've had a chance to think it through."

"Can we meet tomorrow during lunch?"

My lunch break was the only unscheduled half hour I had all day. Not giving it up. "I don't do assignments during lunch."

He studied me impassively. "You want to meet outside of school?"

"I know it's a sacrifice for you, but yeah." He had beautiful eyes, dark brown and fringed with thick lashes. That was the second personal thought I'd had about Ash today. I strained away from him and inwardly cursed Mundy.

"How about tomorrow night?"

"Sorry. I'm working."

"Could we Skype after you're done?"

"My shift runs from seven p.m. until seven *a.m.*"

His forehead scrunched with curiosity, but when I didn't clear up that mystery for him, he opened his iPad again. "What about Friday after the final bell?"

"I have Webmaster's Club."

"Fine. Why don't you tell me when you're free?"

Time to cut the pissiness. This was a major grade. "How about this afternoon? I could be done here in thirty minutes."

"Doesn't work for me. I'm on my way to a club meeting."

Whoa. One of my responsibilities as the school's student webmaster was to update the master calendar. There weren't many extracurriculars that met today. "Dance Team, Horticulture, or Comic Book?"

"Comic Book. Is that a problem?"

"No." Ash had this rigidly planned life, with every single moment designed to impress on his college applications. Comic Book Club didn't quite fit. "How about tomorrow, immediately after school?"

He nodded as he stood. "Where?"

"In the gazebo at the town park."

"Why the gazebo?"

"Neutral ground. No audience."

"Works for me."

I waited until he'd left to boot the desktop. I'd only managed to check out a couple of scholarship sites when the door to the lab creaked. Quickly, I closed the browser, just as someone stopped directly behind me, reeking of raspberries and vanilla.

I didn't have to turn around. "Do you need something, Tiffany?"

A delicate snort was her response. Tiffany wanted to be looked at. I glanced over my shoulder. She stood behind me, wearing the unofficial uniform of the dance team, a shirt in neon coral and the kind of shorts that violated the dress code for everyone except girls who bounced around in pep rallies.

Tiffany's sole attempt at originality came from the miniature bronze sculptures dangling from her earlobes. "Cute earrings," I said.

"Thanks." She hoisted a camera bag onto the table, drew out a media card, and popped it into my computer's card reader. "Here are some candids."

Photography was Tiffany's third love, right behind herself and the dance team. Uncool as it was to be in the Journalism Club, she'd had to join to find an outlet for her work.

I paged through the images, mostly of students from the first two weeks of the school year. There were the requisite shots of the football players and cheerleaders. A dozen or more of Sawyer. But Tiffany had also taken several shots of less obvious subjects. Friends hugging after a summer apart. The head custodian taking a smoke break behind the cafeteria. A teacher setting up an experiment in the chemistry lab.

The collection showed serious talent. Our web site had plenty of space in its "Campus Candids" gallery. I could use at least half of her photos. "Do you have permission to publish these?"

"All of them, but I want to ask about the last one."

That was strange. I maximized the last image.

It was the best shot of the bunch—a masterpiece in black and white. Mundy Cruz sat cross-legged on the wooden bench in the front schoolyard, chin resting on fists, eyes closed, a killer smile curving her lips. Beside her, Cam reclined, his head thrown back in laughter.

I focused on Dr. Holt more closely. He always looked that

happy, even in class. This semester was the only time I'd taken art. Until I'd started babysitting the Fremonts, fine arts hadn't been interesting to me. But now that I wanted to be a school-teacher, drawing seemed like an important skill to be exposed to.

My timing was good, because Dr. Holt had enthralled our class from the first day. His every word inspired confidence in our ability to create art. The tiniest gesture from his beautifully slim hands urged us to dig deeper.

Smiles of approval were his secret weapon. After earning one, we'd work our butts off to earn the next. The committed art students were hoping Mrs. Banik stayed home with her baby, so he wouldn't have to quit.

"What do you think?" Tiffany sounded cautious.

"It's an amazing shot." With a few taps of the keyboard, I copied the images into a staging area.

"Are you worried about posting that one? They look too friendly for a student and teacher. Will people wonder if there's something going on?"

"There *is* something going on. Campbell Holt is Mundy's stepfather."

The news rippled through Tiffany like an electric shock. "How come people don't know that?"

"I guess they can now. It isn't a secret." I gave her a thoughtful look. She could've flung that image on the Internet and made things uncomfortable for a day or two. It was cool that she'd asked first. "I'm glad you checked, though, before things got embarrassing."

She shrugged off my comment. "Do you think she'd let me use that in my portfolio?"

"Portfolio?"

"I'd like to make a career of photography. Maybe go to college."

Whoa. Tiffany wanted to go to college? That was surprising. Her dad was a real lowlife who treated her and her mother like a pair of mindless fluffheads. He might spoil his little princess with small things, but the big things? He controlled those with a grip of steel. No way would he let her escape the future he had mapped out—which was hostessing in his seafood restaurant down at the beach, avoiding ass-grabs from dirty old men with large expense accounts.

Like me, Tiffany had to be investigating colleges behind her father's back. Well, he wouldn't hear about it from me. "Good luck with that."

Her gaze met mine. A desperate kind of hope flickered in her eyes. "Thanks. I'll need it."

Dad roared up around four and waited for me get in, a huge smile on his face.

I smiled back. "Are you liking your new job?"

"Sure am. Mr. Cooper says I'm a natural at it." He screeched out of the parking lot. "I even caught a shoplifter today. She was white, too."

Did he really just say that? "Shoplifters come in all colors and sizes, Dad."

He continued as if I hadn't spoken. "The break room has free snacks. Good ones. Oh, and guess what, baby girl. Mr. Cooper is having a problem with the computer in his office. I told him you'd take a look."

"You what?" I gaped at my father. He was chewing on a

toothpick, staring through the windshield as he drove through town. "Why would you say that without asking me first?"

"He needs help, and you're smart with computers." He scowled. "I don't like your attitude."

"It's not attitude, Dad." I ought to take a breath and start over. This might go better if I acted curious. "Has Mr. Cooper called whoever installed the system?"

"They charge by the hour, and they're real expensive. If it's something easy, you could figure it out fast and save him some money."

"What kind of problem is it?"

"Dunno."

"What kind of computer?"

"Dunno. Does that matter?" He pulled onto the highway and floored it.

"Yes, it matters. He could have a machine that I don't know anything about." I gritted my teeth. I had to be honest here, and it would piss off my father. "Sorry, but I'm not the best person. The problem could be a real time suck, and I'm too busy right now."

"Doing what?"

Really? Did he ever see me lying around with nothing to do? I was awake at dawn and going strong until midnight. Why would I want to spend my precious time off at yet another job? "Besides babysitting three nights each week, I'm taking three AP courses. The homework never ends." *Then there is the college search.*

"You can spare a couple of hours. I promised."

Spare some hours? I didn't do that for myself. "You shouldn't have promised."

"He's expecting you Saturday morning at nine o'clock." Dad's hand snaked out cobra-quick and latched onto my wrist. "It's my first week there, Eden. Don't screw this up for me."

I went still. With four miles to go, I should drop the subject until he cooled down. "Can you let go of my arm, please?"

When his fingers relaxed, I slipped my wrist from his grasp and scooted closer to the door.

"Your mom got another job."

"What?"

"Yeah. At the convenience mart where the highway dead-ends near the beach."

It was a scuzzy place on a lonely stretch of road. If I'd tried to dream up the worst alternative for her, my brain would never have imagined a job this bad. "When does she start?"

"Last night."

Of course. Marnie had worked a shift while I was with the Fremonts, so that I wouldn't know. "Tell her to quit."

"Like I can stop your mom when she's got a bug up her ass." He shrugged. "She clocked out at midnight."

"Holy shit. *Dad*."

"She wants to pay you back for the car." His lip curled. "She doesn't count on me lasting long at the hardware store."

God, he was a jerk. He'd planned this conversation carefully, knowing exactly what to say and when to say it, in order to manipulate me into doing what he wanted. And it was working. The thought of Marnie at that place made me sick. "I'll give Mr. Cooper an hour."

"Thought you might."

· 7 ·

Terminally Embarrassed

Thursday after the final bell, I walked to the gazebo. My route took me through downtown Heron and around the courthouse square. I followed a zigzag path through pools of shade cast by pecan trees—anything to escape the sun broiling my head. When I reached the sloping meadow in the middle of the park, I was sticky with sweat.

There was no sign of Ash. Good. I'd have the place to myself for a while.

The gazebo rose six feet above me, like a fat white cupcake resting on a carpet of faded green. In the summer, the town band used it as a stage for concerts. Otherwise, the gazebo sat empty, waiting for picnics, playtime, or whatever else a kid could dream up.

I climbed its twelve wooden steps and flung my arms wide as I twirled under the high-domed ceiling. When I was a little girl, I had come to the gazebo on rainy days, wearing a princess night-gown and glittery tiara—both handmade by my lady-in-waiting,

The Right Honorable Countess Marnie. Since nobody else would brave the weather, we could enjoy afternoon tea and dancing, totally alone.

My best childhood memories had happened here. Why had I suggested this place to Ash?

A board creaked behind me. I stopped twirling and faced my Darcy. He was standing a few feet away, expression neutral, eyes masked behind shades.

"Sorry I'm late," he said.

"I hadn't noticed."

Ash dropped a folder onto the wooden bench that hugged the gazebo's perimeter. With a flick of his hand, he opened the folder, lifted two stapled sets of paper, and held one out to me.

I accepted it with a frown. "What's this?"

"A script for the MIM."

There were several pages, covered with text in an extra-large font. I skimmed my set, reading as Ash/Darcy asked Eden/Elizabeth to prom. "What happened to *The Twilight Zone*?"

"It's the voice-over at the top and the bottom."

"And everything in between is a basic rewriting of the proposal scene?"

"Yeah, I decided not to go too far out there. Since we're the first team to do one, we don't know what Ms. Barrie is looking for. We can give her something straightforward and add a little edge with my Rod Serling imitation."

"Anything left for me to do?"

"What?"

"This is *your* script and *your* imitation. You've done all the work."

"Not really. We'll perform it together on Monday."

"So I can read the lines you wrote."

"Fine. What did you bring?"

"My notes."

He exhaled noisily. "What's the issue, Eden? Someone had to write a script. You didn't. Let's use mine."

"It's a *team* project, Ash. I'm half of the team." I looked at his pages again. In addition to the voice-over stuff, he'd given himself the best lines in the rest of the scene. What a surprise. In Ash's version, Darcy sounded more balanced than he did in the book. Ash's Lizzy sounded silly to reject such a splendid offer.

Maybe, like Darcy, that's what Ash thought. Life was easy for him. He was rich, built, and friendly. Had he ever worried about losing his home? Did he know how it felt to be terminally embarrassed by his parents? Were girls so eager for his attention that anyone who wasn't must be an idiot?

He'd had a glimmer of an inventive idea and backed away from it. The remainder was an accurate yet conventional adaptation of Austen's words. I knew we could do better. "No, don't think so."

"Why?"

"I want an A."

"Wow." His lips tightened. "I suppose you've come up with something great."

"Actually, no." Ash and I were the smartest kids in the class. We had to be more imaginative. Kneeling on the bench, I faced into the park, as if inspiration would be out there somewhere in the sunlight filtering through the trees.

He slumped onto the bench a couple of feet away, extended his legs, and wiggled like he was about to take a snooze. "How about I sit here while you take over?"

"I'm good with that."

His head angled in my direction, the shades firmly in place. It was hard to be creative with him watching me.

He waited a minute before asking, "Anything yet?"

"No."

"Could I make a suggestion?"

"Could you be quiet instead?"

"Nice." He looked at the dome. "At this rate, we'll get there Monday and have to wing it."

"Uh-huh." I slipped an arm around a pillar and hugged. What could we do? Because we couldn't show up in class with nothing prepared.

Or could we?

Maybe . . .

"You're right, Ash. We can wing it."

"What?" He snapped into a sitting position. "You're joking, right?"

"An improv." Possibilities floated in the murky fog of my brain. "It could be intense."

"It could fail."

I pushed away from the bench and backed into the center of the gazebo, unable to contain my excitement. "Nobody would expect *us* to do something unrehearsed. It's brave."

"It's insane."

"Sorry. Ignoring you." Fragments of the concept slowly crystallized. We could prepare three or four strategic sentences. Around them, Ash and I would react naturally. The unknowns would keep the tension high. "We could have an outline."

"No, Eden. The MIM is ten percent of our final grade. We can't do something that *might* work." He got to his feet and took a step closer to me. "Would you just do a read-through of my script?"

"What are you scared of?"

"There are too many things that could go wrong."

"Like what?"

The silence lasted a long moment, disturbed only by the distant shrieks of children in the playground.

"Ms. Barrie might think we haven't made an effort."

"You're the poster child for overachiever. She knows better than that."

"What if my mind goes blank?"

"I'll jump in."

"What if your mind goes blank?"

"We'll fill the void with adoring glances and smoldering sighs." I couldn't hide my frown of irritation. His excuses made me more determined to have my way. "What is wrong with you?"

"It's too risky."

"Which is why, if we pull it off, we're guaranteed an A."

"We won't pull it off. So, no, we'll do my script."

"Okay. Bring it with you on Monday to class, and I'll give it another look."

"If we don't rehearse it, then it's like an improv."

"That thought had occurred to me."

He muttered something that sounded like *crap*. It was probably the closest he'd ever come to swearing. I felt honored.

"Fine, Eden. Let's hear your plan for the improv."

"In the book, Darcy offers Elizabeth marriage, which is something she wants desperately, just not from him. How do we make that modern?" The only thing I wanted desperately was to get out of this hellhole of a town, and Ash could have no effect on that.

His face hardened into angles and planes, smooth as marble. "In my script, I ask you to prom."

Not something I wanted, but our audience would understand. "Sure. We can use that." I stared at him, wanting to tune into his reaction, but all I saw was my reflection in his shades. "After you beg me properly, I'll say *no*."

"I'm counting on it. What's next?"

"Some name-calling, back and forth."

"My mind won't go blank on that one."

There were so many synonyms for *arrogant jerk*. Which to choose? Bastard? Prick? Asshat? The trick would be to figure out what Ms. Barrie would let me get by with. "Then you can remind me what a sacrifice it is to ask someone . . ." I bit my lip and looked away.

Why hadn't I thought of this before? Like Lizzy, I had parents who were embarrassing. I would never bring them up on my own, but Ash could. He was perfect for the job, a Mr. Midas whose touch turned everything to gold—sports, grades, projects. If he had any flaw at all, it was his lack of humility. "You can remind me what a sacrifice it is to ask out the daughter of a slut and a redneck."

He whipped off his shades. "*No.*"

"You have to."

"I'm not saying that."

It would be agonizing, but once the deed was done, it would be out there. The thing that had been laughed at behind my back would've been said in my presence. It wouldn't make people change their minds, but it might make this topic boring enough that it would wither and die.

We had to do this. "It's the kind of risk Ms. Barrie expects."

"Ms. Barrie wouldn't want us to—" His lips clamped shut.

"She expects us to be brilliant. She wants us to dig deep and set the bar for her excellent idea."

"We're going too far, Eden."

"No, we're not. The proposal scene is about misjudging a person. It's about Darcy loving a girl in spite of her background. It's about Elizabeth rejecting what she wants most over a misunderstanding. We can make this real. We can *be* Elizabeth and Darcy."

He remained silent for so long I wondered if he'd forgotten where he was. A breeze ruffled the black silk of his hair. "Please, Eden," he said, the words so soft I had to lean forward to hear. "Let's do it my way."

"We've been on enough project teams before to know that we won't fail."

"This feels different."

"It's okay, Ash. I want you to do it."

He stood over me, his gaze studying my face with such care that it felt like a caress. "I don't get you."

"You're not supposed to."

With a tense nod, he slipped on his shades. "It's a bad idea, but I'm not arguing anymore."

"Good. Then—"

The beeping of his phone interrupted me. He pulled it from his pocket and tapped out a text in response.

I craned to read upside down.

Be right there

His eyebrow arched. "Do you mind?"

"Your mom's checking up on you?"

He flushed. "She worries."

"Uh-huh."

"Yeah. Gotta go." He grabbed his folder and thudded down the steps.

It was good to be alone, so I could think through the MIM. I sank onto the bench and hugged my knees to my chest, my mind racing.

"Eden, do you need a ride?"

I glanced down to the meadow below. Ash waited on the grass. What had he asked again?

Did I need a ride? *Yes.*

Would I let him drive me to the trailer park? *Never.*

"No thanks."

He shrugged and turned to go.

"Ash?" He paused but didn't look back. I enunciated clearly, to make sure he heard. "No hard feelings afterwards. I promise."

✦ 8 ✦

Whatever University

Heron High had a home football game Friday night. Our pep rally started at two and raged in noisy chaos for an hour, after which most of the student body dispersed. I headed for the computer lab, fully expecting to be the only student to show for Webmaster's Club.

It was silent except for the hum of fluorescent lights. I logged in to the To-Do-List account and checked its e-mail. Fifty messages. There were content changes for the web site, event notices to add to the school calendar, and an interview with the vice principal to post on the Faculty Facts page. I would be busy for a couple of hours.

A chair squawked in the lab's office. "Eden?" Mrs. Barber yelled.

"Yes, ma'am." I could get away with calling her Gina at family events, but she wasn't actually related to me. At school we were formal.

"What're you working on?" she said, her voice drawing nearer.

"The usual updates. Do you have anything for me to do?"

Mrs. Barber crossed the room and sat on the table beside my desktop computer, sipping from a can of Diet Cheerwine. "I have an important project for you, but it might take a while to finish."

My heart sank. Dad was supposed to pick me up at five. "How long?"

"If you do it well, a couple of months." She dropped a large, thin envelope on the table next to me. The label read *Peyton Scholarship Program.*

Yes. The Peyton meant a full ride for four years at the University of North Carolina. Honors college. Study abroad. No restrictions on my college major. It was highly competitive and prestigious as hell.

This scholarship would be a huge win for me. I could go to one of the top colleges for special education in the country. The money would become a much smaller issue. And I wouldn't be all that far from home. I liked the idea of being an easy drive away from Marnie.

It was the perfect solution.

I'd never invested a lot of effort into dreams. When daily survival took everything I had, flexibility was more practical than hope. But this? The Peyton? It scared me how much I wanted it.

"Thanks." With shaking hands, I ripped the envelope open and pulled out the half-dozen loose sheets. The application requirements were predictable. A resume with outstanding grades, extracurriculars, leadership, and SAT scores. An essay. Recommendation letters from a teacher and a community member. And then . . .

Big problem. A consent form signed by a parent or legal guardian for applicants under eighteen. Like me. Would Marnie be able to talk Dad into signing it?

"Eden, do you need me to speak with Byron?"

My reaction had been visible on my face. I had to watch that. "No thanks. I'll handle it."

I'd worry about the parent part later, because there was another hurdle to get past. It was virtually impossible to become a finalist without the support of my school, and Heron High was limited to one endorsement. The Honors Committee would only invite a few students to apply. Since Ash and Upala were planning to go out of state, that left Dwayne Key as my main competitor. My academics against his sports.

Besides being ranked number one in the class, I had more AP classes and amazing SAT scores, but my extracurriculars were a major weakness. Webmaster's Club was the only school-based activity I'd had since my sophomore year, although I did have essay and poetry contest wins and I'd placed well in my age category for a couple of 5K races.

Dwayne was ranked fourth in our class, which would hurt him compared to me, but the rest of his resume was solid. The tennis team. The senior rep to the Student Council.

Who was on the Honors Committee this year? That could make a big difference in whether they cared more about academics or "being well-rounded." Would this year's committee give me credit for my jobs? The chair was supposed to make sure that they did. Otherwise, poor kids wouldn't stand a chance.

I looked at Mrs. Barber. "Has the Honors Committee been named?"

"As of this morning."

"Do you know who's on it?"

"I do, since I'm the chair."

Whoa. Yeah. "Congratulations." Mrs. Barber loved me, and

she was *the chair.* She'd insist that the committee count my work history. And there were my superior academics . . .

This was good. Very good. "Who else?"

"Ms. Lee, Mr. Applewood, and Mrs. Parsons."

"Mrs. Parsons?" At Gina's resigned nod, I looked away. That was good for me, too. As the head of athletics, Mrs. Parsons had been my track coach for a year and liked me pretty well. But she was also the person who had given Ash his only B. I'd heard that "transfer" students never got A's from her. No one could prove it, but it was generally accepted that Mrs. Parsons made it easier for local kids to win school honors—by hurting the chances of anyone "not from around here." Dwayne and I didn't have to worry about that, though. "She's a strange choice."

"She insisted."

The principal must have caved. That was interesting. Wonder what she had on him? "How soon will you hold interviews?"

"Mid-November."

I nodded but inside I was smiling. I might not be popular with kids my age, but I would do well in interviews with teachers. And the essay? I wasn't worried. I was a better writer than most. "There's plenty of time to prepare."

"Yes." She bit her lip. "Unfortunately, I'll have to recuse myself from voting on the endorsement, Eden."

I blinked in surprise. "Why?"

"Tiffany is one of the candidates."

Tiffany Barber? How did that happen? I knew she had a crapload of extracurriculars. Dance Team. Vice president of Student Council and the Journalism Club. But her grades had to be the best-kept secret in the high school, because I hadn't realized they were that good. "How is she getting this past her dad?"

"I don't know. She realizes that she'll have to work it out." Her lips twisted. "He's competitive. That might be enough to do the trick."

"So she must be ranked in the top five in our class." Which was an absolute stunner.

"I can't confirm that." Gina shook her head at me. "This will be a hard decision. All four of you are strong."

"Four?"

"You, Dwayne, Tiffany, and Ash."

What?

That couldn't be right. Ash wasn't in the running. Everybody knew where his top pick was. "Ash is applying to Stanford."

"He won't know whether he's been accepted until December, and Carolina is one of his safety schools. Ash is seeking the endorsement, too."

The Peyton consumed me Friday night.

The news about Ash was a blow. I'd finally found a full-ride scholarship to a college I'd give anything to attend, and now it might slip through my fingers and go to Ash, whose parents were rich enough to send him anywhere he wanted.

I wouldn't have worried much about Tiffany and Dwayne. The label of valedictorian would've been hard to beat, especially once the teachers knew that I had to sacrifice extracurriculars for a job. But Ash was different. If our school system had chosen weighted GPA instead of unweighted, he would be valedictorian. And he had leadership, clubs, and sports. He looked better than me on paper. The committee was likely to endorse Ash. Then Stanford would admit him, and he would turn the Peyton down.

This wasn't fair. How dare he!

What must that be like—to pursue a scholarship simply because you wanted it? I had no other way to afford a school like Carolina. It terrified me to think what would happen if I didn't get the Peyton or some other scholarship like it. I was smart. I was good. I would make an amazing special-ed teacher, and I could lose it all because Ash wanted to pile up prestigious awards that he would never use.

I wasn't sure how much more of a battering my heart could take.

The rest of the evening was spent assessing the probability of me winning the endorsement now that Ash was in the running, and I had to admit it was close. But I wasn't giving up. If there was an angle I could exploit, I would find it.

Dad woke me early Saturday morning to leave for the hardware store. We arrived there at nine o'clock. Five minutes later, I was done.

Mr. Cooper's problem turned out to be easy. He'd gotten his font size uncomfortably small and hadn't known how to change it. Fortunately, his desktop computer used Windows. I'd fixed it immediately and then taught him what to do if it happened again.

"So, you're good now," I said, sliding off the chair.

"Yes." He patted me awkwardly on the shoulder. "Thank you."

"You're welcome."

"Let me pay you for coming." He reached in the petty cash box and handed me a ten.

"Thanks." I would never admit it to my dad, but I'd enjoyed this.

"Look, Eden." Mr. Cooper cleared his throat. "Would you like to work a few hours each week and help me with computer stuff? Things like typing in data and running reports?"

I would've been tempted if I had any time, but I didn't. "That's nice, Mr. Cooper—"

"She'd like that," Dad said from behind me.

I turned to him, eyes narrowed and pissed. *No*, I mouthed.

"She'll call you next week." He was looking past me to his boss. "If it's all right, I'll take a quick break and drive Eden home."

"Sure, sure." The old guy bobbed his head. "Thanks again, honey."

I remained silent on the way back to the trailer, too upset to speak without yelling.

As he turned onto our lane, he said, "This could be a great job for you."

"I'm old enough to decide what's right for me, and in this case, I don't have time." Why couldn't he get that through his thick head?

"You're not busy on the weekends."

"I study like crazy on the weekends. I have a tough semester."

"If you do good with the computer, Cooper might keep you on after you graduate."

"I'll be gone after I graduate."

Dad scowled as he pulled into the driveway. "And where the hell do you think you'll be?"

"At college."

"Cape Fear Tech isn't that far. You can commute."

I did not want to get into this with him. "I won't be attending a community college."

He cut the engine. "I don't know what else you have in mind."

Marnie's car wasn't here. Dread flickered in my gut. My dad

and I were on the brink of a fight, and she wouldn't be here to defuse it. I unclipped the seat belt, gripped my bag, and slid from the truck. I'd made no secret that I was leaving Heron and heading to whatever university handed me the most money. He'd always ridiculed my plans, but that hadn't stopped me from pursuing them.

"Don't walk away from me, Eden. I haven't finished talking to you."

I unlocked the front door of the trailer and stalked into my bedroom, slamming the door behind me. I'd just flopped onto my bed when there were two sharp raps at my door. I watched as it swung open.

He loomed in the doorway, nostrils flaring. "Just where exactly do you think you're going to college?"

I rolled off the opposite side of the bed and stood, facing him across the barrier. "I'm working on it."

"I ain't paying for you to leave."

"I never expected you to, Dad. I'm the girl who bails out her parents, remember? You're threatening me with a weapon you don't have."

He crossed his arms and stared at me through narrowed eyes. Curiosity replaced anger in the set of his jaw. "How do you plan to get the money?"

"Scholarships. Grants. Whatever it takes."

"Will they need to know about our income?"

"Most of them, yeah."

His upper lip curled into a triumphant sneer. "Then you gotta big problem, baby girl."

That reaction alarmed me. "Why?"

"I haven't been too careful about filing our taxes. You can't give the government a reason to take a look."

After dinner, I slipped out of the house, ran across the back deck, and jogged the short distance to the wooden pier jutting into Heron's Bay.

Maybe other people looked down on us since we lived in a trailer park, but they didn't know what they were missing, because I had the bay. Our lot had three hundred feet of frontage, endless wildlife, beautiful sunsets, and the soft, sweet lap of waves against a shore that was all mine.

In the two years since we'd moved into Heron Estates, I'd become addicted to this spot. I could creep out, day or night, and come to the end of the dock. I would sit, legs dangling, while the world around me waited, quiet and still. It made me feel small but important. I liked that thought. I fit here. The bay soothed my pain and brought me peace.

I needed that tonight. My big plans had depended on financial aid, and I would've qualified for lots of it—merit and need-based. But nearly all scholarship programs required that I fill out the government's FAFSA form, and it was designed to suck in tax information automatically. I was screwed.

By cheating on his taxes, my dad had stolen my future, and I had no idea how to steal it back.

· 9 ·

Bag Lady

Marnie outdid herself with a late Sunday breakfast. Boone had driven up from Wilmington to spend the day, and she expressed her approval with food. We all benefited.

I didn't talk during the meal. There was no chance to since Boone had plenty to say. He was working as an EMT and taking classes at the community college. Currently, he was in between girlfriends, but that wasn't likely to last long.

While Boone and Marnie cleaned up, I put on my running shoes and hit the 5K trail along Heron's Bay. I'd been on the track team my freshman year and had done well at a few of our meets. That had all ended when my dad got laid off from the nuclear power plant. Extracurriculars were expensive, and my parents had needed me to earn income at whatever job I could find. I'd traded running for busing tables.

This trail was another of the reasons I was glad that I lived in Heron Estates. It was beautiful along here, especially on a day with gorgeous weather.

When I got back home, I found my family sitting in the den, drinking beer and watching a football game. As I slipped past them, my dad said, "Your brother likes Cape Fear. It's a good school."

I ignored the comment. After showering, I changed into shorts and a tank top and hid in my bedroom. With the curtains drawn, the space was dim, clean, and in perfect order. Just what I needed to concentrate. I sat cross-legged on the carpet and reached under my bed.

My fingers closed around a folder of paper that I couldn't let my dad know about. I'd spent an hour on Saturday at the county library, printing off everything I could find about private scholarships. Without FAFSA, public financial aid was out, and most of the private ones required it too. But there had to be something available for me. Right?

I sorted through the information I'd collected on private aid and organized them into two stacks, in- and out-of-state. Of the private scholarships in-state, there were only three that didn't require FAFSA. The Peyton was one of them.

Yes.

I had to win it, and getting my high school's endorsement was practically mandatory. I had to do everything in my power to make that happen.

Tires crunched on the gravel driveway of our lot. Who was coming by at three o'clock?

A car door creaked and slammed shut. The visitor climbed the steps and clumped across the porch. There were five raps on the front door.

I debated whether to move. In theory, I should be the one to answer, since no more than six feet separated me from the door being rapped on.

Rap, rap.

Yes, it should be me. In theory.

The TV went mute. "No need to move your lazy ass, Eden," my brother shouted, his footsteps booming nearer. "I'll get it."

I shoved the folder back under my bed.

The front door was wrenched open.

"Hey," Boone said in his impress-the-pretty-girl voice. "How can I help you?"

"I'm Mundy Cruz. Is Eden here?"

Whoa. I stood, financial aid forgotten.

"Yeah," Boone was saying, "I think she's at home." He peered at me, aware that the front door blocked Mundy's view. "Sis?"

I walked over and punched him. "Got this."

He punched me back. "You have a guest."

"I can see that." I blinked at her, shocked and disturbed and elated. "Why are you here?"

"I thought we could hang out," she said. "May I come in?"

My brother nodded. I did not. She went with Boone's response and stepped onto the fake marble square that served as our foyer. There was a corduroy bag slung over one shoulder.

"I'm Boone Moore." He hadn't backed up and was, therefore, crowding her. "Eden's brother."

"Hi, Boone." She smiled.

He jerked a finger toward the love seat. "That's our dad."

"Hi, Mr. Moore."

Dad nodded, his eyes never leaving the television. Marnie had disappeared.

I waved Mundy into my room as I made a face at my brother. "Bye. Drive safely if I don't see you again."

"I'll let you know when I leave."

"Not necessary." I shut the bedroom door and leaned against it as the volume on the football game ramped up again.

Mundy had tossed her corduroy bag onto the pillows of my bed, messing them up. She was now standing by my bookcase, checking out my things.

I waited rigidly by the door. I wasn't used to having people in my room.

She reached for a picture frame decorated with chipped seashells and multicolored sand. "Who is this with you?"

The photo showed six-year-old me with Marnie in our Easter finery. "My stepmother."

Mundy put it down and grabbed a second frame, her eyebrow arching in inquiry.

"Heather." My bio mom sat on the hood of a car, holding me at four on her lap, laughing into the camera. "A month after that photo was taken, she abandoned us."

We'd had macaroni and cheese that night. And broccoli, which she'd burned. The smell was horrible. Heather had set the table for three. When my dad asked her who wasn't eating, she'd said, "I'm not. I have other plans." A few minutes later, she was gone. She never returned.

Just like that. Said good-bye to two little kids and a husband because she had "other plans."

Mundy shook her head, set the frame down, walked over to my bed, and fell backwards until she was lying in the middle. "This is fabulous."

I stared at her, arms crossed.

She rolled her head toward me. "Something wrong?"

"The quilt is wrinkled."

"Yes, it is. I'm sure that'll change the minute I leave."

"It'll change before you leave."

She laughed. "You might as well sit. I'm going to be here a while."

I slid down the door until I was sitting on carpet. "How did you find me?"

"Your stepmom. I called. She gave me directions."

"She didn't bother to mention that detail." Marnie had conspired on this surprise. No wonder she'd disappeared. Payback was hell. "How'd you get Dad's cell-phone number? Through Dr. Holt?"

"I'd rather not say. To protect the guilty."

"You went to a lot of trouble." Which was arguably nice, in a screwed-up way.

"I sure did." She flipped to her belly and propped her chin in her hands. "Are you ready for the MIM?"

"I guess." It was weird to see her from this angle, as if she were a disembodied head floating above my yellow quilt.

"What're you doing?"

"An improv."

Her eyes widened. "Ash Gupta and Eden Moore have planned something that isn't tightly controlled and scripted?"

"Yeah." Why'd she have to put it that way?

"Bold choice for the two of you." She tapped a fingernail against her lips, her brow scrunching in concentration. "What are you wearing?"

"I haven't thought about it."

"You're playing Elizabeth Bennet. You have to look the part."

Did I look like the kind of girl who wanted to talk fashion? "I'll figure it out."

"Please, not your normal stuff."

"What's wrong with my normal stuff?"

"Elizabeth Bennet was a member of the gentry. Not a bag lady."

Bag lady? Mundy had better read the expression on my face. "What fails to meet with your approval?"

"You wear big plaid shirts, like an old guy going off to fish."

"They're comfortable."

"Your jeans don't fit."

"They won't fall off. I tie them on." Goodwill hadn't had much in my size on my last visit.

"Of course. Jeans that are three sizes too big can be forgiven if they're *tied* on." She scooted to the end of the bed, hooked my desk chair with her foot, and rolled it closer. "It's time for a Mundy Makeover. You'll hardly recognize yourself when I'm through."

"No thanks."

"This isn't an offer. It's an order."

"Do you honestly think that crap works with me?"

"I'm very good. You'll be gorgeous." She patted the chair. "If you turn me down, you'll be eaten up with curiosity, wondering if I was right."

Her expression dared me. I held out for a few seconds and then caved. "You get fifteen minutes."

"I get as long as it takes." She scowled at the bare surface of my dresser. "Where's your makeup?"

"I don't have any."

She strained backwards until her fingers snagged the corduroy bag. "Glad I came prepared."

"You don't wear makeup either."

"I don't need to." She emptied the bag's contents onto my bed. There was an entire artist's palette of eye shadows. A dozen shades of blush. Loose and pressed powder. Lipsticks, pencils, and glosses.

I frowned. This didn't make sense. "How can you know what you're doing?"

"My mom's an actor. I'm her makeup artist."

"What kind of actor?"

"She's done regional theater in California. You've never heard of her, though. She's also a drama professor at the community college where Cam's been teaching art." Mundy organized a set of sponges on my dresser before selecting several metallic tools whose purpose was fearsome. "I'll leave some of this stuff for you."

A war erupted within me. I was fine the way I was. No use trying to screw with nature; she'd had her say.

Yet I did feel nervous about being in front of the classroom. I'd be sharing the spotlight with the perfectly beautiful Ash. Stared at by fifteen other students. Verbally assaulted. Judged.

I studied the array of objects with a mixture of dread and longing. What if Mundy were as capable as she was confident?

Okay, deep inside, I knew how amazing it would be if this makeover went well.

After she had everything arranged, Mundy pointed at the chair. "Sit."

The two warring Edens compromised. I sat obediently while maintaining an attitude of doubtful resignation.

Mundy picked up a pair of tweezers.

I eyed them unhappily. "What are you planning to do with those?"

"Pluck your eyebrows."

"Why?"

"Because they're ugly."

"You didn't learn your conversational skills in the South."

"No, thank God. Now hush."

She worked without speaking. I kept my eyes shut since I was skeptical about how this would turn out. Marnie never wore makeup. Heather had worn too much. I sided with my stepmom on this issue, so I was wary.

Of course, I could always scrub my face afterwards if I didn't like the result.

Once the tweezing was out of the way, the makeover wasn't too bad. I dozed while Mundy brushed, dabbed, and powdered.

She tapped my shoulder. "Where's a hairbrush?"

"Top right drawer of the dresser."

Mundy had a feather-light touch as she tamed my damp hair. It was soothing.

"Done." She spun the desk chair around until I could see the mirror over my dresser.

I concentrated on my reflection. A prickly sensation fluttered over my skin. Mundy hadn't lied.

It was as if the good parts of me had been highlighted while the bad parts faded away. My eyes looked enormous and vividly blue, framed with thick lashes and smoky lids. There was a rosy glow to my cheeks and mouth. My face seemed less gaunt and angular. I could hardly believe it was me. "I'm in awe of your skill."

"The raw materials made it easy."

"Yeah, right."

"Humble doesn't suit you." Mundy frowned, hands on hips. "Okay, costume next."

"The makeup is enough." I couldn't take my gaze away from the mirror.

"The makeover isn't done. Where's your closet?"

"Behind there." I gestured toward the cranberry curtains draping the opposite end of the bedroom from ceiling to floor.

"Wow. Nice."

"Yeah, my dad did that. He can do anything with his hands."
The original closet had been too tiny to be worth anything, so
Dad had made me a curtained storage area with special lighting
and built-in cabinets.

Mundy disappeared from view and rummaged through my
clothes, making distressed noises. "Is this all?"

Why had I let her back there? Here was proof that my new
look had distracted me. Otherwise, I would never have given her
permission to glimpse the entirety of my public wardrobe. Five
pairs of jeans, one pair of khakis, ten shirts, and a black skirt.
"That's all you have to work with."

"What about shorts?"

"I don't wear shorts to school."

"Most of your stuff makes me cringe."

With her back to me, she would miss my scowl, but it would
likely still be there when she turned around.

She drew out a hanger. "Unbelievable. I found a pair of jeans
that might actually fit."

I knew exactly which pair she meant. They did fit. Too well.
"Marnie's fault. I've never worn them."

"You will tomorrow." She tossed the pair onto the bed. "Where
are your camis?"

"Middle drawer in my dresser."

Kneeling, she slid the drawer open, pawed through it, and
pulled out several items. "Aqua cami. No overshirt."

"You're kidding, right?"

She smiled at me.

"No, Mundy. Not going to happen."

My resolve must've sunk in because she nodded as she stood,
clutching tank tops. "We'll layer tanks, then. White under ice
blue. Your eyes will pop."

So would my breasts. "No, I'll feel naked."

"Elizabeth Bennet would've wanted to look as good as possible."

"I won't be comfortable."

"Your comfort isn't what we're going for." The wide-eyed excitement left her face, replaced by something akin to sympathy. "A lot of girls would go through painful plastic surgery to get a body like yours."

I looked away. I'd inherited this body from Heather. It wasn't something to be proud of. It was something to hide.

"You're playing a theatrical role," Mundy said. "You've got to use every asset, especially the natural ones."

As much as I didn't like her conclusion, I couldn't fight her logic. I had to be a modern Elizabeth. She would've done everything she could to look attractive. So would I, within reason.

I tried to imagine what my classmates would see tomorrow. Tight jeans and tanks, revealing a waist, ass, and breasts they didn't know I had. Bare arms. Makeup. I'd feel ridiculous. Exposed.

Yet it had been my choice to do an improv. Since it was part of the role to look good, I would. "Fine, but I'll wear a big shirt for the rest of the day."

She smiled. "Sounds like a plan."

After straightening my room and packing my overnight things, I left with Mundy, who dropped me off at the Fremonts on her way home. I walked into a quiet house. The kids were fed and in their pajamas, both parked on the den carpet, glued to their favorite DVD. I peered at the counter on the player. There was another hour left.

I pulled Mrs. Fremont aside. "Do you want me to put them in bed at the normal time?"

She didn't meet my gaze. "If you wouldn't mind."

I would, actually. I hated being the one to wrench Kurt away from a movie. "Why are you leaving this to me?"

"I can't take much more today."

"That bad, huh?" I swallowed hard. "Go on. I've got this."

She shuffled away guiltily. Seconds later, the garage door slammed.

"Fifteen minutes," I warned. The statues in front of the TV ignored me.

I curled up on the leather couch with a textbook. But after reading the same page twice without taking in any information, I snapped the book shut and watched the grandfather clock, my tension growing with each tick.

"All right, guys, bedtime. You have school tomorrow."

With a noisy huff, Marta clicked the remote, tossed it onto a table, and rose. Kurt leaned forward, fumbled for the remote, and smacked a button. The movie came back on.

Crap. He was going to be a problem. "Kurt, we're done for tonight."

He didn't budge.

I walked around the table and touched his shoulder. "Come on."

His hand flew up and raked fingernails along my arm.

I screeched as I stumbled backwards, landing on my butt. Blood welled up in reddened streaks on my aching forearm.

"Kurt, what are you doing? You hurt Eden." Marta snatched the remote away and clicked the movie off again.

"Give it back." He lunged for his sister.

Her frightened gaze skittered to mine before she dodged

behind a chair. My heart started racing. Kurt had had meltdowns before, but they were rare when I was around. The steps to get him to chill out didn't sound that hard, but I'd never had to use them by myself.

Say his name often. Speak with calm authority. Don't give in.

How was I supposed to do all that?

He crawled on his hands and knees, shrieking in odd barks, moving closer to where his sister huddled behind a chair.

First I had to rescue Marta. With a confident expression that hardly matched my feelings, I ran to the chair, planted myself between brother and sister, and said, "Marta, go."

She took off for her room, still clutching the remote.

He crawled after her.

"Stop acting this way, Kurt." I caught him by his elbows and hauled him to his feet.

His legs went liquid. It was like cradling sand. He slipped through my arms to the floor.

As much as that pissed me off, I had to be the grown-up here. I had to get myself under control. "Get up, Kurt." My voice was firm, but I'd have to work on the calm part.

"No."

"If I need to, I'll carry you to your room."

"No." He lay on his back, his feet churning wildly.

"Yes." Careful to avoid any flying limbs, I scooped him up. "It's a school night, Kurt. Time for bed."

He bellowed with rage, arching his back and bucking in a strange spiraling kick.

Down we went, rolling and grunting in the hallway.

I was wrestling a six-year-old boy, an unrecognizable creature that I loved. "Kurt," I said, my voice barely above a whisper, "calm down."

The words seemed to incite him to greater fury. His fists flailed about. When one brushed my hair, he wove his fingers in and yanked with all his might.

I gritted my teeth against a scream, not quite successfully. He yanked harder.

"Kurt. Stop. Now." I flipped him onto his belly, locked one of my legs over both of his, and pulled his hand away from my head. Strands of hair fluttered from his fingers.

He went still.

My joints ached with the effort to hold him gently. "Good. You must chill." Was the reminder for me or him?

"No," he said, but the intensity had lessened.

"You're doing better, Kurt." I spoke in bursts as I tried not to think about the agony of my scalp. "We'll lie here until you're okay."

He buried his face in the carpet and sobbed, his shoulders shaking.

We sprawled there, the two of us, for a couple of minutes. After the AC kicked off, the house grew quiet. The door to Marta's bedroom opened, and feet padded down the hall to the bathroom.

I eased my hold. Nothing happened—a hopeful sign. "If I let go of your hands, will you scratch me again?"

A muffled "I won't" wheezed past my ear.

I curled on my side beside him, breathing as hard as he did, cheek against the rough carpet, face a few inches from his.

He sniffed.

"What's wrong, buddy?"

One fist scrubbed at his eye. "I don't want to go to school."

The words grated against my ears, plaintive and unexpected. "I thought you loved school."

"I don't." He smashed his fist against his forehead again and again.

It broke my heart to see that. "Kurt, don't hit yourself." I rocketed into a sitting position and drew him onto my lap. His body stiffened, but he didn't fight to be free.

We sat there silently in the hallway. Moment by moment, his body relaxed. When at last he slumped against me, I staggered up, carried him into his room, and knelt beside the bed. "I'm listening if you want to talk about school," I said, smoothing the covers over him. Something was off here. Did his mother know what it was?

"It's very bad." He hiccupped his way into a sob, eyes closed. "Eden, I'm sorry I hurt you."

"I understand, but don't do again. Okay? It's not all right."

"Okay. Will you rub my back?"

"Sure." I perched on the edge of the bed and patted his back until his breathing gentled into soft puffs.

I said good night to Marta and went to sit quietly in the den, staring into the fireplace, wondering if I really did want a career filled with an hour like the one I'd just spent. Was teaching right for me? More importantly, was I right for it?

· 10 ·

The Same Dazed Regret

Mrs. Fremont dropped me off in front of the high school at the last moment Monday morning. I hurried through the school, with one of my father's old plaid shirts covering me from shoulders to knees. The only sign of my Elizabeth costume was the jeans peeping below the shirt's hem. They were as tight as leggings.

With each step closer to the senior hallway, every spare muscle on my body quivered harder. What had I been thinking? In a few minutes, when I yanked off Dad's shirt, it would be my version of naked. My classmates would see what I'd tried for years to hide. Would I ever be able to fade into the background again?

It was a horrible possibility.

I made it to Ms. Barrie's room without making eye contact. Mundy was in her seat.

She leaned across the aisle. "How are you?"

"Here." The word came out as a croak.

"You're nervous, which is good. My mom always says an actor who's too calm will suck."

"Then I'll be a star." I shrugged off the big shirt.

"Wow, Eden. You look—"

"Not now." My fingers feathered over the scratches from Kurt, their livid red marks glowing against my fair skin.

"What happened to your arm?"

"I don't have time to explain."

"Take this." She handed over a silver cuff bracelet.

I slipped on the shiny camouflage and grunted my thanks.

Ms. Barrie stood and made one quick announcement. Then she rapped on her podium. "Ash and Eden, you're on."

He unfolded from his desk and faced the door. I ripped off my ponytail holder, combed my fingers through my hair, and channeled Elizabeth Bennet.

Chairs squawked and notebooks fluttered as I walked to the front, but no one said a word. Not sure if my classmates were stunned by my appearance or just used to being mute in the presence of Ms. Barrie.

Probably both.

With a curt nod at our teacher, I said, *"Pride and Prejudice* by Jane Austen. Volume two, chapter eleven. An improvisation."

There was an odd stillness in the room—a quiet so complete it was as if everyone held their breath.

Ash turned, stiff and forbidding. His gaze landed first on my face, swept down my body, and raised to my face again. There was no change in his expression, except in his eyes. They widened with shock. The good kind.

The shock went both ways, because he looked really good to

me too. He wore black jeans and a dress shirt, pristine white and molded to the muscles of his chest and arms. If this was his interpretation of the twenty-first-century gentleman's best clothing, I approved. Ash—the gorgeous, modern Darcy.

A fine, tall person, handsome features . . .

The silence stretched, the classroom faded, and we simply stared, studying each other. Was this how Elizabeth felt? Overwhelmed by the sight of him as she fought to resist?

"Eden, you look amazing."

Pride flowed warm and sweet through my veins. I liked the compliment better than I should have. "Thanks, but you didn't come here to say that."

"No, I didn't. It's just . . . I've come to say how much I ardently admire and adore you."

It was the most predictable way to begin this scene, and I hadn't expected it at all. "You admire me?"

"Insane but true." He moved closer, until we were nearly toe to toe, his spring-fresh scent washing over me. "Go with me to the homecoming dance."

"Homecoming?" I repeated. Why had I been downgraded from prom to a dance? "Is this a joke?"

"I wouldn't joke about asking you out."

"Then where did you get the idea that I might be interested in you?"

He crossed his arms over his chest, one brow arching until it disappeared behind the hair tumbling over his forehead. "If we're in the same room, you're watching me."

"You can't know that unless you're watching back."

"You take the same classes I do."

"Like all college-bound seniors at this school."

"You've shown up in the media center on Mondays when I've been there with my study group."

Whoa. He'd noticed that last year? "Pure coincidence, although it's predictably arrogant that you thought you were the cause." I looked up at him with Lizzy's haughty disdain. "I'm sorry, Ash. I don't want to hurt your feelings, but I won't go out with you."

"You're turning me down? Without even thinking about it?"

"I don't have to. I wouldn't date you if you were the only guy asking."

"I *am* the only guy asking."

"How can you possibly know that?"

"Nobody else would dare."

His claim shuddered through me. Murray Fielder had dared, and it'd been a disaster. Had Ash forgotten, or had he used *dare* on purpose? "What's that supposed to mean?"

Remorse clouded his eyes. "I don't want to say."

Well, he would have to. This was the climax of the scene. He couldn't back down. I wouldn't let that happen. "Coward."

"Excuse me?"

"Just say it, Ash. Or do we need to wait until you text your mommy for permission to speak?"

"Fine, Eden." Humiliation hardened his face. "You avoid the rest of us. You're the last one in the classroom and the first to leave. You dress like a street person and shut down conversations by swearing. If no one asks you out, it's because you won't let us forget you're trailer trash."

Even though I'd been anticipating something like this, the reality of his last statement punched me in the gut. I took a quick step back and stumbled. Ash's arm whipped out and locked around my waist, his hand warm and steady at the small of my back. I reached for him, my fingers connecting with the solid muscle of his upper arm. We stood in a near embrace, breathing hard.

Trailer trash? I thought I'd been prepared for whatever he might say, but I was wrong. Ash had gone off script, and I could hardly take the pain.

How can someone go off script in an improv?

No, this wasn't an improv anymore. It was Ash and Eden, shredding each other. "I would've never guessed you had the balls to say that. But as charming as this discovery is, it doesn't change my decision. I'd rather stay home alone than dance with an arrogant asshole like you."

The warm pressure left my waist as he slowly disentangled his arm. "My mistake," he said, his voice soft yet distinct. "I'm sorry for wasting your time. Have a nice life."

The squeak of his shoes was the only sound in the room. He stalked to the open door and leaned against its frame. I looked at my hands, my hair swinging forward to curtain my face.

When the class broke into applause, I flinched. I'd forgotten where I was and that they were there.

I looked at Ash, visible to me but not to the rest of the class. He stood in profile, head thrown back, breathing through his mouth.

What had we done?

"Eden," Ms. Barrie said. I blinked at her. She motioned me over.

"Yes, ma'am?"

"Are you all right?" Her tone was quiet and concerned.

I nodded, not meeting her gaze.

"Go to your seat then." She turned and called, "Ash?"

Her voice sent a jolt through him. He ducked his head and turned back to the room.

I shuffled to my seat, slipped on the plaid shirt, and tried to convince myself that this grade had been worth the cost.

There was an assembly before lunch to ensure that students understood the perils of saturated fat. On our return from the auditorium, Mundy spewed a nonstop stream of consciousness, oblivious to my lack of participation.

"The MIM was fabulous. It seemed real."

I jammed my fists in my pockets and ignored the crowd, the noise, and Mundy. The scene hadn't been real. *It was fiction, people.* Jane Austen wrote it two hundred years ago. It was her premise. Her emotions. Ash and I had merely been the vessels.

Except it hadn't felt like pretend. The words just flowed, and some of the things we'd said had crossed the line.

"When Ash caught you with one hand and you hung on? That was intense. It's a wonder someone didn't tell you to get a room."

"Shut up, Mundy." My whole body ached. I didn't want to be here.

"Your dialog was perfect. I can hardly believe it was un-scripted."

"Stop."

"The bit about coward/trailer trash? Amazing. Your expressions were angry and hopeless at the same time. Academy Award performances."

"Shut the hell up."

She whirled around and looked uncertain. "What?"

I halted, staring at her with blazing eyes. "Could you try to tune in?"

"Wow, uh—"

"Ash and I said horrible things to each other, and I hated it."

"I didn't realize—"

"Now that you do, could you drop it?"

"Okay. Sorry." She gave me a pained smile. "If it helps, you looked stunning."

"*Mundy.*" I shook my head at her, annoyed but also relieved that she'd raised the other touchy subject. "The makeover was a bad idea, and I wish I hadn't let you talk me into it. For the rest of the year, it'll hang over me. I'll be stared at every day, while people wonder when I'll appear next in Heather's body. I don't want that kind of attention ever again. Got it?"

She nodded solemnly.

I exhaled a noisy breath, glad that was behind us, although she was right about something. I had felt angry and hopeless when he'd called me trailer trash, and it still gnawed at me. The MIM wasn't really over yet. I wanted to apologize to Ash, and I needed him to apologize to me.

"Ash is about to walk by."

I spun around and searched the crowd until I found him. It was clear that he'd seen me, for his gaze was focused carefully on the sidewalk. His Indian friends surrounded him on three sides, like a walking fortress. As they passed Mundy, he glanced my way, the tension in his face mirroring mine.

"Ash, we need to talk."

Everybody froze.

"I don't think that would be wise." His voice was tight.

Maybe not, but I wasn't backing down now. "Three p.m. today."

"I always have study group on Mondays."

"I know."

When he faced me, his friends closed ranks around him. There was a long silence. I kept my expression blank, unwilling for them to see how much this meant to me.

Upala murmured, "Let's go."

He shook his head, as if rousing from a dream. "Where?"

"Same place," I said, not wanting the others to know.

He gave one sharp nod, spun on his heel, and charged up the stone staircase leading to the building's side entrance. His entourage followed.

"Wow," Mundy said. "That was . . . bold."

I'd call it crazy, but it had to be done. Now, if he would just show up.

It was quiet in the park, too early for school kids to have gotten here yet and too late for babies needing naps.

The gazebo was empty, as I'd hoped. I plopped on the floor, my back against a pillar, sitting directly opposite the steps.

I'd walked. He had a car. How come I was here and he wasn't? Had he thought better of meeting with me?

I glanced at my arm. The scratches looked human-inflicted and painful. It was a good thing that Mundy had lent me her bracelet.

Closing my eyes, I tried to relax, weary beyond belief.

The slamming of a car door startled me awake. There was a minute of silence. A soft tread on the steps. He hesitated at the top, taking a moment for his eyes to adjust to the shade.

"Hi," I said.

"Hello." He crossed the space and dropped to the floor a couple of feet away. We both faced the entrance, staring at the trees that dotted the park.

"Ms. Barrie spoke to me on the way out of class," I said. "We'll get an A."

"I could've found that out tomorrow."

Anxiety rolled over me. His tone reflected the same dazed regret I felt. "I'm about to be honest with you, and I want you to be honest with me."

"We started that game earlier today."

Crap, he didn't have to make this any harder than it already was. "Please, Ash."

"Fine." He shifted uncomfortably.

"When I said no hard feelings, I lied."

"Got that."

"The MIM became personal."

"Like you said before, Ms. Barrie expected us to dig deep. We're both used to doing whatever it takes for our grades." His voice was tinged with bitterness. "I should've refused to say those things. It's not who I am."

"I don't think you're a coward."

His head turned until our gazes met. "I don't think you're trailer trash."

The comment made my eyes burn. We had to get through this, but it was tough. "You sure about that? Plenty of people do."

"Not me. You're too . . . complete."

It was a strange word, and I liked it a lot.

"I'm sorry." We said it in unison and looked away.

It grew quiet again, except for the sound of laughter in the distance. We didn't speak. Just sat there.

He stirred. I turned toward him and waited for him to turn toward me. He didn't.

Guess it would be left to me to keep this happy conversation flowing. "I haven't heard from Heather in over four years."

"Who?" He looked bewildered.

"My trashy bio mother."

He winced. "Do you know where she is?"

"She didn't leave a forwarding address." I shrugged. "The improv was more effective than anything we could've scripted."

"Agreed." He rose to his feet. "Is it okay if we never talk about this again?"

"Fine with me."

When he held out his hand, I grasped it tightly and let him pull me up.

Neither of us let go. His fingers stayed wrapped around mine. Warm. Strong. We stood there, inches apart, staring into each other's eyes.

"Eden, you are . . ."

What? I am . . . what?

"You're not what I imagined." He released my hand and gestured vaguely. "I'm glad you did this—cleared the air. It was good."

I nodded. The praise felt nice.

"Can I give you a ride home?"

I would accept his offer this time. In this heat, I didn't want to walk the mile to where Marnie worked. "Do you know the nursing home on the east side of town?"

"Sure." His smile was relaxed. "Let's go."

✦ 11 ✦

Ancient Formals

I pushed through the main entrance of the high school and halted at the top of the steps, yielding to a burst of optimism, especially on a day like today, with the weather hinting at autumn's approach. Mild temperature. Light breeze. Carolina blue sky with picture-perfect clouds.

It had been over a week since the MIM. Mundy's makeover hadn't stuck; that was too much effort. But Ash and I had hung onto civility, and I had a glimmer of hope about a scholarship that my father couldn't screw up.

I was feeling good.

Below me, on the front schoolyard, rested a wooden bench. A plaque proclaimed that it had been somebody's old Eagle Scout project. Remarkably, its softly weathered boards had remained relatively uncarved and ungraffitied since.

Mundy sat in the center of the bench, head bent over a book. I detoured in her direction.

"Hi," I said, and waited until she looked up. "Why are you here this late?"

"Waiting on my dad to take me home." She scooted over and patted the empty space next to her.

I plopped down. "What are you reading?"

"*Lord of the Flies.*"

"Why?"

"It was time." She flipped the book shut and slid it into her bag. "The homecoming dance is two weeks from Friday."

Oddly, the transition from an island full of malicious kids to a gym full of snarky classmates made perfect sense to me. "I update the master calendar on the high school web site. I know when dances take place."

"What do you plan to wear?"

Uh-oh. School dances and I didn't mix. "I'm not going."

"Why not?"

"Zero interest." I'd attended a dance with my friend Jordan our sophomore year and hated it from the moment I walked into the gym. It was loud, crowded, and stank of raging sweat.

"You'll go this year."

The confidence in her tone sent a tickle of wariness down my spine. "Why would I do that?"

"To prevent me from doing something inappropriate."

Not possible. There weren't enough hours in the day. "Like what?"

"I don't know, but I'm new. I'm bound to mess up if you're not there."

"You're bound to mess up whether I'm there or not."

"See, I knew it. You'll come." She tossed her head smugly.

That's not what I said. But Mundy was right. I would go, because I was uneasy about what she might do—and proud that she'd invited me. "You have other people you could hang out with at the dance. Why ask me?"

Her gratified expression faded into something more pensive. "I've been around a lot of different kids since I moved here. One thing they all have in common is how much they enjoy talking about their problems. Complaining has become a major-league sport. But their problems are so trivial compared to yours. Life could be crushing you, yet it doesn't. You have real reasons to complain, and you don't. That's what I want to be a part of."

I looked at the sky, blinking at the moisture stinging in my eyes. "Got it."

"Good." She gave a little laugh. "So we're going to the dance. What do kids here wear? Jeans?"

I'd given in with hardly a fight. "Girls wear dresses. Guys wear sports jackets."

"Great. Who will we dance with?"

I shook my head decisively. "I might show up, but I won't dance."

"Why not? Are you afraid no one will ask?"

"I don't fear things that will never happen."

"If you wear something strapless, guys will ask just to get a better look."

Holy crap. She never gave up. "I'm not letting a guy at this school get that close to me, on the dance floor or anywhere else."

A motorcycle rumbled to a stop in the parking lot. The biker, encased from head to toe in shiny black gear, looked our way. Mundy stood and gathered her things. "There's Cam. Gotta go." She squeezed my shoulder. "It's a date. We'll take my car, and you can sleep over afterwards at my house."

A whole night off? I hadn't had one of those since school started. "Sleep over?"

"It'll be fun. Okay?"

"Okay."

I got home from school as my father was walking out the front door, wrapping on a tool belt. "Hey," I said, stopping in surprise when he didn't move out of my way.

"Mr. Cooper wants to know if you could come in this weekend."

"What for?"

"He needs help with something he calls *quick stuff.*"

"You probably mean QuickBooks."

"Yeah."

I knew it well enough, but how much time could I spare? A few hours?

Dad caught my upper arm with his rough, thick fingers. "Please, Eden."

"Fine. Sure." What was this really about? Why did he care so much? Maybe he was struggling to keep himself together at work, and I was insurance. It would be worth finding out. "I could come in Saturday and see what he needs. But no promises, Dad. If it's complicated, he might need a professional."

He gave a sharp nod, released my arm, and stepped off the porch, cutting across the yard toward the center of the trailer park.

I entered the front door and shouted, "Marnie, where are you?"

"Back here," came the muffled reply.

I followed the direction of her voice and the scent of lemon-fresh cleaner. Her tiny butt was backing out of the bathroom.

"Have you quit your second job?"

She stood and stripped off rubber gloves. "I don't have enough to pay you back yet."

"So that would be a no."

She squeezed past me and disappeared into the pantry. When she returned, she carried a mop.

I blocked her path. "Please, Marnie. I care about you more than I care about the money."

"A few more weeks and I'll be good."

"And in the meantime, you put yourself in danger."

"There hasn't been a holdup there in over a year. I feel safe."

"No, you don't, so stop pretending."

Her smile flashed, then faded. "Thanks for worrying, sweetie. But really, it's okay." She nudged me out of the way and stopped in the bathroom entrance.

"I could come to the store with you on nights I'm not with the Fremonts."

"Not necessary." She stretched up to kiss my cheek. "You're a good daughter. Now, unless there's something else, I need to mop."

"I'm going to the homecoming dance." I waited for her reaction and got exactly what I expected.

"Oh, sweetie, that's wonderful. With Mundy?"

"Yeah." I should be pissed about being blackmailed into going, but I wasn't. More like resigned. Yet it did present a problem. "I don't have anything to wear."

"Can Mundy lend you something?"

I laughed. "Not unless she buys her dresses two sizes too big."

"When is it?"

"October third."

"A couple of weeks. I have an idea." Marnie dropped the mop and practically skipped to the master bedroom. Sifting through hangers in the closet, she pulled out a large floor-length garment bag. "Let's see what we have in here."

I didn't have to ask what was in the bag. It was her collection of ancient formals. One of my favorite activities as a little kid had been to put one on, slip into a pair of tacky pumps, and clop around our apartment.

Unfortunately, what was fun as a kid didn't feel fun anymore, especially since I was a big girl now and my stepmom was three inches shorter than me.

Marnie unzipped the bag and pulled out five gowns in different styles, lengths, and colors. *Ugly* styles, lengths, and colors.

I had a sick sensation in the pit of my stomach. "That gives me several choices," I said with all the enthusiasm I could muster. Which wasn't much.

"Pick whatever you like."

I reached for the best dress, a pale pink gown in satin and lace, and held it up. A vague memory tickled. "Where have I seen this one?"

"I wore it to my wedding."

Oh, yeah. An image swam around in my brain and slowly sharpened. Dad, Boone, and I had stepped off an elevator at the courthouse. Marnie had waited there in a magical pink dress with a white rose tucked behind one ear. She'd looked like a fairy princess to me.

"Dad brought flowers."

"They were pretty."

I'd been in kindergarten. Only the four of us attended. Not even Marnie's family showed up. Dad had carried a big floral box. It held a bouquet of white rosebuds for Marnie, a wrist corsage for me, and two boutonnieres for the guys.

The ceremony hadn't lasted long. Afterwards, Dad took us to

the fanciest restaurant he could afford in Wilmington. We sat by a window overlooking the water, and I spilled ketchup on the tablecloth.

"Do you have any pictures?"

"No. We forgot that little detail." Marnie took the hanger from my hands and held the dress against me. "Do you want to wear this one? I could alter the bodice."

"It's perfect the way it is." I didn't understand why she would be willing to cut up her wedding dress, and I wouldn't let her. I pulled out the cocktail gown that Marnie wore to fancy parties. "Plum is more my color." The halter dress included a beaded jacket, which would get left behind.

"I don't know if it'll fit right," she said, her forehead creased in concentration. "Go and try it on."

When I returned from the bathroom, she zipped me up while I stared in the mirror. The halter top was snug, and the hem was higher than I'd ever worn with a dress. "I don't know."

She tugged at the seams along my hips. "You have a nice butt."

"Uh . . ."

"I could make the bodice strapless."

"No." I scowled at her. "You know me better than that."

"You have great boobs, and you're always hiding them behind big shirts."

"This conversation is so wrong."

She laughed. "You'll be hot."

I wrapped my arms around her and gave her a hug. "Thanks, Marnie. I'll wear the dress, no changes."

She nodded against my neck.

· 12 ·

Stark Lines

This assignment had sounded easy enough: *sketch your hand*. Then I tried it and learned something I'd never noticed before. A human hand had a lot of joints and skin folds.

I frowned at the sheet of art paper lying on the table before me. Something wasn't quite right yet. I concentrated on my left hand. The nails gleamed like tiny half moons along my fingertips. I added them to the drawing.

Dr. Holt stopped behind me. "Tell me about the hand, Eden. What does it want to say?"

The question puzzled me. Could drawings talk? A protest leapt to my lips, then died away at the encouragement on his face. I stared at the page and listened. The hand lay there in stark lines, muted and clenched.

My throat ached. I had a lot to be frustrated about right now. "It's pissed."

"Yes, it is. Nice work." He turned to Mundy. "Let's see how you're doing."

I looked at hers and winced. If she spun the paper upside-down, she'd have a passable cow's udder.

"So, uh, Mundy. What's your hand saying?"

"You can't tell?"

"Moo?" Dr. Holt clamped a hand over his mouth, which did nothing to hide his laughter. With a happy snort, she punched him in his side.

I looked around the room. Nobody looked up. Nobody cared. Obviously, Tiffany got the word out.

As we were leaving class, he called her over. I glanced back once more before heading to chemistry. They whispered in rapid-fire dialogue, their heads bent over her phone.

Mundy caught up with me at the lockers. "Are you busy this afternoon? I thought we could do something together while Cam attends a staff meeting."

"Sure. I have the car today. I need to get a few items for Mar-nie at the drugstore. We could go to Charlie's Diner afterwards for coffee."

"Good. Let me text him where to pick me up."

After school, I drove to the courthouse square and pulled into the last shady parking space. Mundy headed to Charlie's while I did my shopping.

It was breathlessly hot for mid-September. I hurried past Cooper's Hardware Store, stepped over a couple of dogs panting on the sidewalk, and waved at the two retired farmers sitting behind them.

It was cool inside Pettit's Pharmacy. I went straight for Marnie's favorite shampoo, which was heavily marked down. After grabbing a bottle, I pointed my cart toward the section with household cleaners.

Looking down one aisle, I spotted Sawyer. We'd known each

other since the summer before first grade when we played Mr. and Mrs. Peacock in "Noah's Ark" in Vacation Bible School. But that wasn't why I liked him. For my eighth birthday, I'd invited my entire second-grade class to my party. Only five kids came, and one of them had been Sawyer. I hadn't forgotten.

He was standing in the middle of the aisle, staring in bewilderment at the shelves, a shopping list dangling from one hand.

I stopped beside him. "Hey. What's up?"

He gestured toward the array of products in front of him. The feminine-hygiene products.

"Do you need help?" I smothered a laugh.

He groaned. "I didn't know there were so many kinds."

"For your mom?" At his nod, I lifted his hand to scan the list. "Let's see what she wants." Mrs. Atkinson had given fairly explicit instructions, leaving nothing to chance. I located the correct package.

"*Sawyer.*"

We both whipped around. Three of Sawyer's baseball teammates descended on us. Horrified, he glanced at the object in my hand before shooting me a pleading look. I tossed the offending package into my cart.

"What's happening, man?" one of the buddies asked as they all went through their hand-slapping, fist-bumping routine.

"Hey, man. Nothing much . . ." Sawyer nodded at me as he took off with them.

He was still talking with his buddies when I walked outside. As I passed by, I stumbled and dropped one of my bags—whose contents, naturally, spilled on the sidewalk. Sawyer, ever the gentleman, rushed to my side.

"Here, let me help." He crammed my stuff—and a five-dollar

bill—back into my shopping bag, except that one particular item had somehow transferred to his.

"Thanks," I said, loud enough for Sawyer's friends to hear.

"You're welcome." Glancing over his shoulder, he leaned closer to whisper, "I owe you one."

"I think you do." It was a debt I never expected to collect.

Mundy sat in a booth in the diner's big picture window, hands wrapped around a cup of tea. A mug of coffee awaited me. On the tabletop between us rested a large slice of Charlie's most popular pie: lemon chess.

She eyed it suspiciously. "The waitress said you like that."

Norah knew me well. I'd worked here before getting the job with the Fremonts. "You'll like it too."

"What's that crispy stuff on top?"

"Cornmeal."

"The waitress said you'd want a cup of coffee with that."

"She's right."

Mundy watched me take my first bite before asking, "Did I see you talking to Sawyer Atkinson?"

"I ran into him at the drugstore."

"You're almost smiling. Why? Do you like him?"

"Well, yeah."

"Normal 'like' or more than that?"

"Normal 'like.'" My almost-smile turned into a full smile. "Sawyer's a great guy."

"I would've guessed that a baseball jock would be the last person you'd say that about."

The smile disappeared as I looked out the window. I didn't want to have this conversation. "Someone told you about Murray."

"Yeah."

"What did you hear?"

"What do you want me to know?"

Down the street, I could see Sawyer with his teammates as he leaned against his restored Vette. "Murray asked me out. Eventually I said yes. We spent twenty minutes together. Done."

"What happens on a twenty-minute date?"

"It wasn't a date, because I ended it before it began. He drove me to a truck stop and parked in the farthest corner of the lot. When I asked him what was going on, he unzipped his jeans and told me to pay in advance. I, um, declined the offer." Remembered humiliation heated my face. Reluctantly, I met her gaze. "Then I got out, called Marnie from inside the truck stop, and waited until she picked me up."

"That isn't how his version of the story goes."

"Not surprising." I frowned into my coffee. "Does his version include the part where I punched him in the nuts?"

There was a snort of laughter, quickly choked off. "He left out that detail."

I took a sip from the mug, warmed by the one satisfying memory of that horrible night. I'd been naïve to accept. Naïve to go. Naïve to hesitate long enough for him to grab my ponytail and encourage my head in his preferred direction. But his scream of pain? Yeah, that salvaged some of my self-respect.

"Why him, Eden?"

If only she knew how often I'd asked that of myself. "He moved here our freshmen year. I thought that might make him different. Might make him worth taking a chance on. He was persistent, so I agreed." He'd started his campaign in midspring. I was alone and tired and—

"When did you find out it was a dare?"

"The next week at school."

"Was it Sawyer?"

"Who dared Murray?" At her nod, I shook my head emphatically. "When Sawyer found out, he got royally pissed and ripped into the whole baseball team about it. The talk died down after that."

She frowned as she dipped the tines of her fork in the pie and took a tiny bite. Then another and another.

Yeah, I knew she'd like it.

"Mmmm." She licked the fork and pointed it at me. "Do you get along with your stepmom?"

How did Mundy make the transition from Murray to my stepmom? Had his confrontation with me at the Labor Day picnic become a thing too? "Marnie and I get along very well."

"So why do you call her by her first name?"

"I don't. Her name is actually Marlene. We're not sure how my five-year-old baby brain created Marnie, but it appears to be a compromise between Marlene and Mommy." I pointed my spoon back at her. Mundy's turn. "You don't use Cam's last name. Is your dad still in the picture?"

"He was a helicopter pilot in the military. He died when I was two. I don't remember him."

Now I felt like an ass. "Sorry."

"Thanks." Her brow creased. "Cam's been in my life so long, he *is* my dad, but I feel like I should keep some link to my father."

"Sure." This conversation hadn't been all that cheery. Might as well keep the drama going. "Heather called Marnie before they'd ever met and told her she could have us."

"That's awful."

"Yes, it is." I might not share DNA with Marnie, but she was a way better parent than either of my biological ones.

When her phone buzzed, Mundy took a quick look at the screen and then slid from her side of the booth. "Gotta go. Cam's here. I've already paid the bill."

"Mundy. Really." I was relieved. Dessert wasn't in the budget.

"Don't want to hear it."

I nodded and pulled the pie over.

Mundy threw her arms around me in a tight hug. "Heather did the right thing." She turned and ran from the diner.

"Yeah," I said. "I know."

· 13 ·

Enthusiastic Vigilance

It was homecoming week. Energy buzzed around the school. Teachers were bowing to the excitement by keeping the homework light. That was fine with me.

Monday evening I drove to the Fremonts' house, parked the car at the curb, and let myself in. Since it was Mrs. Fremont's day off, the kitchen and den were spotless. Kurt and Marta were in their rooms when I strolled by.

Mrs. Fremont stood in the master bedroom, frowning at her reflection in a full-length mirror.

"Are you ready for your big date?" I asked her.

She blew out a nervous breath. "I guess." With a quick turn sideways, she sucked in her gut and peered at the mirror again. "Do I look fat in these jeans?"

"Do you want the truth?" I laughed when she rolled her eyes. "You look gorgeous."

"Thanks." She walked into her bathroom.

"Would this be a bad time to ask you for a favor?"

"What do you need?"

"A recommendation. I'll need one from my employer when I start applying for scholarships."

Her head popped out again. "I don't like to think about you going to college. How will we live without you?"

My smile froze. I didn't like to think about that part either.

She nodded and disappeared back into the bathroom. "I'd be delighted to write you a recommendation."

"Thanks. I'll let you know the details later." I crossed to the door in time to see her apply lip gloss. I was ready to be protective over her first post-divorce foray into the dating scene. "So, tell me about your date. How old is the guy?"

"Thirty-seven."

"Where'd you meet him?"

"At the hospital."

"Ah. Another medical professional."

She smiled. "Maybe."

"Sounds promising."

"It is."

There was a little boy shriek from the hallway. "Eden, why are you here? Mommy doesn't work tonight."

I looked at his mother with a questioning look. She shook her head. The kids didn't know.

"Well, Kurt—"

He slammed into me, arms locking around my hips. "Did you come to have supper with me?"

Yay. He'd handed me a great solution. "I did. I was in the mood for McDonald's, and I thought you and your sister might want to come along."

"What about Mommy?"

"It'll be more special with the three of us."

"Come on. Let's tell Marta."

I had both kids buckled in and was about to slip behind the wheel of their SUV when Mrs. Fremont poked her head out the garage door. "Eden, can you come over a week from Saturday for a couple of hours? I have a staff meeting at the hospital that morning."

Mrs. Fremont's boss held a lot of meetings. It didn't seem fair to call people in on their days off, particularly when many lived a long commute away, but Mrs. Fremont never complained. "I can do that. What time?"

"Nine-thirty?"

"Nine-thirty is good."

"Mom?" Marta called.

"Uh-huh?" Mrs. Fremont stole a look at her wristwatch.

"Do you think you and I could do something special that Saturday? Eden could stay longer with Kurt."

Mrs. Fremont exchanged glances with me. I nodded.

She looked at her daughter. "What did you have in mind?"

"I don't know. Whatever you want."

"How about manicures?"

"Oh," Marta said with huff of excitement. "Manicures would be awesome."

It was a date.

On the drive to the restaurant, Marta bubbled happily about her upcoming event with her mom. Kurt hummed and kicked his car seat. It didn't take long, though, for the conversation to switch to food. Our selections engrossed us.

McDonald's was packed. After picking up our order, we located a table near the playground. Marta snuggled on the bench beside me while Kurt sat across from us, his back to the craziness.

I stirred my yogurt parfait while surveying the rest of the dining area. I'd almost completed my sweep when I spotted Ash. He held a tray with a serious amount of food and two drinks. A little boy waited beside him, clutching his belt.

There weren't many places left to sit. His gaze slipped past mine, then returned. I waved him over and pointed at the empty table next to us.

"We have room," I said when he got within earshot.

"All right," the little boy yelled and climbed onto the seat closest to Kurt. "I'm Raj, and I'm four."

"Hi, Raj, I'm Eden, and these are my friends Kurt and Marta."

Like me, Ash sat on the bench side of the table, his hip nearly bumping mine. I scooted over to give him more room.

It had been three weeks since the MIM. We were hardly friends now, but the peace had held so far. I'd even spoken up a couple of times in project-team discussions to agree with what they were doing. He'd noticed my attempts to "collaborate," if the quick smiles I'd received were any indication.

Kurt was glaring at Ash. "Who is that guy?"

I met Kurt's gaze calmly. He didn't like change or strangers all that much unless he'd had some advance notice. "Ash and I go to the same school."

"Why is he here?"

"Uncle Ash is taking care of me tonight," Raj said. "Why are you here?"

"Eden wanted McDonald's food."

Ash choked on a laugh as he tore into an apple pie.

Kurt turned sideways on his seat and stared at a wall while he ate his hamburger. Raj became consumed with ripping open ketchup packages and squeezing the contents onto a flimsy paper napkin.

"Eden," Raj said in his piping voice, "my uncle told his friend Dev that you have a great rack. Where is it? I want to see."

I snorted sweet tea up my nose, then grabbed a pile of napkins and held them to my mouth. It did nothing to suppress my laughter.

Ash dropped his flaming face into his hands.

The kids watched us in astonishment.

I nudged him in the side with my elbow. "Me too, Ash. Where is it?"

"Please," he hissed.

It was hard to regain control. Normally I would be pissed by a comment like that, but I couldn't be when it was Raj who'd said it. He was an adorable kid, asking what he wanted to know. It was one of the things I'd learned to love about babysitting.

"Uncle Ash, can I play now?"

"Yes." He said it so fast that I started laughing again.

Raj tapped Kurt on the shoulder. "Wanna come?"

Kurt, his eyes huge, looked at me for guidance.

"Go ahead."

His lower lip rolled out. "My dad says that only little kids are supposed to use the playground at McDonald's. He says I'm too old."

Mr. Fremont was such a jerk. Much as I'd like to smack the man, I wouldn't contradict a statement by a parent, which meant I'd have to work around it. "You could be the playground monitor."

"What's that?"

"If anyone breaks a rule or gets hurt, you come and tell me."

"I would be good at that job."

"I agree."

He pushed Raj off the seat. The two boys raced for the

playground. Ash stood and circled around to the other side of his table to clean his nephew's glops of ketchup.

Marta cupped a hand around her mouth and whispered in my ear, "That guy is cute."

"You think so?" I whispered back.

Her face scrunched uncertainly. "Don't you?"

"Oh, yes. Definitely."

She beamed at him. He blinked and smiled back.

"Thanks for inviting us over," he said.

"You're welcome." Marta hopped off her seat. "May I help you bus the table? I know how."

"That would be great."

I left the two of them to the chore and went to check on the boys. Raj frowned at a slide while Kurt maintained enthusiastic vigilance over the three other toddler occupants of the playground.

"Done, Eden," Marta sang out. "Time to play beauty shop."

I returned to the bench and waited dutifully for her to set up. While she unzipped her sequined purse, Ash flopped down beside me.

"Beauty shop?" he asked.

"She loves to style my hair." It seemed a simple enough way to make her happy. All I had to do was rest while she braided, curled, or threaded ribbons through my hair. There was something quite relaxing about the process.

We didn't talk. I sat sideways on the bench while Marta knelt behind me, brushing my hair with extreme care. Ash watched the production intently, craning to see better as she attached sparkly clips about my head.

"How do they stay in?" he asked.

With a shy smile, Marta held one out to him. He flicked it open and closed a few times, his forehead creased in concentration. "It's well designed," he said, handing the clip back to her.

She nodded. "And pretty."

"That too." He grinned.

She sighed happily, which I completely understood. He had a dazzling smile. Such perfect white teeth.

"I'm letting Eden borrow the silver one on Friday."

His gaze met mine. "Are you going to homecoming?"

"Yeah," I said.

"With a *friend*," Marta added.

"I didn't think you . . ." He paused.

There was surprise in his voice, and a trace of something else. Irritation, maybe. "I don't usually go, but Mundy is insisting."

He nodded and looked away, his eyes focusing on something over my shoulder.

Raj and Kurt ran up and skidded to a stop beside us. "We're done," they said in unison.

Kurt added, "Too crowded now."

Ash made a soft grunt and rose. "Time for us to go."

"Wait," Raj said. He leaned on my leg. "I've never touched yellow hair before. Can I touch yours?"

The request echoed through me, honest and innocent. "Of course, you may."

"Raj—" Ash's voice sounded choked.

"It's okay," I said.

The little guy petted my hair. "It feels the same, but it doesn't look the same."

Marta held out the brush. "Want to try?"

"Yeah." Raj gestured for me to sit straighter and then stepped between my knees. "I'll try not to scratch your ear."

"Thank you."

Raj brushed with precise strokes, his lips pursed.

Ash shuffled his feet. "Raj, we have to leave."

His nephew nodded and handed back the brush. "How did I do?"

"You were quite gentle, and you didn't get near my ear," I said as I stood too.

Ash caught Raj's hand in his. "Thanks again." With a nod, he wove through the tables, his nephew skipping to keep up.

Kurt scowled. "I'm not sure if I like the big guy." He punched me in the hip. "What about you, Eden?"

I nodded, my eyes tracking Ash all the way until he disappeared through an exit. "I'm not sure either."

· 14 ·

Flame Out

Mundy decided to skip the homecoming game. She claimed that she didn't like football. I suspected it was more about not trusting me to try hard enough with my appearance. While everyone else was screaming their heads off at the stadium, we were at her house. Preparation, for her, was serious business.

After a decadently long shower, I returned to her bedroom, awaiting the second Mundy Makeover of my life. I'd been in her room fifteen minutes when the door burst open. A little boy, dressed in footed superhero pajamas, raced to my side and asked, "Who are you?"

"Eden." I remained still, careful not to move while Mundy was brandishing a curling iron near my head. "Who are you?"

"Destin." He crawled onto my lap.

Boldness, apparently, was a genetic trait. I gingerly slipped my arms around him and adjusted him into a position more comfortable for me and safer for him. His hair tickled my chin, damp and baby-shampoo sweet.

"Destin," Mundy said from somewhere behind us, "don't wiggle. I might burn Eden's scalp."

"Obey your sister," I said in a loud whisper. He giggled.

Another face appeared in the mirror, a much older and nearly as beautiful version of Mundy. The woman had the same startling blue eyes and shiny black hair, except hers hung in a thick braid to her waist.

"Hi, Mrs. Cruz-Holt," I said with absolute certainty even though we'd never met.

"Please call me Clarissa." She squinted at my hands. "Are your nails painted?"

"No, ma'am."

"I'll be right back."

They didn't ask permission in this family. They simply did things. Another genetic trait.

Destin slid off my lap and followed his mother out the door. Only a small portion of my neck was burned in the process.

When they returned, Clarissa had a half-dozen bottles of polish and a small stool. Destin had nothing but suppressed energy.

My transformation progressed at a steady pace. Mundy did most of the work, comments flowing in a never-ending stream. Clarissa perched beside me, monitoring her daughter's efforts while painting my fingernails purple.

After patting Marta's silver clip into place at the back of my head, Mundy knelt in front of me and scrutinized my face. With a pleased smile, she nodded. "You're done. Sit here and let your nails dry. I'll change." She disappeared into her walk-in closet.

When she came out again, there was an excited flush to her cheeks. She wore a silky emerald dress that stopped at midthigh, with long, tight sleeves and a mandarin collar. The dress looked prim until she spun around. The back was nothing but sheer lace from shoulders to waist.

I gasped. "Sh—"

Her mother clapped her hand around my mouth.

Mundy looked at me wide-eyed. "I'm completely covered."

"Not exactly how I'd describe it," I said through her mother's fingers. Clarissa laughed and backed away.

The other girls at the dance would have plenty of skin on display, except closer to the slutty end of the spectrum. Mundy would stand out in a good way.

"We have to leave soon. It's your turn to dress." She sat on the edge of her bed and slipped her feet into bronze heels.

I headed into the closet to slip on Marnie's plum dress and waited as Clarissa zipped the back. Closing my eyes, I concentrated on the feel of the fabric, which was wonderful. Cool and sleek. If I looked as good as the satin felt, it wouldn't be a miserable night. I still planned to blend into the shadows, but at least I wouldn't look bad back there.

I walked out and twirled before my friend. Her nose wrinkled.

"You have to lose the ballet flats."

I glanced down. They were fine. It was more important that my feet didn't hurt. "Why?"

"They're ballet flats." She exchanged disturbed glances with her mother. "What do you have?"

"Let me check."

When she returned, Clarissa showed me a pair of pumps. They were silver, peep-toe, and had four-inch heels.

I shook my head. "Absolutely not."

She held out a second pair in satiny black. They looked like the kind of shoes that ballroom dancers wore. The heel was higher than I liked but not terrible. I slipped them on and felt pretty. "These'll be fine."

We were ready.

We still arrived late.

After the crisp freedom of the night, the gym yawned like a mildewy, sweaty barn. The dance committee must've saved the ticket revenue for a future event because they'd spent nothing on this one. There were no decorations anywhere. No streamers or fake ivy or twinkling white lights. Refreshments had been dispensed with, too. The committee had paid for music, a hard-to-miss part of a dance. All other expenses had been spared.

A few couples stomped in the center of the gym to rap music. Everyone else clustered in small groups on the sides, in the stands, or against the walls.

Mundy and I found a spot on the bleachers. While I squirmed around, trying to determine how to sit in this dress without flashing people, she focused on the dance floor.

"Hardly anyone's dancing."

"I'm sure the DJ knows what he's doing."

"People should be willing to try something new." Her lips twisted.

"We've only been here for five minutes. Give it a chance." I looked away, hoping she would drop it.

The next song switched to country, which drove a complete change on the dance floor.

She leapt to her feet. "Come on. Let's go."

"To do what?"

"Dance." She clearly didn't care whether I went with her, because she sauntered onto the gym floor and stopped a few feet apart from the crowd, making her more noticeable. With flapping arms, she twitched in her own little universe, totally out of rhythm with the music.

If I'd been guessing, I would've expected her to be a competent dancer. Instead, she was bad—so bad we couldn't even laugh at her. A dancing Mundy Cruz was a horrific train wreck we had no choice but to gape at.

This was my fault. I should've punctured her tires and saved us all the grief.

I couldn't let her stay out there by herself, but if I joined her? The thought made me shudder. I had to find Mundy a dance partner, but who?

Above me on the bleachers, Ash's entourage sat in a clump off to themselves, watching Mundy like everyone else. Except Ash. He stared at me.

Why was he here? I wouldn't have thought that dances were his thing unless . . .

Ash was the secretary of the Student Council. He had to be here, which explained why his friends had come, too. Could I ask him to help me?

Nope. I wasn't asking Ash Gupta for anything.

Who else? There weren't many people that I could imagine helping me. I didn't want to be in anyone's debt.

Debt!

Where was Sawyer Atkinson?

I spotted him under a basketball goal, shoulder to shoulder with Tiffany, surrounded by a bunch of other popular kids, staring at my friend in fascination. Yeah, I'd found my solution. Sawyer was one of the few guys at the school who could dance with me and have no repercussions. He was so amazingly popular that everyone would overlook it.

Tiffany would be pissed off, but that didn't matter anymore. I had to give this a try.

My footsteps slowed as I got near him. Murray was there too, and he spotted me first. Maybe I should keep walking and pretend I hadn't come over here on purpose.

"Eden," he said in a way that made my skin crawl.

Sawyer elbowed him out of the way. "Enough, Fielder." It had an electric effect on Murray as well as the rest of the group. They turned as a unit.

When I stopped, Sawyer drew closer to me with a smile. "Hey."

"Hey." I smiled back nervously. Now that I was here, could I actually ask him? I'd feel like a complete fool if he said no in front of all of these people. "I need a favor."

"How can I help?"

Before I could respond, Tiffany stepped between us as she made an exaggerated study of my dress. "Nice color. Reminds me of the dress that Marlene wears to weddings."

I glared at her. Had she really used Marnie to score against me? Yeah, not getting away with that. My mouth said, "Thanks." My eyes said, "Bitch."

Tiffany grasped Sawyer's arm and pressed her cheek against the sleeve of his sports jacket. "Is Mundy your date?"

"At least I have one."

She went rigid. The others laughed.

I looked at Sawyer, took a deep breath, and held out my hand. "Dance?"

Without hesitating a second, he pulled free of Tiffany and linked his fingers through mine. "Thanks for rescuing me."

While her face burned with humiliation, the laughter continued. I didn't have a chance to see more, because Sawyer was dragging *me* onto the floor.

Even though he'd always been nice to me, I'd heard that Sawyer, as captain of the baseball team, could be harsh on the field. This was the first time I'd seen that side of him in action. I almost felt sorry for Tiffany. Almost.

Once we reached the crowd in the center, he launched into some moves that looked really good. I swayed beside him, positioning myself between him and Mundy, so that it seemed like the three of us were together. Before much longer, a couple of his teammates appeared near us with their girlfriends. Mission accomplished.

When the song ended, he smiled down at me. "That was an easy favor."

"You're not done yet." I clutched his wrist and closed the distance to a still-twitching Mundy. "I need you to dance with her."

"Shit. I don't know—"

"Feminine hygiene," I said.

The DJ announced the next selection. A love song from the eighties. A mass of students surged to the floor.

Shaking his head in resignation, he touched her shoulder.

She stopped twitching and blinked dazedly. "What?"

He offered his hand. "Dance with me?"

She considered him coolly before transferring her gaze to me. "Did you put him up to this?"

"I did."

"Why?"

"You're so bad, you're embarrassing me."

"Why not ask me to leave the floor? I'll still be a bad dancer with him around."

"He's good enough for both of you."

Sawyer crossed his arms. "Do you ladies need me to give you some privacy?"

She ignored him. "I'm trying to get everyone to stretch their boundaries."

"It's a stretch to imagine you and Sawyer together."

"Why?"

"You're not his type."

Irritation sparkled in her eyes. She wrapped her hands behind his neck and pulled him toward her.

"Whoa. Careful," he said, smiling as his fingers splayed against her lace-covered back.

"He's not my type either," she murmured and laid her head on his shoulder.

Right on cue, the music swelled and slowed. The lights dimmed. Couples merged into one.

Except for me. Oh, yes. Having relinquished my dance partner, I now found myself alone in the center of the dance floor.

Did I mention *alone*?

A voice spoke behind me. "Eden."

I glanced over my shoulder. Ash stood there, looking completely hot in a black dress shirt and black pants. Instead of smiling, he brooded at me, which was completely hot too. "Are you here to save me?"

He didn't answer—just held open his arms. I stepped into them and allowed myself to be pressed to his chest. The fabric of his shirt felt silky beneath my cheek.

For the moment, I would go with this. Out here, with a wistful song and other swaying couples, there was no room for the emotions that should have had me pushing him away.

I couldn't gauge what kind of dancer he was. After all, how much skill does it take to hug someone and shuffle back and forth? But it was nice. My first slow dance, and it was with Ash Gupta.

The music ended, but he didn't pull away and neither did I. "Ash?" Upala asked.

We both looked to the side. She and Dev were standing next to us, staring pointedly at Ash. The three of them exchanged glances for several seconds. He shook his head at them, looked down, and settled me more firmly in his arms. Another love song started.

Dev and Upala moved together stiffly, hovering nearby, their faces wary.

I was content where I was, leaning into Ash, feet barely moving. His hands lowered from my waist to my hips.

What was happening? This was me and Ash.

I raised my gaze to his. He stared down at me, his expression fierce and hungry. Shivering, I broke away, hungry too for something I couldn't name.

The music faded. A microphone squawked and the DJ said, "We're taking a break. Back in ten."

I gave Ash a hesitant smile, because he was looking at me in a way I'd never been looked at before and I didn't know what to do with it. Shouldn't I just leave? I glanced around for Mundy. It was her turn to rescue me.

"Ready?" Dev prompted Ash, gesturing toward the bleachers and their group.

Ash and I followed his two friends from the dance floor. But when we reached the side, his hand remained glued to my waist, holding me next to him.

"Be right there," he said to the other couple, his voice firm.

They frowned at him and then rejoined the rest of the entourage.

I looked up at him, puzzled by everything that had happened in the past few minutes. Why hadn't he bolted yet? Why hadn't I? "Your friends hate this, don't they?"

"They think—" His lips clamped shut.

Reality twisted in my gut. I knew what they thought. "They think you're a hero for reaching into the gutter and pulling me out, but that you're overdoing it."

"Yeah."

His agreement stung, but dishonesty would've stung more. "Sorry, but tonight you have to share the rescuer honors with Sawyer."

"Eden. That's not the reason I did it."

"Okay, why?"

"I wanted to dance with you."

A sweet thrill ignited inside me, only to flame out at the look of utter torment on his face. He hated whatever it was he wanted from me. That hurt. "How convenient that I gave you an excuse to hide behind."

His head snapped back. "Crap."

"Ooh, *crap*. Now there's an edgy word."

"Why do you say things like that?"

"I *think* things like this all the time. Be glad you got to hear it."

"Right. Thanks." Jamming his fists into his pockets, he turned away.

"Ash?"

He paused, shoulders stiff.

There was something going on and if I let him leave, I would lose the chance to learn what it was. "Why did you want to dance with me?"

He shook his head, once, twice, as if he were arguing with himself. "During the whole time I've known you, you've never let anyone get near you, but that's changed recently. You've allowed me to see more, and I thought . . ." He took a sudden step into my personal space, tension crackling off him in waves. "You look incredibly beautiful tonight, and you seem open, like maybe you wouldn't mind being touched. I want to be the guy you let in," he said in a rush, as if the admission pissed him off. His gaze drifted to the halter of my dress before sliding up to focus on my mouth.

What did *that* mean? Did he wonder what it would be like to kiss me?

I looked at his mouth and wondered the same thing myself. If we were somewhere private, would I want to kiss Ash?

Wait, dammit. What was wrong with me? He ignored my existence most of the time. He might ruin my best shot at Carolina. What kind of idiot was I to put *kiss* and *Ash* in the same sentence?

I had to leave before I didn't recognize myself anymore. "I need to find Mundy."

"Will you go out with me?"

I froze.

Okay. Rewind that. What? "Did you just ask me for a date?"

"Yes." He stood there unsmiling, his jaw so tense that it looked like it might crack.

I gaped at him, shocked and amazed and terrified. This was a guy who'd only dated two girls to my knowledge, both from his "ethnic clique." His circle of friends kept to themselves at school and hung out with no one else when they weren't. How did he go from being that exclusive to dancing with me and asking me out, practically overnight? It didn't make sense. "Is this a joke?"

"I wouldn't joke about asking you out."

Whoa. It was the MIM all over again. The trailer trash girl and the rich, beautiful boy in front of everyone—except this time it was a gym full of students and they couldn't know what we were saying.

Or could they? Was I being too trusting? Did some of them already know? Like his friends?

What a sickening thought. Could this be another dare?

Please. I didn't want that to be true. Not from Ash. He was a good guy. Wasn't he?

No, I couldn't fall for it. Ash and Eden dating? It was . . . impossible. "I don't think so, Ash. Not interested."

He closed his eyes briefly and gave a sharp nod. "My mistake. Sorry I bothered you." He stalked away and melted into the crowd.

· 15 ·

A Complete Revelation

Saturday at the Cruz-Holt house was calmer than I expected. When Mundy and I finally got up, the rest of the Holts had left on unspecified errands. We had the whole place to ourselves.

By noon, we were sitting in the living room, with hot, sweet tea and still-warm, frosted, homemade cinnamon rolls awaiting us on the coffee table.

I burrowed deeper into their burgundy velvet sofa. Mundy's family was living in Grampa Holt's monster house. It was listed on the historic register, with verandas and twelve-foot ceilings and rooms decorated in stark but comfortable IKEA chic.

My eyelids drifted down. Since I never had a morning off, I was content to lounge around, stuff my face, and stay quiet. Mundy, of course, was not.

"Do you want your toenails purple or silver?"

I licked cream cheese frosting from my finger. Yum. "Any other options?"

Silence greeted my question. Had I discovered a way to shut

her up? If only her silence weren't so obnoxious. I glanced at the other end of the couch. She scowled.

Okay, whatever. "Purple."

She hauled one of my feet on her lap and unscrewed the top off the bottle of polish. "Eden?"

"Hmmm?"

"We need a plan."

"For what?"

"To get you a second chance with Ash."

Hadn't we completed this same discussion around two a.m.? "Do you have an off switch?"

"No." She laughed while holding my pinky toe in a viselike grip.

I'd wait until she was done. No reason to distract her at such a key moment.

With a flourish, she recapped the bottle and relaxed into the cushions. "One foot done."

I wiggled my toes. Not too shabby. "What's the point when it'll soon be too cold to wear sandals?"

"You'll feel different with painted nails."

"Right."

"You will. It makes you bolder." Her eyes widened meaningfully. "Bold enough to ask Ash out on a date."

"It was a joke."

She shook her head. "Don't think so."

After hours of Mundy wearing me down, I didn't believe it either. "How can you be sure?"

"He's better than that."

She was right. He was one of the good guys. But maybe . . .

"Charity?"

"No. Going out with Eden Moore would be too risky for it to be charity."

"Whoa, Mundy. Don't hold back on my account."

"Listen to me. I know what I'm talking about. Ash likes you."

I tried to take that in and couldn't make it fit. "I don't think I should go out with him." Which would be why I'd refused him the night before. Mundy and I had covered both facts numerous times since midnight.

"You should." She smiled back at me from the other end of the couch. "Now that you've had time to think it through, admit the truth."

Like I knew what the truth was. My brain was so noisy and opinionated that it drowned out my heart. "Which is . . . ?"

She moved my finished foot out of the way and gripped the other one. "You like Ash Gupta back."

Did I? The way she meant?

I propped my head on the armrest, stared at the ornate brass light fixture above us, and thought about what it had felt like to be around him last night. I'd liked dancing in his arms and the touch of his hands. Would it have been the same with any guy, or was it important that the guy had been Ash?

Dancing with Sawyer had been gentle fun. Dancing with Ash had been a complete revelation.

"We're both fighting for the Peyton Scholarship, and I want him to lose."

"You're overthinking this." She shook her head at me, as if lecturing a child. "Pretend that you're not rivals. Let's list some reasons for you to go out with him."

"Like what?"

"He's hot."

"Shallow, yet true."

"He's smart."

"Intelligence is the problem. We wouldn't be competing if he were average."

"He's rich enough to spend money on you."

I laughed. "I have nothing to compare that to."

Triumph gleamed in her eyes. "It's your turn to list something."

"It was nice of him to rescue me on the dance floor."

"See, four reasons. That's three more than most of us care about."

Eden and Ash. On a date. It was crazy. "I still can't believe he asked. His friends would be horrified. And his parents. And mine."

"I can understand why his parents would hate you . . ."

"Thanks."

". . . but why would yours hate him?"

"He's Hindu." I hoped she hadn't notice the hesitation. It was more than religion. My dad would hate for me to date an Asian, especially Indian and especially Ash. My dad lost his job at the power plant when a director converted 10 percent of the jobs to robots. Ash's father had been that director. "We'd have to keep it a secret."

"This is so Romeo and Juliet. I love it."

"How comforting, considering how well their story ends."

"Both feet done. Don't move for five minutes." Mundy slid the second foot from her lap, stood, and stretched. "What are you thinking?"

I was thinking that I did want another chance. "I rejected him on the dance floor in front of everybody."

"Nobody knows but the two of you."

"And you."

"They probably thought you were fighting."

"We were." But it had been because I was insecure about being a dare. And there was the resemblance to the MIM, except last night I'd done the lines as the real Eden. "How do I get him to ask again?"

"You have to ask him."

"Me?"

"You'll be fine. It's all about the approach."

Okay, stuck in neutral here. "Me ask him?"

"If only we knew enough about him to know where he hangs out . . ."

"He's gone to the media center for years on Monday afternoons."

"And he's noticed that you've noticed. The media center is the perfect place to beg."

Was she crazy? No way. "In front of his friends? I don't think so."

After I finished my homework for the weekend, I spent the rest of Sunday afternoon working on my Peyton application. Sitting on the carpet in my bedroom, with a legal pad on my lap and a pen in my hand, I thought about the essay. *What unique experiences and characteristics will you add to the college community at UNC?* I'd written about one hundred words and scratched out half of them.

"Where's your mom?"

I jerked in surprise. Dad stood in my bedroom door, gym bag in one hand and stinky towel in the other. He dropped both on Marnie's favorite braided rug.

"I don't know."

"What are you doing?"

"Writing an essay." I tried not to take a deep breath. Gross.

He leaned over to peer down, sweat dripping from his chin to splat on the paper. "What about?"

I fought the urge to cover the page with my hands. No need to make him overly suspicious. "Does it matter?"

He yanked off his tank top and swabbed it under his armpits. It was vaguely disturbing to have a father who worked harder on his body than the guys on the football team.

"It doesn't look like you got very far." He reached down to snatch the pad from my hands.

I clawed for it but no luck.

The longer he read, the harder his breathing got. "What is this for?"

It had to be obvious. I rose to face him. "The Peyton Scholarship."

"Dammit, Eden." He kicked his gym bag out of the way and stomped into the kitchen.

I followed and snagged the legal pad the moment he put it down. I didn't want to risk him throwing away what I'd written so far.

He slammed his hand against the countertop. "I'm tired of saying it. You can't go away to college."

It was insane for him to believe that he could prevent me, but I refrained from pointing this out. "I think I am."

"You got it good here. We want you to stay." He ran a hand over his sweaty, shaved head. "You can go to Cape Fear, get a job at the hardware store, and babysit the Fremonts. You'd have a lot of money saved after a couple of years."

I couldn't stop myself from doing calculations in my head.

He was right. At the age of twenty, I'd have an associate's degree that would transfer. No debt. A bank balance. And I could still take care of Kurt and Marta. That almost made it tempting.

But this town . . . It was poisoning me. The people around here believed I was nothing, and as long as I lived here, that's all I would ever be.

If I could scrounge together a way to pay for college, I was getting out of Heron. I had to. "Sorry, Dad, but I'm sticking with my plan. Like I've said."

"What is out there that you want so bad?"

I watched as he wrenched the fridge door open, his movements jerky. Why was he being so insistent about this? "I want to be a teacher."

"A teacher? What a waste." The fridge door banged shut. The pull top on his beer can tinked. "Teachers don't make shit. You'd get more money bartending at the beach." He took a slug from his beer. "You've got the kind of body that earns big tips."

Maybe if I tried hard enough, I'd forget he ever said that. I turned to leave.

"Are you going to do it?"

"Do what?"

"Don't fuck with me, Eden."

My mouth disengaged from my better judgment. "If I win the Peyton, I'll attend Carolina. If I don't, I'll find somewhere else."

"You're an idiot if you think you stand a chance at that scholarship. White kids don't win anymore, not unless you change your name to something no one can pronounce."

I shook my head, hot and shaky and all kinds of embarrassed. Why did he have to open his mouth and let slime like that slither out? One day, he'd do it in front of the wrong person, and it would be bad.

He crushed the can on the kitchen counter. For several tense seconds, he stared me down. "Don't be asking me to sign your dumbass forms."

The threat clamped around my throat and squeezed. I'd been hoping to avoid this discussion until Marnie worked on him. "You have to."

"I don't *have to* do anything."

"Please. I can't apply without your signature."

He brushed past me. "Tough."

I caught his arm. "Dad, don't do this to me. I have to get out of this town."

"Like Heather," he mumbled.

"No. I am nothing like her."

"Sorry, baby girl. I'm not ready for you to go. Don't expect me to do anything to help." He yanked his arm from my grasp and disappeared down the hallway.

· 16 ·

Mighty Vocabulary

Monday afternoon arrived. It was time for the get-a-date-with-Ash plan to launch.

I sat in the media center at a table with my back to the door, shaking with fear. In ten minutes, this horrible thing would be over, one way or the other.

Mundy reached across the table and patted my hand. "Ash and his friends have come in."

I didn't turn around to see. Instead, I rubbed moist palms against my jeans and practiced deep breathing. Inhale. Exhale. Inhale . . .

Not helping. Deep breathing made me dizzy.

"They took over a table. There are five of them. Ash, Dev, Upala—"

"Got it, Mundy." Four witnesses to my humiliation. Or victory. Lucky me.

"Ash nodded at me."

"Lovely. Maybe you should be his girlfriend."

"Go."

"My legs won't move."

"Coward."

"Yep." What was wrong with me? Why did I care what his circle of friends thought?

Well, I did, so I'd have to drag Ash away from them. "I'll find somewhere quiet to talk."

"Let him pick where."

"Why?"

She gave me a pitying look. "You have to involve him. It makes guys happy to think they're in charge."

I rose. "You are scary."

As I approached, his friends fell silent one by one, their expressions ranging from surprise to hostility, but I was a girl on a mission and it was too late to stop. "Ash," I said in a tone resembling a bullfrog.

Ash went still, his face blank as if I were a nothing. "What?"

"Can we talk?"

"Go ahead."

"In private?"

He stared at the table for several seconds, then shot to his feet. "Where?"

"Wherever you want."

"Biographies." He took off without a backwards glance.

I trotted after him. He'd picked the perfect section, shelf after shelf of dusty, musty books no one ever read. It would be deserted.

When I caught up, he waited in the farthest corner, straight and tall, arms crossed. I stopped a couple of feet away and shuddered as his scathing gaze raked me from head to toe.

"All right, Eden. What do you want?"

Excellent question.

I wanted *him.*

I wanted *us.*

Had I lost my mind? This was Ash. The Stanford-bound dick who was ruining my future over a scholarship endorsement he would turn down. The guy who, no matter how good he looked to me, would be battling me to the last breath for the honors we both wanted. When had my attitude gone from contempt to *I can't think of anything else?*

And why would he want me? I was the girl that everyone ignored unless they needed to raise the average on a group assignment. The girl that guys had to be dared to touch.

I inhaled. Exhaled. It didn't help to calm me. "I'll be honest—"

"You were honest on Friday night."

"Please, Ash, hear me out." In the entire time since he'd arrived as a freshman, we'd barely tolerated each other. Yet, six weeks into our senior year, things were noticeably different. I didn't understand why, but I was anxious to see where they might lead. "I'm trying hard not to screw up what I have to say, but I might anyway because the words are coming out as fast as I think them."

"Like the improv?"

I winced. We didn't have such a happy track record with improvisation. "Something's changed between us this semester. There have been times where we'll be throwing out ideas about projects, and I'll look at you, and it feels like you *know* what I'm thinking. Like our minds are connected. And during the MIM . . . It was supposed to be Darcy and Elizabeth, but maybe it was us." This speech would be easier if he didn't look so grim. "Being around you hasn't been the same since. I don't know where this is headed or whether I want to follow, but I can't help wondering."

"Go on."

"You can be such a control freak. You get on a team, and you want to take charge and roll over everyone."

He snorted.

"A month ago, I thought it was arrogant. Today it's exciting. How'd that happen?" I trembled, afraid that I hadn't gotten through. "This is crazy."

"What's crazy?"

"You and me. We've known each other for three years. I've always thought you were gorgeous, but we've never been friendly. We've never talked about anything that mattered." I searched his face for some sign he shared my confusion. "How did we get *here?*"

His arms dropped to his sides as he took a step closer. "For me, things began to change around the MIM. What we said was real and wrong and painful. Then you made us apologize to each other. To get the toxic stuff behind us. It was amazing and brave. I haven't stopped thinking about you since."

"And?"

"I want more."

"I do, too." He had that look on his face again, the same one he'd worn Friday night, like I was something extraordinary, like I wasn't the antisocial brain taking up space in the back of a classroom. "Ask me again," I whispered.

He remained quiet for so long I began to worry. What was going on inside his head? It was awful. Putting myself on the line and dangling in the silence. No positive feedback. Was this what I'd put him through at the dance?

"Why don't you ask me?"

"Fine." I took a deep breath, cleared my throat, took another deep breath. All I had to say was *Will you go out with me?* Simple, one-syllable words. Strung together in a fairly standard pattern. Yet it was horrible. Nerve-wracking. I wavered on my feet, felt the bookshelves cut into my side, and held onto them for support.

Was this what guys went through when they asked girls out? I'd never realized how much courage it took when the answer wasn't a sure thing. "Go out with me?"

Really? I couldn't even speak in a complete sentence?

He studied my face for what seemed like forever. "Yes."

"What? Yes?"

He smiled then, finally. A beautiful, sexy smile. "Yes."

Holy crap, he made me breathless. "How . . ." Oh, where was my mighty vocabulary when I needed it? "Great."

"When?"

"Okay. Yeah." There were decisions to be made, but who made them? Was this my date? Or was it his? He'd asked first, but then I'd asked. "Uh . . . Saturday?"

"Saturday works for me."

"Where?"

"Your call."

Relief made me light-headed. I gave him a mock frown. "Are you saying that I have to make the plans, since I asked?"

"Yes."

Mrs. Fremont asked me to watch Kurt from nine-thirty to three. I couldn't let them down, especially Marta. Plus, there was the cost. How much did I have to spend? Would coffee out be enough? Nah. I had to do more but how much more? "Do you know the diner on the town square? Charlie's?"

He nodded.

"Could you meet me there for breakfast?"

"Sure." He laughed, low and happy. "Are you driving?"

"I don't have a car."

"I can pick you up."

Ash—picking me up? He would see where I lived. My dad would go psycho. And Marnie? I didn't know about her. She'd spent the past three years hearing me trash the "arrogant asshole Ash." She'd listened—usually without comment—and never said anything racist, but I couldn't be sure if she let Dad do the talking for her, or if she didn't want him to know how she really felt.

Either way, I couldn't let them see me with Ash. "You can meet me at the diner. Is eight too early?"

"Eight is perfect."

· 17 ·

The Wiser Option

On a normal day, four seconds was about the maximum amount of time I spent picking out clothes. Saturday was a big exception.

I had some tough criteria. The fabric had to withstand the potential damage that inevitably followed from whatever activity Kurt chose to play. The outfit had to be ordinary enough that my parents wouldn't wonder what was up. And I wanted to look good for my first date.

I settled on shorts (necessitating a shave—ugh), lacy gold camisole, and a lavender overshirt (buttoned when around my folks, unbuttoned when around Ash.)

What should I do about my hair? A ponytail was too unspecial. Loose was too suspicious.

"Marnie?" I called.

She emerged from the shadows of the master bedroom, rubbing her eyes. "What, sweetie?"

"Could you do something with my hair?"

"I'd be glad to. What did you have in mind?"

"A French braid."

It took her about a minute to whip my hair into a braid. She was too delighted to ask questions.

I rode with my dad downtown. We parked near the hardware store.

"Hey," he said, yawning. "Maybe I'll head over to the diner with you. I could grab a cup of coffee."

Nope. I could not permit a chance meeting between Dad and Ash. "It's almost eight. You don't want to clock in late."

"You're right." He scowled. "They'll have coffee in the break room."

I strolled along the sidewalk, not increasing the pace until my father had disappeared inside the store. The timing was just right. As I was nearing the diner, a faint hum throbbed up a side street. Ash's blue convertible BMW Z4 circled the town square and parked in front of me. He slid from the driver's side.

"Mornin'." I cringed at my husky Southern drawl. I thought I'd rid myself of that.

"Hi." He whipped off his shades and looked me over head to toe, smiling slowly.

Holy crap, he was perfect.

Who was I kidding? Eden Moore with . . . this? I spun around and hurried to the diner.

He made it there ahead of me and opened the door, which left me all achy and charmed inside. I picked a booth in the back. He slid across from me and skimmed the menu.

"What do you recommend?"

"Everything." The smell of country ham frying had me wavering about a stack of pancakes.

Charlie's daughter Norah approached, notepad in hand. "What can I get for you?"

I looked at Ash. Since I'd budgeted twenty bucks for this outing, I'd better let him order first. "Go ahead."

"Oatmeal deluxe . . ."

I relaxed. Five dollars. I had sufficient funds. Pancakes and ham for me.

". . . yogurt, strawberries, and decaf coffee with creamer, please." He snapped the menu shut and handed it to the waitress with a smile.

My heart sank. After his meal plus tax and tip, I would have little left over. "Whole wheat toast with peach preserves and hot tea."

Norah's eyebrows shot up. Since I used to work here, she knew that toast and tea were more of an appetizer for me. I bared my teeth at her meaningfully.

She shrugged. "Okey-dokey, hon." Then she was gone, and it got quiet.

I unrolled silverware wrapped in a paper napkin and carefully set my place.

He tapped his fingers on the table. "So . . . hi."

"Hi," I said without looking up. With precise movements, I adjusted the knife until it lay at a right angle to the table's edge. What were we supposed to do? With our orders out of the way, the two of us should move on to whatever it was couples did on a date. If only I knew what that was.

"Have any plans today?" Ash said.

It was a start. "I have to babysit."

"Where?"

"For Kurt."

"Good."

It was my turn to ask him something, right? But my brain went blank. I tried not to fidget and wished I could dream up some clever conversation.

Eight days. It was astonishing how quickly everything had turned around. Eight days from dance to date. Eight days from *thanks for rescuing me* to *what am I doing here*. It scared me more than I'd expected.

He'd consumed me nearly nonstop since homecoming. While I was studying, thoughts of him hammered at my brain, demanding attention. His smile. His voice. I replayed conversations we'd had as well as conversations that had only existed in my head. I'd been practicing for days how to be cool and smart and alluring. Now, those practice sessions deflated like leaky balloons. I had him all to myself, and I didn't say a word. Just sat here on my side of the table, a tentative smile on my face, wanting to talk and not doing it.

"How long will you be with Kurt?"

"Around six hours."

Silence again. I didn't know how to do this.

Ash did. He'd dated Sarita Patel last year and Rekha Srinivasan before that. They were beautiful and talented and good at everything they tried. His parents had probably loved them, exactly the sort of girls they would want around their son. The only reason he wasn't dating one of them still was that they were both in college now.

Norah appeared at the table with two mugs. I added four teaspoons of sugar to mine. I needed calories I didn't have to pay for.

The interruption gave me a moment to collect my thoughts. It didn't help. There weren't any to collect.

I was terrified of making a bad impression. Keeping my mouth shut seemed the wiser option. Maybe I should start out with safe topics and progress from there, except I couldn't think what those might be. Not college applications. Not past relationships, which would be short for me since I'd never had one. And definitely not families.

The silence dragged on. I'd looked forward to being with him, and we sat here like strangers.

"Do you babysit a lot?" he asked.

Whoa. I'd been scouring my brain, trying to think of something to ask about his life. It hadn't occurred to me to keep talking about mine. "I only babysit Kurt and Marta. Today is special, since I usually stay overnight. Mrs. Fremont is a single mom. While she works a graveyard shift, I sleep at their house and get the kids ready for school the next morning."

"Is that why you come in late on Wednesdays?"

"Yeah. She's a physician's assistant in the ER. She can't always leave her job on time."

"Which hospital?"

"In Wilmington."

"My mother works there."

"Your mom is her boss." Mrs. Fremont had a lot of respect for Dr. Gupta, calling her fair and hardworking and one of the best doctors around, but the staff meetings on Mrs. Fremont's days off? They sucked big time.

"She's mentioned my mother?"

"Yeah." I swallowed hard. Might as well get the ugliest fact out of the way. "My dad used to work at the power plant."

"Did he quit?"

"Laid off."

Ash gave a shake of his head as realization settled in. His father had fired mine. "Wow."

I played with a salt shaker and wondered what topics could make this conversation worse, but there weren't any.

Our food arrived. Ash sat back, silent and expressionless, as Norah checked to see if we were set. After she left, though, he didn't make a move to eat. Just regarded me steadily across the table.

I smiled, shrugged, and picked up a triangle of toast. It had to be buttered heavily, with extreme care and attention.

"Eden, our parents don't have to be part of this."

"Yes, they do." Why didn't we go ahead and give up? This thing between us was ridiculous. "Yours would hate finding out that you were on a date with me."

"They would, which is why I haven't told them." He poured creamer into his coffee and watched the white wisps curl. "Have you told yours?"

I shook my head.

"If we want this badly enough, we won't let our family and friends get in the way." He slid his arm across the table, his hand open in invitation. "We *are* going to do this, Eden."

"How?" I linked my fingers through his.

"Keep it between you and me as long as we can."

It was hard to think around the velvet slide of his thumb across my palm. "Mundy knows. She's jumping for joy."

"Besides Mundy, then." He released my hand and reached for his spoon.

The ice was broken. My earlier weirdness faded.

The rest of the meal was spent in nonstop conversation. We never ran out of things to say. I wouldn't be able to remember a single word later, but I loved it while it lasted.

Norah stopped by to refill our mugs and leave the bill.

Ash picked up the ticket and reached for his wallet.

"No way." I snatched it from him.

He gave me a challenging look. He must've planned to fund our dates, whether from old-fashioned chivalry or my obvious lack of income, I couldn't tell.

"I asked. I'll pay." I lifted my chin. We were equals in this relationship. That's just the way it had to be.

His lips twitched. "Okay."

We left soon afterwards, since I had to arrive at the Fremonts by nine-thirty. Marta was peeking through the curtains as we pulled up.

"Thanks for the ride." I smiled shyly, not sure what happened next. Would he kiss me? Did people kiss after breakfast dates? Since I asked, was I supposed to initiate it?

He reached across the space and cupped my face with both hands. "Will you go out with me next Saturday?"

"I'm free all day."

"All day sounds good." He stared at my mouth and then looked into my eyes, as if seeking permission.

Oh, yes. He had permission.

Our lips touched.

I couldn't think. Instead, I closed my eyes and yielded to my other senses. The scent of spicy cologne. The faint taste of coffee. The warm pressure of his fingers.

Mostly, I wanted to focus on the feel of his mouth moving over mine. So many contrasts. Sweet and hot. Firm and soft. The kiss lasted forever and ended way too soon.

Today, I'd had my first date and my first kiss. Ash could become addictive.

He pulled back enough to smile down at me. "Do you want me to pick you up?"

"What?" His question might have to wait until after I recovered.

"Next Saturday?" He kissed me again—soft, sweet, and brief. "We could drive to Jacksonville and hang out."

"Yeah." I looked away from him, embarrassed by my reaction. It ought to take more effort to turn me into a quivering pile of stupidity.

"Your address?" he prompted.

"Uh . . ." If this car pulled into our neighborhood, it would grab attention. Even if my folks weren't home, the residents would note and report his presence. I wasn't ready for any rumors yet. I needed us to become strong before others began the attack. "I'll meet you at the gazebo."

· 18 ·

A Mere Backdrop

Monday morning was torture at school. When I entered the English classroom, Ash glanced at me without interrupting his conversation with Upala. I could've been anyone.

Okay, I got that we had to keep this a secret, but I hadn't thought about how hard it would be to go through the entire school day like nothing had changed between us.

I flopped into my seat and scowled at the back of his head.

Mundy was already there. "How was your date?"

"Amazing."

"Did he ask you out again?"

I nodded.

"You don't look happy."

"Saturday is five days away." I focused on her face. It seemed as if she'd been crying. "Is something wrong?"

"Grampa isn't doing well."

Before I could respond, Ms. Barrie stood. "Open your books . . ."

The rest of her statement was drowned out by the sounds of students following her instructions. I leaned over and whispered, "Hey, Mundy. I'm sorry. Is there anything I can do?"

She shook her head as she got out her book.

After talking with her between classes to arrange a coffee date later this week, I walked into statistics class. Written on the white-board was "Project Teams Today."

Really? Ninety minutes, sitting beside *him* in a circle, trying to act normal? Not possible.

"Let's get started," Ash said, tapping his pencil on a notepad.

I sighed noisily.

He turned to me. "Is there a problem?"

Mundy's distress had heightened mine. "Do you ever get tired of being in charge?"

Dev and Upala exchanged glances and then looked at Ash.

He kept his gaze on me. "Does someone else want to take over?"

There was silence.

He nodded at Dev. "Do you want to?"

"No, I'm good."

Ash looked back at me. "Eden?"

I rolled my eyes. "Go ahead."

The rest of the period didn't get any better as frustration brought out the worst in me. I objected to whatever he said. Didn't matter if it was lame or brilliant. I found flaws.

The rest of the team watched me in shock. I'd always been the stir-things-up-at-the-end girl. I had challenged Ash before, but never this much throughout. By the end of the period, all conversation had dropped to the two of us arguing and the other three staring at their notes.

When the bell rang, I leapt to my feet, pushed my chair back into its row, and took off for my lunch break.

Ash intercepted me in the hall outside the cafeteria, his entourage fanned out behind him. "Eden, got a moment?" His face was tight.

Dev and Upala openly grinned, as if he was a teacher who had the right to rip into me.

Yeah, I knew that was wrong. "Whatever."

He placed a hand on my back and nudged me out of earshot. "What was that all about?" His voice was low and controlled.

"Camouflage for what I really wanted."

He studied my face for a long moment. "What did you really want?"

"To have your whole attention."

"Oh, you had that."

He deserved a better explanation, and I wanted to give him one. But what if it was too much, too soon? Insecurities bloomed inside me, and I forced them down into their corners. I had to trust this thing between us. Ash had asked me out on a second date. This wasn't one-sided.

I stared at the top button of his shirt. "I wanted to be alone with you. I was afraid that my feelings would be obvious unless I hid them behind the pissy attitude."

"I was fooled."

"Good. Then the others were too."

"Yes, they were. Eden?"

I raised my eyes. He wasn't exactly smiling, but the tension had eased. "Yeah?"

"We'll be alone Saturday. All day."

"That's a long way off."

He glanced at his friends and back at me. "How are you getting home today?"

Okay, this might have potential. "The bus."

"I can take you."

My dad would be around. I couldn't let him see us together, but turning down a few minutes with Ash? Not going to happen. "You could take me to the nursing home."

"When does your stepmom's shift end?"

"At four today."

His lips curved into a wide smile, slow and sexy. "Then we'll have to think of something to do for an hour."

Holy shit. I'd better leave before I flung myself into his arms. I started to back away. "We could discuss those lame ideas you suggested in statistics."

"Lame?" His eyes narrowed. "I thought you said that was camouflage."

"My attitude was, but your proposal sucks." I yanked open the cafeteria door and slipped inside, happy that we didn't have to wait until the weekend to be together.

I quickly learned that Ash's school nights were tightly scheduled. Since I spent mine on homework and babysitting, hanging out during the week would be a challenge.

It didn't take long to discover that there was virtually no place on campus where a couple could be alone, especially when the two people involved had the Honors Committee scrutinizing all aspects of their lives. Heron High's administration had my respect for how well patrolled the facilities were.

Fortunately, Ash and I were the two smartest students at the school. We were creative. We were figuring things out.

Like . . . Tuesday. I stuffed a change of clothes into my backpack and then hid with Ash in an obscure corner of the town park until I had to leave for the Fremonts. He told his parents he was studying with a friend.

Yeah, we were studying all right. Just not academics.

There were moments when I didn't recognize myself and wondered if my classmates had noticed too. Maybe I should blame it on Mundy. I had purple toenails, which made me bold. And a guy who thought I was beautiful, which made me bolder. Could anybody tell the difference?

Thursday after school, Sawyer flagged me down on the front sidewalk. "How are things going?" he asked when he caught up.

There we had it. Proof. I was open to the universe, and Sawyer could tell. "Things are good. What about you?"

"Fine." He strolled beside me, slapping one fist against the other palm. He looked at me and immediately looked away, as if he was ramping up the courage to say something big, which intrigued me, since we'd known each other long enough that he should've been comfortable with babbling about anything.

"Would you say that you're good friends with Mundy Cruz?"

"Yes." It was a rhetorical question. Sawyer saw us everywhere together.

"I think she's amazing. And hot." He stopped, his face split by a wide grin. "And amazing."

Oh, man, he had it bad. I could empathize. "I'm guessing you think she's amazing."

"Yeah. Is she dating anyone?"

"No." Uh-oh. My heart sank. I could feel what was coming.

"Does she ever talk about me like—you know?"

She hadn't mentioned him in that way. Not once. Should I give him false hope?

Much as I hated to be the person to squash him, I couldn't bring myself to lie. "No. Do you want me to ask her?"

His smile twisted. "No. Thanks."

I watched him walk away, his attitude dejected, and it made me sad. I was adored by someone, and I wanted everybody else to be adored too. Maybe I should drop a few hints with Mundy anyway, even if she had said Sawyer wasn't her type.

Ash had never been mine either, until he was.

"Eden?" Upala stepped in front of me, a determined look on her face.

Every muscle in my body locked down. I would not react. I would not give into the desire to run screaming away and not listen to whatever she had to say, because there could only be one purpose for her to approach me. And if she expected to learn anything about that topic, she would leave disappointed. "Uh-huh?"

"What's going on with you and Ash?"

"Ask him."

"We have. He won't say."

"I won't either."

She shook her head, her eyes pitying. "No matter what it is, it can't last. When his parents find out, they'll stop it."

The statement echoed inside me, unwanted but familiar. I'd had the same thought often. "Why haven't you told them your suspicions?"

"The members of our study group have many secrets. We're hoping that Ash gets tired of you before any of us risk speaking out."

Mutual blackmail. Nice. "Thanks for the warning." I turned to go.

She reached for me. I gaped at the sight of her fingers wrapped around my wrist.

Upala looked down, too, and gasped. She jerked her hand away, as if afraid of being contaminated.

I kept walking.

"You are not worthy of him."

I paused and glanced over my shoulder. "Who could be?" Her eyes narrowed in surprise. I gave her a nod and continued down the sidewalk.

Not worthy. As hard as I tried to shield myself from that idea— to reject it from my body—the damn thing snuck back, doing its best to worm its way inside.

No. She was wrong. They were all wrong. Ash and I were good together. I wouldn't give up that easily.

The computer lab was deserted when I entered it before school Friday morning. Not even Mrs. Barber had arrived yet. The custodian let me in before disappearing through the emergency exit door for a cigarette break.

I booted one of the desktop computers and combed through my webmaster e-mail. There were several messages from Tiffany, each with attachments.

"They're candids," she said from behind me.

"Yeah, I can see that." The volume of images made me tired, and it also pissed me off that Tiffany had managed to slip into the lab without me noticing. "Why don't you tell me your favorites?"

"The third one."

I clicked it open. It was a shot of the dance team, moments before they were about to run onto the football field at a halftime show. One of the girls looked like she was about to have a meltdown and several others had gathered around, giving her a pep talk. The color, the lighting, and the framing of this image were all wonderful. Tiffany was improving with every photo she took. "That one is good," I said and uploaded it to the web site's staging area for Mrs. Barber's approval. "You get better at telling a story with each shot."

"I've been thinking I might be good at photojournalism." She eyed me warily. "They have it as a major at Carolina."

"Is that why you want the Peyton?"

"If I won the Peyton, I could study abroad. Daddy would never pay for me to do that."

"I can imagine." I felt a twinge of sympathy for her. Her parents had a decent amount of money, but that didn't matter when her father ruled the checkbook.

"Look at the last image, Eden." Her voice held a weird edge.

When I opened it, I instantly knew why Tiffany was nervous about my reaction, and she was right to be.

This shot had been taken during the fire drill on Wednesday afternoon. Students were standing outside the main building. There was a small group of emos looking bored. A couple who looked as if they were on the verge of a breakup. Two kids standing in their own isolated worlds, one defiant, one simply alone.

Yet all of those students served as a mere backdrop for the two couples in the right foreground.

Mundy was pretending to punch Sawyer in the arm while he was giving her a mock scowl. I was trying not to laugh. Ash was watching me with unguarded adoration.

I shivered. The photo was layered and charming and the most nuanced thing Tiffany had ever done. The kind of shot that could get her some attention. No way could I allow its use. "There are five students at the high school who haven't signed a photo release," I said as I deleted the image. "One of them is me."

"You can give permission."

"I could, but I won't." I logged out of the mail app.

"Eden, I need this for my portfolio."

"You know I would rather take the pictures than be in them."

"You can make an exception. It's the best thing I've ever done."

She was right. If only it hadn't included me and Ash. That look on his face? Both beautiful and disastrous. "You'll take others."

Clogs clip-clopped into the lab. "What's going on?" Mrs. Barber slurped from her coffee mug.

"Eden won't upload my best candid."

Mrs. Barber quirked an eyebrow at me in question.

"I'm recognizable." I cut a glance at Tiffany. "I could crop myself out of it." As well as Ash.

She looked horrified. "No. The composition would be ruined."

"Then we're done here." I slung my backpack over my shoulder and stepped past my teacher.

"Aunt Gina!"

"I'm sorry, Tiff," I heard Mrs. Barber say as I left the room. "There's nothing I can do."

· 19 ·

Marginally Perpendicular

Saturday morning, Dad dropped me off at the Fremonts on his way to work. Once his car had disappeared around the corner, I jogged the half mile to the gazebo. Ash was waiting for me. *Hello there* kissing ensued under the domed platform.

He spoke nonstop on the drive to Jacksonville. I didn't mind. I basked in the warmth of his voice, didn't pay much attention to what he said, and focused instead on the touch of his fingers curled around mine.

A light drizzle was falling when we parked at the mall. Ash clasped my hand and ran with me through a back entrance. He took us straight to center court, stopped, and smiled expectantly, his body humming with excitement.

"What?" I scanned the scene. Shoppers milled around, dragging cranky kids. Marines from Camp Lejeune clogged the food court.

"The rink?"

The mall had a small ice-skating rink with a half-dozen people looping around. "What about it?"

"Let's go."

"Uh . . ." I eyed it warily. "I've never tried."

"You'll be fine. I'll be beside you."

Ten minutes later, we were on the ice, both standing, him because he was crazy-good, me because he was holding me up.

"What do you think?" he asked after we completed our first lap without mishap.

"Still not sure."

"Let's see how you do on your own." He gave a little push and released me.

I slid forward a few yards, arms outstretched. Slowing to a stop, I concentrated on his instructions to move again. Push left. Push right.

Yay. My head was still five feet above the ice. I wanted to tuck my freezing hands into the pockets of my jacket, but I was afraid to move my upper body in any way.

"Keep going," he yelled.

I nodded over my shoulder at him. Catastrophe struck so fast, I had no chance to react. My skates went up. My ass and head went down. Bang.

Déjà vu. I lay flat on my back with Ash bent over me, offering to help—except this time, the "floor" was frozen.

He lifted me onto my skates. "Are you all right?"

"Maybe." I clutched his hoodie, sorry that I was too sore to enjoy the excuse for exploring his chest.

"I won't let go again, not until you're positive you're ready." He brushed icy slush from my butt. I was too sore to enjoy that either.

A grunt was the only reply he got from me. It took all of my concentration to keep myself above the ice.

We pushed off again, arms intertwined. There was, I soon figured out, feminine-wiles value in clinging to him with helpless abandon. But my natural competitiveness eventually took over. I wanted to be good.

After three laps around the rink, I graduated to holding hands with Ash as he skated backwards in front of me. Since I now felt secure, this was fun. Skating was oddly isolating for us. Even with dozens of other people on the ice, we were alone in our own little world.

I had reached enough of a comfort level to risk looking at him instead of my feet. "Where did you learn to skate so well?"

"Boston." He smiled. "You're doing fine."

I gave him a hesitant smile, not sure I agreed but willing to progress some more. Reluctantly, I dropped one of his hands.

An out-of-control skater swooped past, surprising us with a near miss. To avoid a collision, Ash changed course without warning. When I balked, our hands separated. Before I realized what had happened, I was on my own, wobbling but marginally perpendicular to the ice.

I smiled at him, childishly pleased. "I didn't fall."

"Staying upright is an important goal in skating."

"A goal I have achieved." I gestured him closer. "Don't disappear, though."

"I won't." He drew up beside me, adapting to my pace.

One more incident-free lap gave me the confidence I needed to attempt a conversation. "How long did you live in Boston?"

"Fourteen years."

I would've never guessed. He didn't have a Yankee accent at all. "Were you born there?"

He nodded. "My mom went to med school at Harvard."

Ah, yes. My stepmom cleaned toilets. My bio mom married men. Ash's mother saved lives. Lovely. "Why did your family move here?"

"One of my sisters lives in Wilmington. My parents wanted to be closer to Priya and Raj."

"You have more than one sister?"

"Yeah. My middle sister lives in Charleston. She and my parents aren't communicating well right now."

"Why?"

"Neela is living with her boyfriend."

An odd thought struck me, which I blurted without thinking. "Did your parents have an arranged marriage?"

"They did, but it was arranged in America since they were both here."

"Will they expect it of you?"

He looked away from me. "Your turn, Eden. Where were you born?"

So arranged marriage was something he didn't want to discuss. I was filing the topic away for later. "I was born on Wrightsville Beach."

"*On* the beach?"

"Yeah. I arrived quickly. A paramedic delivered me."

"When's your birthday?"

"March twentieth. Why do you want to know?"

"That should be obvious." He took off and raced ahead of me. After performing a couple of show-off maneuvers, he returned. "Ready for some speed?"

"No."

"Ready for a break?"

"Yeah."

We detoured to the wall. Weirdly, once we stopped, my legs didn't seem to get the message. They vibrated with the effort to keep me moving, even though I didn't want to. I would've slipped if Ash hadn't clamped an arm around my waist.

The ice held more skaters now. Some experienced. Most chugging along like I had. A tiny girl in pigtails and a bright green leotard thing went flashing by, doing leaps and twirls.

I had about OD'ed on skating. Facing Ash, I turned my back on the rink and its humiliatingly good, tiny people. "Since your mom went to Harvard, will you apply there?"

"Yeah. It's where she wants me to go."

"What about your dad?"

"My father is pushing me at Duke. They'd be happier if I chose one of their alma maters."

"Why Stanford, then?"

"It's where *I* want to go." He looked down at his hands. "They'll pay for Stanford if I get in, but they'd rather I stick closer to home."

What must that feel like? All he had to worry about was getting in. The funding was guaranteed. "Have you picked a major?"

"Political science. That's why I'm going after four colleges with top-ranked programs." He shifted until our hips pressed together. "Where will you apply?"

"Carolina."

He cocked his head, as if waiting for more, but I just smiled tightly.

"Anywhere else?"

"No definite plans yet." College visits were expensive. Even at schools offering a free ride without FAFSA, I wouldn't seriously consider accepting until I'd seen the campus in person. For each road trip, I'd have to babysit a night or two to raise the money. That might not be an issue for him, but it was for me. "I'm still researching my options."

"Have you looked at any private colleges? They'll throw money at you."

"Not enough." This topic was edging toward dangerous ground. I couldn't avoid it any longer. We had to have the scholarship thing out in the open between us. Dread filled my gut. "If I don't get a Peyton, I might have to go to Cape Fear for two years."

His eyes narrowed as he considered my statement. His expression changed clearly and rapidly from curiosity to concern to suspicion. "What are you trying to say?"

The dread in my gut grew stronger. My body knew I was about to get myself in trouble, but I couldn't stop my mouth. The words gushed out. "If you get the endorsement, my college plans are screwed."

"Wow." His gaze dropped to the ice. He picked at it with the toe of his blade. "What's the point of telling me this? Are you hoping I'll get out of the way?"

"That would be great, actually."

My response gave him a jolt. His head snapped up. "Do you really think I'd drop out because of you?"

"I think you might drop out because it's the right thing to do."

His expression morphed into the haughty-Darcy look he did so well. "Being named a Peyton Scholar is a huge honor. It would please both me and my parents."

"It would please me to get a college degree." I wanted to kick something. It was as if Mr. Center of the Universe was deliberately ignoring the truth. "Why bother with Carolina when you're going to Stanford?"

"I haven't been accepted."

"But you will be. How can you doubt it? And the moment you get your acceptance letter, you'll blow off the Peyton endorsement after robbing me of my best chance to escape Heron."

"If you wanted to escape so badly, you'd have more schools on your list than Carolina."

I clamped my lips together. There was no good comeback without telling him things I didn't want him to know.

He pushed away from the side, glided to the middle of the rink, and made slow circles on the ice. I watched him, mesmerized by the repetition, debating with myself over what to say next. If I didn't tell him my situation, he couldn't understand me. But I didn't trust him yet, at least not enough. This was our second date. There might not be any more.

He braked, then zoomed back to the side. "Is this why you're going out with me?"

"Shit, Ash. How could you think that? I'm with you because I like you. No other reason." Apparently, he didn't trust me either. The ice rink had stopped being fun, with its looping skaters and the cold and the insanely good Ash. I inched along the wall, determined to reach the gate without falling.

He whooshed past me, skating backwards. "Where are you going?"

"I can't be around you right now."

"Mature."

I flipped him off as I stepped from the ice. This date was officially over. I headed for a bench and flopped down, fuming.

My first skate was unlaced when Ash's jeans-clad legs appeared in front of me.

"What are you doing, Eden?"

"Taking off my skates."

"Then what?"

"I'm going home."

"I drove."

Major detail I'd forgotten in the midst of my tantrum. I couldn't call my folks. They were busy today, besides the obvious questions I wouldn't want to answer. Maybe Mundy would come.

I exhaled loudly. This was silly. Ash brought me. He ought to drive me home. When necessary, I could be an expert at the silent treatment. "I'm hungry. I'm about to look for something to eat."

"Me too." He sat next me, his thigh touching mine. "May I join you?"

I met his gaze. Bad decision. Longing rippled through me, dissolving the anger. He was so . . . perfect. I wanted to be with him, not be mad at him. "Yes, you may."

He slid an arm around my waist and leaned his forehead against mine. I didn't know how long we sat that way. It was nice just to be held.

"Is this our first fight?" I asked.

"Not even close. More like our fifty-first."

"And not likely to be the last." I wiggled away from him. "Let's eat." After removing the second skate, I tramped over to the vendor to trade for my shoes. Ash was right behind me.

I nudged him. "What kind of food do you like?"

"All kinds. My mother doesn't like to cook. We usually eat takeout." His mouth hovered close to my ear. "Tell me what you want."

Eating out for us was so rare that anything classier than a diner was an impossible dream. So I wanted somewhere that I would never go on my own, and he *had* asked. "Italian. With a waiter, a tablecloth, and real silverware." I wouldn't feel guilty if this was more expensive than he'd planned. Our first-date breakfast had set me back a higher percentage of my income than this would likely cost him.

He caught my hand. "Come with me."

The restaurant looked like something out of a romantic movie. Dimmed lights. Tables lit by wine bottles with candles stuck in them. Waitstaff wearing black vests and bow ties.

"This is wonderful." I opened the menu, read the prices, and snapped the menu shut. He would spend more on our meal today than I earned each night. "Have you eaten here before?"

"Often. The pasta primavera is awesome."

Often meant he got the prices. Whoa. I took his suggestion, waited until our order was placed, then stared at him with determination. "We have to finish our discussion."

"No, we don't."

"How can you doubt that Stanford will accept you?"

My question upset him. He toyed with his fork, tapped his fingers on the table, looked at me, and frowned. "My SATs might not be good enough."

Interesting. Even after the high-school guidance counselor had told me I had the highest score in the senior class, I'd never wondered about Ash. "What did you make?"

"Twenty-one hundred."

Whoa. No wonder Stanford wasn't a slam dunk. "Take it again."

"I have." He held up three fingers. "I freeze. Every time."

Mr. Amazing Grades wasn't always amazing on exams. Last month, this story would've made me ecstatic. Now, I wanted to hug him and make it all better. "You'll still impress them. You have lots of AP classes. You'll get in."

"I hope you're right."

"Ash?" I couldn't get over how persistent he was. "Your parents want you to stay on the East Coast, and you're not confident you'll be admitted. Why are you pushing so hard for Stanford?"

"It's a great school—" he began, as if reciting a familiar speech.

"Stop." I shook my head at him. "Don't tell me the story you're telling everybody else. Duke and Harvard are great schools too, and you're not drooling over them. What's the real reason?"

He pursed his lips and looked out across the restaurant. "No one in my family has gone there."

I laid my hand on the table, reaching out to him. "And you'd be far enough away that people from here can't get to you easily."

His gaze flicked back to me. "Yes." He curled his fingers around mine, a big smile lighting his face. "You should see the campus. I love everything about it. The buildings. The energy. The weather. It feels like *my* school."

I watched him speak, thrilled that he was excited, subdued that he'd be on the opposite side of the country from me, upset that I cared so much after two dates.

Our salads arrived. I released his hand, glad of the excuse to be busy, and dived right in.

He sat back in his chair. "Are you okay?"

"Sure," I mumbled around a mouth full of lettuce. "You'll love it there."

"Eden, you have to apply somewhere besides Carolina."

Well, that was a topic I could address with absolute confidence. "I'm not sure what I can afford."

"You'd qualify for financial aid, wouldn't you?"

Confession time. He'd given me something personal. It was my turn. "I might qualify, but I'll never get any. I can't use FAFSA."

"Why?"

"My dad doesn't want the government to know his business."

"The government already knows his business."

I speared a slice of plum tomato and watched the salad dressing slide off. "Doesn't matter. Dad won't cooperate."

"Wow. You're screwed."

"I believe I mentioned that earlier." I smiled at Ash over the drippy, waxy, candle-in-a-bottle—incredibly happy to be with him.

"Carolina has a top-rated poli-sci program, and their grad school in public policy is also one of the best. I want the Peyton endorsement, Eden, and I won't cut you any slack."

"Oh, yeah? Well, I'm going to win. Just a warning."

"Don't think so." His eyes held a determined gleam.

I held out my fist, and he bumped it.

Game on.

✦ 20 ✦

A Predictable Affair

Iarrived in the media center after school on Monday with a specific mission. Find Heather.

It was a desperate choice. I didn't really want to contact her, but I needed a parent's signature on my scholarship forms. She might do it to spite my dad. And at this point, I didn't care as long as I got my chance at leaving this hellhole of a town.

Heather would understand that.

Her last known location had been California. Four years had passed since we'd spoken, so she could be long gone, but maybe. I tried her third husband's name. It was distinctive. Howard Stebbins.

I found him in Sacramento. A couple of searches later, I pinpointed his address. The other name on the deed was Taylor Mabry. Guy or girl?

Howard and Heather weren't married anymore. That meant divorce decree. I went looking and found what I needed quickly.

Heather Anne *Moore*? She still used Dad's name. Or was it the name of her kids?

We were *not* her kids. We belonged to Marnie.

I pushed away from the computer, my hands dropping into my lap. That tiny bit of information upset me more than I could've imagined. Her maiden name was Young. Simple to remember. But she kept Moore.

Her choice didn't make sense, yet I didn't want it explained. Not now. Not ever. I changed my mind. There would be no contact with Heather. I'd rather forge my dad's signature a million times over than ask her for anything. After logging off, I fumbled with my backpack, preparing to leave.

When the door to the media center swished open, I glanced up to see Ash enter with Upala. He claimed a nearby table, never once looking my way.

We hadn't been alone together since Saturday. Had the argument about the Peyton put a strain on our relationship? Two days seemed like forever.

I released my backpack, watching him intently, as if the force of my will would cause him to turn around and look my way. Upala frowned at me. I lowered my gaze to the computer screen. Maybe I should do some research for chemistry.

No, my brain was too fragmented to think. I needed to feel. I needed to be wanted.

Too distracted to stay focused, I glanced up again. He wasn't there. I scanned the room in time to see him disappearing into the Biographies section.

Oh, yeah. Never could tell when information on Teddy Roosevelt might come in handy.

Ash was waiting for me in the A's section. Poor John Adams would be sick of us before long.

I hesitated at the far end of the aisle. His expression was solemn. Why? Had I screwed things up?

"Come here," he said.

I was going to melt. Really. If a bookshelf hadn't been there to prop me up, I would be pooling on the floor. After shuffling along until I was few inches away from him, I gripped a metal shelf and hung on. "What do you want?"

"To touch you."

I exhaled a happy breath. I hadn't ruined anything. Life went back into balance. "I'm okay with that."

He reached out, caught a stray lock of my hair between his fingers, and tugged me closer. "We don't have another date planned."

"True." I shivered, hoping he was about to correct that oversight.

"How about this weekend?"

There was a Barber cousin getting married Saturday afternoon. "My folks are attending a wedding at Hammocks Beach. Marnie wants me to go, but I could skip it."

"You'd be free the whole afternoon?" At my nod, he said, "Invite me over."

"I don't know . . ." Ash in our dinky trailer? His garage had to be bigger than my home.

"I need to be alone with you."

His request made me nervous. "There are other places to be alone."

"I don't want to risk getting caught." Ash closed the gap between our bodies. "I'd like to see where you live."

I flattened myself against the bookshelf and watched him, mesmerized. Waiting. He braced his hands on either side of my shoulders, effectively trapping me in this spot. I felt feverish. "This is hot in ways I don't want to examine."

"Yeah?"

Nodding would have to do, because I seemed to have lost the ability to speak. His mouth hovered . . .

I shut my eyes, leaning into his kiss, focusing on nothing but the taste and touch of our lips and tongues.

"Invite me over," he whispered.

This was a major step for me. "I'm not sure."

"Please." Another kiss.

I wanted to be alone with him, too. Somewhere that didn't involve imminent discovery or our American forefathers peeping from the shelves.

But my home? Could I do it? Could I let him in?

It was hard to think that anything could go wrong when we were together and happy like this. "Okay."

He smiled against my lips. "Saturday then." The next kiss was hard and brief.

Even after he drew away, I stayed where I was, clinging to the shelves. My eyes opened as he reached the end of the aisle. He turned the corner without looking back.

I slid to the floor, a puddle of joy in Biographies, and wondered how I would make it through the rest of the week.

Mundy didn't show up for school on Tuesday. Neither did Dr. Holt. I was worried, but either the other teachers didn't know or they weren't allowed to say. Ash called her on his phone, but she didn't answer.

Dad's cell was buzzing on the kitchen table as I entered the trailer after school. I answered. "Hello?"

"Eden," Mundy said, her voice thick with sobs. "I need your help."

My whole body went on alert. "What happened?"

"Grampa Holt died last night. Around midnight."

"Oh, Mundy. I'm so sorry."

"Cam and Mom are at the funeral home. I have to join them." She coughed.

"What can I do?"

"Could you come over? Destin is taking a nap. If he wakes up and you're here, he'll be too excited to get upset."

"I'll be over as soon as I find a car."

When a yawning Destin thumped down the stairs, I was able to keep him happy with a bowl of peach ice cream and the promise of a playdate at the park. A couple of quick phone calls expanded the group of boys to three. Ash had a babysitting gig with his nephew, and Mrs. Fremont was glad to turn her little guy over to me a couple of hours early.

I pulled into the parking lot right behind Ash. Introductions weren't necessary. Raj and Kurt remembered each other. Destin, having descended from the same extroverted gene pool as Mundy, joined in without hesitation. Hardly a minute passed before the boys were running around on the grass, playing some incomprehensible game with rules made up on the fly.

Ash and I sat side by side on a picnic table. While he maintained a vigilant watch over three boys, I admired his profile. An appropriate division of labor.

His lips twitched. "What are you doing?"

"I enjoy looking at you."

"You're giving me an ego."

"Like you didn't already have one?" Really, though, he deserved to. Ash was a nearly perfect guy. He held doors for me and listened to what I said. He was fun to talk to, since he'd been a lot of places and seen a lot of things. Even his arrogance made sense. If he hadn't had a clue about how awesome he was, he would've been totally lacking in self-awareness, and that would've been annoying.

He could have anyone he wanted and look who he went after. "I wish I knew why you're interested in me."

Ash shifted on the picnic table until he faced me fully. "How can I resist you?"

"The other seventy-something kids in our graduating class have managed."

"Which is exactly the way you want it."

"How do you figure that?"

"You protect yourself from relationships, Eden. It took a lot of patience and determination to get past your defenses, but I'm glad I tried, because I found this amazing girl waiting for me. You're generous and loyal and fair. When you commit to something, you give it the best that you've got, and that includes the people you care about. There just aren't many of us because you don't have the time."

Tears burned behind my eyes. "I will always find the time for you."

"I know, and I get how lucky I am," he said, linking his fingers through mine. "You're so clear about what you want from life—"

"You are, too."

"True, but I have my parents and friends to help me, and you're doing this alone." He kissed the back of my hand. "I'm humbled by how intensely smart you are. Nobody at school comes close. Not even me."

Wow. Did he really believe that?

"I like to watch you think. You see the connections that the rest of us miss. I love how you can be scared by a decision and take the risk anyway." His lips brushed the corner of my mouth. "I'm in awe of you."

This praise was making me itchy. We had to flip it back to him. "Someone from your circle of friends would be a more logical match for you."

"I don't want to date anyone from my circle of friends."

"Upala's smart and talented. She dresses preppy like you."

"What is wrong with you today?" His eyes narrowed on me. "Want to know what I like about the way you dress? I like that you keep your incredible body hidden and that I'm the only guy who gets to check out the reality. It makes me—" He groaned.

"Makes you what?"

"Uncomfortable."

It took all of my willpower not to look down to see if he was presently *uncomfortable*. I watched the little guys instead.

Ash slipped an arm around my waist. "Why are we talking about this? You chose me. I chose you. That's enough."

I buried my face in his shoulder and gave into the wave of happiness.

"Hey," he said, "I have something for you. No big deal." He drew a small, thin box from the pocket of his jacket.

I ripped into it with savage eagerness. "A phone?" It was an expensive gift. I should be outraged, right?

"It's one of those prepaids. I have my number programmed in. We'll be able to contact each other without anyone knowing."

My concern at the extravagance was instantly demolished by my appreciation for its usefulness. "We needed this."

"I'm glad you see it that way."

What would I tell my folks if they saw me use it? I would have to make something up. The better option was to keep it out of sight.

"Thanks." I slipped the phone into my back pocket and smiled at him with a need so great that it ached.

This silent but glowing thank-you lasted about fifteen seconds, because two small hands grasped my knees, demanding attention.

"Come on, Eden," Raj said. "Play with me."

I straightened with an exaggerated sigh. "Do the Gupta men always get what they want?"

"We do." Ash rose and helped me off the picnic table.

We spent the next hour doing all sorts of silly things. Throwing rocks in the lake. Climbing the play structure. Hunting for squirmy critters. When the boys begged for a game of hide and seek, I gave in quickly, even though I hadn't played in years.

I "hid" in a stand of trees, which by this time of year had few leaves. Raj found me right away and chased me back to "home," his legs pumping for all they were worth. He tackled me at my knees, knocking me to the ground. Rolling over to my back, I lay prone with a wiggly boy pinning me by my shoulders. Or so he thought. I could hardly catch my breath from laughing.

"Look, Uncle Ash. Look. I got her. I got Eden."

Ash's face appeared above me, his eyes wide with concern. "Are you hurt?"

"I'm fine," I said in between gasps. "Raj got me, fair and square."

Destin and Kurt caught up and cheered Raj noisily. The three boys took off running, comparing notes on the best way to wrestle down clumsy babysitters.

Ash sounded worried. "Are you sure you're okay?"

"Yeah. I think it's your destiny to help me when I fall." I sat too suddenly and cringed. Next thing I knew, I was wrapped in Ash's arms.

"I'm better now," I said, resting against him. I gave into the delicious feeling of being wanted and hoped it would never end.

The playdate had been good for Kurt. He was more relaxed this evening. Instead of watching a DVD, he pulled a barstool next to me and climbed up, his knees bumping the tabletop. "I have homework," he said.

"I do too."

"We can do our homework together."

"Sounds like a plan."

For ten minutes, I calculated orbitals and energy levels while Kurt practiced writing the letters *C* and *G*. I had better luck than he did.

Eventually, he tossed down his fat pencil and rubbed his temples in an eerie imitation of his mother. "I'm finished."

"Excellent. Ready for bed?"

"I am."

"Let's go then."

He ran down the hall ahead of me and charged through the bedroom door. As I passed Marta's room, I glanced in. She was curled against a pile of fat pillows, reading from *The Best of Sherlock Holmes*.

I followed him into his room. He was already under the covers. "Good night, Kurt."

"You can ask me about school again. I won't cry this time."

Whoa, progress. I leaned against the doorframe. "Do you like school?"

"No." His eyes followed my every movement. Maybe he wanted to talk but didn't know how to start.

I perched at the end of his bed and nodded with encouragement. "Will you tell me why?"

"I'm supposed to use my inside voice, but I don't have one."

"Is it your teacher who's asking?"

"Yes. She says I'm too loud a lot." His eyebrows beetled into a thick line. "The other kids laugh."

Anger blazed through my veins. If it had happened more than once, did that mean she wasn't demonstrating what she expected? Kurt liked rules and tried hard to follow them.

But even if she'd shown him, why was she correcting him in front of other students? That was terrible for any kid. "Did she teach you how to find your inside voice?"

He shook his head.

"It's the reason you go to school, to learn how to do things you don't already know." I knelt at the side of his bed. "Why don't I teach you what an inside voice sounds like?"

"Do you know how to be a teacher?" He rubbed his eyes and yawned.

"I'll do my best."

We got a short lesson in. He was too sleepy for a long one. Eventually, we got his inside voice to the decibel level of a loud whisper. It was a start.

I gave him a good-night pat, turned out the lights, and wandered to the kitchen, puzzling over what I should do next. Should I discuss the problem with his mother when she got home tomorrow? Text her now?

How about both? Yeah.

One thing I knew for sure. Mrs. Fremont would have to hold a parent-teacher conference soon, and I wanted to crash that party.

Marnie and I made it to Grampa Holt's church on time and sat in the back row. It was as nice a funeral as I'd ever been to, if it was all right to say such a thing. The minister gave a wonderful eulogy. It made me regret that I hadn't met Mundy's grandfather before he got sick. He sounded like a great guy.

The funeral was a predictable affair for our part of the world. First came the memorial service in the church sanctuary, then a long line of cars to the cemetery, followed by a graveside service. Afterwards, everyone returned to the church fellowship hall for the epitome of a Southern funeral reception. Pans of fried chicken. Sides of potato salad, deviled eggs, and pickled okra. A whole table devoted to desserts like banana pudding, sweet potato pie, and red velvet cake.

Mundy and her parents mingled in a daze, too distraught to eat. I filled a plate with a sampler of food and set it near them. They ignored it.

Destin darted about the hall at first, but the heavy atmosphere finally got to him. He clung to my skirt, then my hand, and ultimately to me. I found a rocking chair in a quiet corner and cuddled him on my lap. When Clarissa discovered us an hour later, Destin and I were both asleep.

"Here, I'll take him," she said, hoisting him in her arms. He mumbled and burrowed his face into her neck, his weight immediately slack.

I stood and stretched. "I'll find Marnie."

"She's gone. I asked her to let you and Destin nap for a while longer. You're good with him." Clarissa smoothed Destin's damp curls. "Can you sleep over tonight? Mundy needs you."

"Yes."

She nodded. "Grampa Holt is the only grandparent Mundy remembers. She's taking this hard."

"No problem." I looked around. A devastated Mundy stood on the other side of the hall, attached to a visibly grief-stricken Campbell. The receiving line had dwindled to almost nothing. "Should I drive her home?"

"If you don't mind." She put a light hand on my arm. "Eden, I want you to know . . ." She stopped and took a deep breath.

"What is it, Clarissa?"

"You've been a good friend to Mundy." She gave me a pained smile. "Thanks."

· 21 ·

From His Perspective

Marnie's grandparents and all eight of their kids had single-handedly populated a large portion of North Carolina's Crystal Coast. A month could hardly go by without a birth, death, or marriage. Saturday's wedding would draw my parents an hour away from here. Adding in the ceremony and reception, Ash and I would have hours to be alone.

"Sweetie, are you sure?" My stepmom had fretted all morning that I was refusing to come because I couldn't stand being around her family. And while that was true, it wasn't the main reason today.

"I'll be fine, Marnie. Go." *Go!*

Dad growled, rubbing the small of his back with a fist. He'd pulled a ten-hour shift yesterday and spent most of it on his feet. He was hurting. "Marlene, can we leave already?"

"Yes." She snatched up her purse.

"Do you have any Advil in there?" my father asked. The slamming of the door cut off her answer.

My parents would have to speed if they didn't want to be late for the wedding, but at least they were gone. I watched from the window as they roared down the street. After they were out of sight, I opened the front door and listened for the sound of tires squealing onto the highway.

Finally.

I raced down the lane and around the bend to the clubhouse. Ash's Z4 waited in the last parking spot. He got out as I approached and reached for me.

"Not yet. Someone might see." I gestured toward a trail winding past the playground and picnic area before disappearing into the woods.

Once we were sheltered by the trees, though, I yanked Ash to me, exploring his mouth with mine, trying to take the edge off my hunger.

He eased back. "Whoa, slow down." He pressed a line of tiny kisses down my cheek, behind my ear, along my neck. "We have plenty of time."

I shivered at the slide of his lips over my skin, yielding to his lead. I didn't want to slow down, but he knew better than I did, didn't he? He was the one with experience.

Or was this about control?

It didn't matter. Either way, I was enjoying the hell out of it.

Soon, we were walking side by side, holding hands, as we explored the perimeter of the property. I pointed out the best features of Heron Estates.

"Here, let me show you my favorite place," I said as we emerged from the woods into a narrow meadow.

We made straight for the running trail and followed as it traced the edge of the bay. I pulled him onto the creaking wooden planks of the dock and led him to its end. We stood quietly, soaking up the scene. The water splashed against the pillars and teased the marsh grasses. A heron launched into the sky, searching for another place to hunt, far from human intruders.

"Is this your view?" He sounded as reverential as I felt.

"Yeah. It's beautiful, isn't it?" I pointed at our trailer, visible through a stand of trees. "Come on."

We crossed the lawn, tramped up the steps of the back deck, and slipped in through the sliding glass door. I locked it behind us and turned. "This is my home," I said in a rush of nerves and apology.

He stood in the center of the den and studied the room. There was the old love seat covered with a floral sheet. The homemade curtains and pillows. The plastic flowers on a faux-wood table.

His jaw flexed.

"What's wrong?" I watched his reaction closely.

He relaxed into a more neutral expression. "Nothing is wrong."

It wasn't *nothing*. There was no hiding the discount store furnishings or the cheap carpet. The trailer surprised him, and he was doing what he could to hide it. "You think it's a dump."

"No, I don't." He looked at me over his shoulder. "Are you upset?"

I was more than upset. I was ashamed. It was the nicest home I'd ever lived in. Yet, as I tried to imagine it from his perspective, I knew what he was thinking. *So this is how trailer trash live.*

A weird feeling bubbled inside me, as if my bones were crumbling and my muscles were jumping. I was in danger of barfing at any second. We shouldn't be here. This place shouldn't be a part of our relationship. I'd been an idiot to let him in. "You've seen enough. Let's go. Do you like the beach?"

"Eden, I want to stay." He held out his hand.

I ignored it, crossing my arms over my chest, trying to fight off the wetness burning behind my eyes.

"Come here, please."

When I didn't move, he drew me gently into his embrace. One of his hands rested at my waist while the other rubbed lightly at the base of my skull. I shuddered against him, confused and aching.

"We're good," he said.

No, we weren't. I shook my head.

"What's bothering you?"

I inhaled, dragging in the fresh scent of him. "It's small."

"It's been engineered for efficiency."

I stiffened. "Don't patronize me."

"I'm not. Do you think it makes a difference to me where you live? Because if you do, I'll try my best not to feel insulted."

"It would make a difference to your friends."

"Then it's a good thing that you're not dating them." His mouth hovered near mine. "I just want us to be together. I only see you, not where we are."

I melted a little. He'd said the perfect thing.

"Can we stay?"

I nodded.

He kissed me softly and straightened. "Is the date officially underway?"

"Yes."

"What's next?"

I wasn't sure. Lots of physical contact should definitely be on the afternoon's to-do list, but I didn't know what that meant to Ash. So far, our make-out sessions had seemed fairly tame. Was that because of the newness of us? Because complete privacy was hard to find? Or were they tame because that's where Ash set his limits?

Maybe we should start with something easy. "Do you want a tour?"

"No."

His answer was so fast and forceful that I giggled, for possibly the only time in my life. "Behind me is the kitchen—"

He stopped my nervous babbling with a kiss that promised to last forever. Not that I was complaining.

The warmth of his mouth pulled away. "Eden?"

My eyelids opened. "What?"

"How long before your folks return?"

"At least four hours."

"Where's your bedroom?"

"Uh . . ." A fast transition. "What are we . . . ?"

"Hey." His hands slid down my arms until his fingers could link with mine. "Don't worry. You're in charge."

"This might well be the first time in history that Ash Gupta handed over leadership of a project to someone else."

That comment earned me a hard, delicious kiss. Being a smart-ass was a productive attitude to take with him.

"Okay, then. Follow me." I led the way to my bedroom. It was small but nice. Clean. Everything in its place. I could say, with complete honesty, that I was proud of this room.

He leaned against the doorframe while I walked around, playing hostess. "Here are my desk and my mirror." I glanced at the bed. Okay, not mentioning that. It was obvious what it was. I pointed to my bookcase filled with photos, awards, and other happy stuff. "Those are my favorite things."

He said nothing.

I'm in charge. My arms and legs quaked. What next?

I couldn't bring myself to look at him. "It's perfect for me, although I'll bet you have closets bigger at your house."

"Eden. Don't." He walked over and hauled me up against him until my toes hardly touched the ground.

Damn, I wasn't exactly a tiny girl. His strength was sexy. "How often do you work out?" I asked, to keep the conversation going, because conversation was good. It bought me time.

"I play sports whenever I get the chance."

"Like?"

"Tennis, golf, surfing."

"Surfing?"

He grunted, his focus no longer on the talking. "I like it when your hair is loose," he said, frowning at my ponytail.

"Take it down."

One of his arms supported me while, with his free hand, he reached for my ponytail holder and pulled it off carefully. "I wish you would always wear it this way."

I loved his absorbed expression. "What is it with Gupta men and my hair?"

"It's gorgeous. Thick. Long." He combed some strands away from my face. "It feels like silk. The first time I saw your hair like this . . ."

"At the MIM."

"Oh, yeah. I turned around and there you were with this golden hair flowing over your shoulders and your big blue eyes and that tight tank top. All I wanted—" He groaned and let me slide down until my feet rested flat on the floor again.

"What did you want?"

"I wanted *this.* To touch you. To reach for you without asking because I knew you welcomed my hands on you."

This was getting intense faster than I could handle. I inched away until his arms dropped. Turning, I wandered over to the full-length mirror, trying to see myself through his eyes.

I looked ordinary to me. Medium build. Medium height, with the top of my head barely even with his chin. Blond hair. Fair skin. A face that most people wouldn't notice. Nothing remarkable. Nothing bad.

Were our contrasts the attraction?

He came to stand behind me, wrapped his arms around my waist, and drew me back against him.

Well, hello. He was hard, and he was holding me close, and what did that mean?

His head bent to my neck, his mouth searing my skin.

What were we doing?

Not that I was complaining. Yet.

He nuzzled aside my outer shirt, pushing it to the floor. Then he kissed his way along my shoulder until he reached the strap of my cami. In one smooth move, he hooked the strap with his thumb and peeled it down my arm. I held my breath, paralyzed by heat and fear and wonder.

"Beautiful." His eyes focused on my bare breast with fascination while his hand slid over to cup me. I was thrilled by the need on his face—that my body created this reaction in him.

It also scared me shitless.

I was in charge. I could stop him. All I had to do was say *no*, but the word that trembled out was *"please."*

He fondled my breast oh so gently. Shivers cascaded over me. I sank back into his hold as I look at our reflection, riveted by the sight of dark skin against light, loving the firm, warm caress of his fingers.

The power had shifted in his favor. I was doing nothing to stop his hand and his lips and his body against mine. I was afraid of what came next, yet I wanted to know even more.

I had to stop him.

No, I had to stop *me*. But how?

Do something.

Say something.

"Ash?" His name came out as a whisper.

He grunted without slowing down.

"Have you ever had sex?"

His lips stilled on the curve of my neck. His eyes raised until our gazes met in the mirror. He waited silently.

"You seem to know what you're doing."

"You don't?"

"No."

He straightened, pulled my cami back into place, and released me.

I bent, grabbed my shirt, and yanked it on. "You're not a virgin."

"You are?"

"What the hell?" Cheeks flushed with humiliation, I backed away from him until the mirror stopped me. "You assumed that I'd had sex before? Without asking?"

"I'm sorry." His voice was gruff.

"That's a big assumption, Ash. I don't date. I've never had a boyfriend. There haven't been many opportunities to lose my virginity." I didn't know whether to be hurt or angry. "Have I ever given you any cause to expect otherwise?"

"Murray Fielder has."

That name added instant fuel to my fury. "That's just great. I believe everything Murray says too." I glared down at my bare feet with their bold purple toenails. "How does his story go?"

"Eden."

"What do people think?" There was silence. I looked up at him. He stood rigidly, hands fisted at his sides. "Tell me, Ash."

"According to Murray, on your first date, you gave him a blow job in his truck before you made it into the restaurant."

I shuddered, as if something nasty was creeping down my spine. Turning my back on Ash, I considered what he'd said. I'd known that Murray wouldn't tell the truth. Why should I be surprised at how far he'd stretched it? He thought he was safe. Nobody would've believed me over Murray. "You came here today to have sex with me."

"*No.*" The word that slipped out was soft. Tortured.

"Then why?"

"I came here today because I wanted to be with the girl I can't—" He stopped.

"What?" I looked at him over my shoulder. He was tense enough to shatter. "The girl you can't *what?*"

"I wanted to be with the girl that I can't stop thinking about. The girl who could want nothing more from me than holding my hand—and it would be enough."

Yes. *That.*

My anger dissolved as if it had never been. Closing the distance that separated us, I wrapped my arms around him and felt his lock around me. I adored him. This was where I was meant to be.

His lips brushed my forehead as I burrowed against him. Our embrace felt sweet and safe. I ached to trust it. "I didn't give Murray a blow job."

"You don't have to do this."

"I want you to hear it." I leaned back in his arms. "It's a lie. Murray shoved his dick in my face and said there would be no date if I didn't take care of him."

Ash was silent, his expression hard to read.

"I answered with my fist."

"You hit Murray?"

"In the crotch."

"Wow." Ash winced. "I should've asked you about it."

"Yes. You should have." I snuggled closer and listened to the steady beat of his heart.

Slowly, he pulled away from me. "I'm sorry, Eden." He backed up until his leg bumped the corner of my bed. "I think that I should leave."

"No. Please stay." I followed him and curled my fingers into his shirt. "I don't want you to leave."

He covered my hands with his. "Maybe we should try this another day. I've messed it up."

I shook my head and gave his chest a firm push. He fell back on my bed, taking me with him. We landed, me on top, our legs tangled.

With a smile, I said, "This is where I want you."

"Are you sure?"

"Yes."

"Fine with me," he said, still watching me carefully. "Should we leave? Go to the beach?"

"I like where we are now. Really. You're tall. I was tired of craning my neck."

"I'll try to remember that." With extreme gentleness, he rolled us until we lay side by side. "Eden?"

I shook my head at him. "It's behind us now."

"Forgive me anyway?"

"Yeah." I ran my fingertips along his jaw, exploring its faint roughness. "My first date was with you, Ash. My first kiss. You're my first everything."

"This may sound selfish, but I'm glad your firsts are mine." He turned his head until he could press a kiss into my palm.

I leaned closer to brush my lips against his. He pulled me against him until we touched chest to hip.

"We got each other wrong," he said.

"Yeah. Not sure if that's funny or sad." The misunderstanding had been painful, but what came afterwards was good—like we'd been propelled forward into something much better. "When you said I was in charge, what did that mean to you?"

"You would say stop when we reached your limit."

"I didn't understand that. I didn't know enough to say *go*."

"Yeah, got it. Can we start over?"

"Works for me." I shifted against him, loving the restless way his fingers traced the length of my spine. "We have to finish the sex talk, though."

"If we must."

"I'm in charge, so yeah." I gave a nod, in case the matter wasn't clear in his mind. "What about birth control?"

"I brought condoms."

"Condoms? As in more than one?" I smiled to show I didn't mind. "Somebody expected to get lucky today."

"Planning is key." He smiled back.

"I'm not on the pill or anything."

"If it's ever an issue, I'll handle it."

"It'll be an issue. Someday." My gaze dropped to the brown skin in the vee of his shirt. "I'm not ready."

"Whatever you give is enough."

I loved that he sounded so patient and matter-of-fact. It made me yearn to give him what he wanted. To want what he wanted. Just not yet. "Can we still make out even if we know where it won't end up?"

"I sure hope so." His smile faded. "What's allowed? I don't want to overwhelm you."

Good question. We'd made it past fierce kisses already, but how much farther could I go? "Maybe . . ." It was hard to think when that beautiful face with those sexy eyes looked at me with such longing. "Anything above the waist is fair game."

"Oh, yeah. I can work with that."

I launched an assault on his mouth. It became quickly evident that not only did he have superior skills in this area, but he was also a talented coach.

The make-out session continued unabated until the crunch of tires on gravel penetrated through my pleasure-hazed brain. I broke off a kiss and raised on my elbows, listening intently. A motor shut off, chugging and clicking its way to silence.

"Get up. That's Marnie's car." I pushed at Ash. "You have to leave."

"I thought you said we had hours."

"Something must've happened." I peeked through the curtains. My dad slumped in the passenger seat, fists over his eyes. The driver's side door screeched open.

I crawled over Ash and made sure the front door was locked. He raced behind me to the sliding door and onto the deck.

"Go straight back to the woods. Do you remember the trail?"

"No problem." His lips touched mine.

Footsteps thumped on the front porch steps. "Go, Ash. Hurry."

He tiptoed across the deck and ran the short distance to the trees beyond. I waited until he'd disappeared into their dim cover, then yanked the curtains into place and ran to the laundry room.

A key turned in the lock. The front door opened and closed.

"Eden, we're home," Marnie yelled. The trailer shook as my father trudged its length.

I waited until he was out of the way before stepping out of the laundry room. "Here."

"Your dad's not feeling well. He needs to lie down."

I gave her a happy hug. "Did you get to see any of the wedding?"

"We left immediately after the ceremony. Didn't make it to the reception." She watched me without expression. "What did you do while we were gone?"

"Nothing special."

She turned her head deliberately and looked into my room. I followed the direction of her gaze. My bed lay clearly visible, the quilt rumpled and askew, pillows on the floor.

She stalked past me. "Nothing special looks like an awful lot of fun."

It was close to midnight when my phone buzzed in its hiding place under my pillow. I took a peek.

> Ash: got a moment?
> Eden: yes
> Ash: did they see me?
> Eden: no

My answer was technically true, but Marnie was suspicious. I would tell her soon and hoped that she wouldn't care much that Ash was Indian. And that she would keep it a secret. Dad would care.

Ash: are you free Sunday afternoon?

Eden: yes

Ash: want to go to North Topsail Beach?

Eden: that's kinda public

Ash: we'll be fine. if anybody sees us, we're just friends

Eden: k

Ash: where should I pick you up?

Eden: go just past entrance to heron estates. i'll be around
    the bend

Ash: can't wait. sleep well

Eden: you too

    I powered off the phone and slid it into the pair of jeans that I would wear tomorrow. Nerves quivered through me at the idea of this date. It was the bravest we'd been. The weather was supposed to be nice, and North Topsail was popular, even in the fall.

    Slipping back under the covers, I shook my worries off. Ash didn't take risks. We would be fine. Like he said.

✦ 22 ✦

Imminent Retribution

The media center was mostly empty when I arrived after school on Monday. I sat at my usual table in the back and got out my chemistry book. I could get a few problems out of the way before Mundy joined me to work on an English project.

A few minutes later, Ash and his circle of friends entered in their typical burst of noise. They laughed their way across the room to take over a table several rows from mine. I glanced up and met Ash's gaze briefly. Damn, he was beautiful.

Relaxing my face into disinterest, I frowned down at the textbook, reread the problem, and picked up my pencil.

Someone pulled out the chair next to me and sat. "Hi," Ash said. His arm dropped along the back of my chair as he peered at my pad of paper. "What are you doing?"

I fought my lips to keep from smiling. Had he lost his mind? "What are *you* doing?"

"I have to be near you."

"We have an audience." His friends had stopped what they were doing to watch us. Dev and Upala looked pissed. The other two looked disturbed. "They know, Ash."

"They don't know." He slid the pencil from my grip and wrote something on my paper. "Not for sure."

"Upala spoke to me once."

His face tightened. "Did she upset you?"

"No."

"Did you confirm anything?"

"No."

He relaxed. "She's smart enough to keep her mouth shut."

"You're being reckless. Go back over there."

"I will." He wrote some more.

I glanced down and had to clench my teeth against a sigh of pleasure.

Wish I were touching you
Call me?

I looked at him. We'd been putting my new prepaid phone to use, with almost hourly texts and hushed calls late at night. "Eleven?"

He stood abruptly. "Sounds good," he said, overly loud.

"What's good?" Mundy appeared beside us.

"Life." He held out her chair and pushed her in. With a smile, he left.

I didn't watch him go, preferring to busy myself with pretending to solve a chemistry problem.

"Ash adores you."

"He does."

"You adore him."

"I do."

Her laugh was triumphant. "I knew it."

"I think his friends do too. That worries me."

"Well, stop it." Unzipping her backpack, she whipped out her tablet and smacked it on the table. "English?"

"Sure." She was right. I ought to stop worrying.

I allowed myself a tiny smile. It was time to trust this.

I arrived at school early enough on Tuesday morning to drop by the computer lab. Mrs. Barber wasn't in sight, although the cup of steaming coffee signaled she couldn't be far.

My e-mail was full with over a hundred messages. Odd. The subject line from Mundy leapt out at me. *Check candids page.* I brought up the school's web site.

"Eden?"

The word shivered over me, leaving goose bumps in its wake. I could become addicted to the way Ash said my name. As a little kid, I'd hated *Eden*. My name had been a big joke, which made *me* a big joke, but Ash made it sound lovely and unique.

I scanned the lab until I found him standing in the entrance. "Why are you here?"

"You really have to ask?" He gestured toward the computer lab's office. "Is Mrs. Barber in there?"

"No." My heart thumped in anticipation.

He crossed to the office and disappeared from view. I hurried after him and, boom, collided with his body. His nice, solid, welcoming body.

Ash wrapped me in a hug. "I missed you."

"I missed you, too." Twining my hands around his neck, I drew his mouth down to mine.

"Mmmm," he murmured against my lips. "We'll have to do this more often."

"Agreed." I hadn't expected to be alone with him until later this afternoon. This was an awesome surprise.

"*Eden?*" Mundy's shout echoed through the lab.

Her timing was bad.

"Ignore her," he said, but there was resignation underneath the words.

"Let me check. She sounds upset." I poked my head out the office door. "What do you need, Mundy?"

Her eyes focused on me, wide with alarm. "You haven't checked the candids yet."

"I will."

"Do it now." Her voice rasped. "This is crazy."

Her urgency got through to me. I exchanged a concerned glance with Ash before returning to my chair. The Campus Candids page held several new shots which had been uploaded Monday. I scanned them quickly and found the image she wanted me to see at the bottom.

Holy. Shit.

It was a black-and-white shot, stark in its beauty. The sun had been low on the horizon, preparing to sink behind the dunes at the beach. In the foreground, the ocean had been gray and choppy. A teen couple, absorbed in each other and oblivious to the rest of the world, leaned against a wooden pillar of a pier at North Topsail Beach, the boy standing behind the girl, cradling her in his arms. While he buried his face against her neck, she laughed at the waves washing up near their feet, her fair hair whipping in the breeze.

The guy would be unrecognizable to all but those who knew him well; the sole telltale sign was a white crescent-shaped scar gleaming on his dark thumb.

And the girl?

She was a deliriously happy version of me.

There wasn't a person in the world who would look at this photo and think that couple was *just friends.*

Ash dropped onto a computer chair and rolled it closer. "What's up?"

"The school's web site." Life was about to change.

He made a choked gasp. "Where did that photo come from?"

"I don't know."

"Did you upload it?"

"Of course not. Why would you think that?"

"You're the president of the Webmaster's Club."

"I can delete files from the web site, but only Mrs. Barber can upload content." How had this happened? Had we been hacked? "I can't believe she would've published it without my permission." As I was speaking, I removed the image, but I knew—and he knew—that it was a vain effort. Things like this could go everywhere in an instant.

"Shit." He popped to his feet, his hands clenching and unclenching.

I rose too and reached for him. He flinched. It was like a blow. "Don't act like this is my fault. It isn't."

"I know, but I can hardly think. This is a disaster."

"Hey, guys," Mundy called from the door. "Mrs. Barber's on her way."

I blinked. I'd forgotten Mundy was there.

Ash gripped his backpack and turned to go. "We have to cancel our plans this afternoon. I'll have to tell my parents, and that'll take hours."

I followed him out into the hall, watching as he hurried away. I wanted to scream at him to come back, not to leave me. My body ached to have our perfect little world last for a day, an hour, a moment longer.

"Hey, Eden." When Mundy pulled me into her arms, I slumped into her like I was a rag doll that needed support. "What do you think will happen?"

"I don't know." I shook my head, dazed.

"Come on. Let's go to class." She lifted my backpack and tugged me along. "Time to face the fallout."

Ash didn't appear in the cafeteria, although his study group did. Their anger had a physical feel.

They weren't the only ones glaring at me. Other classmates were throwing speculative glances my way. I wanted to know what they thought, yet I also didn't want to know.

I tried to eat, but that wasn't working either. The atmosphere in the lunchroom was too thick with tension. What was their problem? There were a few interracial couples at this high school. It couldn't be that I was white and he wasn't. Could it?

Maybe it was something else. Maybe I wasn't the right kind of white.

I couldn't take this any longer. Even with Mundy's protection, the glares and whispers were getting to me.

Popping to my feet, I said, "Can you clean up? I have to get out of here."

"Are you sure?"

"Yeah."

I fled, hurrying down the hall, uncaring of the curious stares, completely focused on finding peace. My best option would be the computer lab. It was in a quiet corner of the building, teachers were used to seeing me there, and it was likely to be empty during the lunch period.

But as I rounded the next corner, I halted. Murray Fielder was standing outside the lab, talking with a couple of his teammates. When he spotted me, he jogged in my direction, waving the others on.

I turned to go.

"Hey," he said, stepping into my path.

I tried to move around him. He stepped there, too.

What should I try next? My normal response to Murray was to run, but I couldn't tell what he was willing to do to prevent my escape.

No, dammit. I wasn't taking this. He'd picked the wrong day to mess with me. "Get away from me."

"Don't think I will." He took a step closer, crowding me. "Ash and Eden? Didn't expect that."

I held my ground.

He smiled lazily. "I wish I'd known you preferred dark meat."

"You are a worthless piece of shit." Revulsion threw me into action. I flung myself sideways, trying to get around him, only to skid to a stop when he blocked me again.

"Fielder! Back off." Sawyer ran at us full speed, his shoes slapping on tile.

Murray and I spun around in surprise.

When Sawyer reached us, he pushed himself between me and Murray. "What the hell are you doing?"

"I didn't touch her."

"Is that true, Eden?"

I eyed Murray with contempt. "He's guilty of a lot of things, but assault isn't one of them."

"Bitch—"

Before he could finish, Sawyer knocked Murray back into the wall. They stared unflinchingly. Where Sawyer's expression promised imminent retribution, Murray's held seething defiance.

Sawyer spoke without looking my way. "Go on, Eden. I've got this."

"What?" Murray forced out through gritted teeth. "I didn't touch her."

As I walked away, pretending that I didn't have the shakes, I heard Sawyer say, in a chilling voice, "It takes a special kind of asshole to pick on a girl. I think you have a lesson to relearn."

· 23 ·

A Film of Tears

Marnie," I called out as I pushed open the trailer's front door with a hip. Continuing into my room, I dumped my stuff next to the bed and stood motionless. It had been a horrible day.

Ash left school after third period. I'd tried texting him. There had been no reply.

How had his parents taken it? Not well, probably.

My turn, but I'd make sure that Marnie was alone first.

Had she responded to my call? I hadn't heard her. Maybe she was back in her bedroom. I started across the den, then faltered to a stop.

My stepmom sat on the love seat, lips pressed tightly together. She watched me through red-rimmed eyes.

"Marnie, what's happened?"

"You're dating Ash Gupta."

I staggered as if someone had smashed me with a bat. How had she found out? She should have heard this from me. "Yes, we're dating."

Tears spilled down her cheeks. She choked on a sob. "You should have been the one to tell me."

"I'm sorry. I was going to."

"When?"

"Today." Carefully, I sat next to her on the love seat and braced myself. The accusation in her voice cut with a razor-sharp sting. "Who told you?"

"Desiree Barber."

Tiffany and her mom ought to know better than to take me on. "When did you find out?"

"An hour ago." Marnie averted her face. "How long have you been dating?"

"Three weeks."

"He was over here this weekend."

"Yeah."

A shudder rippled through her. "You don't trust me."

"Yes, I *do* trust you."

"But not enough to let me know about Ash."

"We kept it a secret from everyone."

"Even Mundy?"

Damn. "She knew, but she was the only—"

"Save the explanation." Marnie mopped at her cheeks. "Why, Eden?"

"I wasn't sure what you'd think."

"About what? That your boyfriend is attractive? Rich? Smart? Yeah, moms hate those things for their daughters."

I hung my head, too guilty to reply.

"You thought I wouldn't want you dating an Indian."

No point in denying it. I nodded.

She sprang off the love seat and stalked to the opposite side of the room. "What kind of person do you think I am? I've never said or done anything to make you think I don't like them."

"But Dad—"

"I'm not your father." She sucked in a ragged breath. "There are things about Byron I don't like. He blames all immigrants for losing his job. He thinks awful thoughts, and sometimes they pour out his mouth. But I'm not him." She paced across the carpet, arms crossed, shoulders hunched. When she spoke again, it was in a whisper. "You didn't trust me to be happy for you."

"I'm sorry."

"Not good enough." She headed to the back hallway, stopping to look at me over her shoulder. "You tell your father when he gets home."

"Where is he?"

"At Granny's, fixing her stove."

"I'm not talking to him unless you're here." I perched on the love seat, staring at my hands. Without her around, any conversation with my dad would rage out of control within seconds. My stomach twisted into knots. "He won't listen."

"The time for listening is over," my father rasped from the kitchen.

Marnie and I stared at each other in surprise. How long had he been standing there?

I glanced at his hardened face and swallowed convulsively. He'd heard enough.

She faded into the shadows of the hallway, leaving me alone with him. My heart thudded into overdrive.

Dad crossed to the kitchen table, spun a chair around, and sat. "A white guy wouldn't have you, so you're slumming with an Indian."

I should thank him for leading off with something foul. It flooded me with disgust, muffling the fear. "I guess you'd know about slumming."

"When were you planning on telling me?"

"Never."

"Because you're ashamed."

"No, because you're racist."

He popped out of his chair and walked over to me, halting when the tips of his shoes bumped against mine. "His folks hang out with their kind. White folks hang out with our kind. If that's racist, then we're both guilty."

I stared straight ahead, my eyes on a level with the tool belt slung low around his hips. Did he ever wonder if they stuck together because his kind worked so hard to keep them out?

No, my dad didn't wonder. He was just smug about the righteousness of his point. No use in trying to rebut it. He didn't want to understand my side of the story.

Of course, I didn't want to understand his either.

"I hear his type treat their women like dogs. Is that how the boy treats you?"

"He treats me better than any guy ever has."

"Is the boy banging you?"

The question swirled around me like a toxic wind, threatening to immobilize me. I wouldn't give in. "His name is Ash."

"All right, then. Is *Ash the Indian* banging my daughter?"

From the corner of my eye, I noticed a movement in the darkness of the hall. Marnie hovered nearby.

"I don't ask you about your sex life. Don't ask me about mine."

"I'll ask you whatever I want." His hand shot out and hauled me to my feet, his fingers biting into my upper arm. "Are you on the pill? I won't put up with little brown babies in my house."

"You're a pig." I yanked my arm from his grasp. "I don't need lectures from the dickhead who knocked up the town slut."

"Whore."

"Loser."

He backhanded me.

I stumbled over the love seat, crashed into the wall, and slid down until my butt met carpet.

Silently I sat there, cheek aching, eyelids floating on a film of tears. In the background, Marnie screamed *"Stop"* at least a thousand times. I wanted to ask her to hush, except it hurt too much to move my jaw.

"Sweetie." She knelt beside me. "Let me help you."

"Don't." I struggled to my feet, moving in stages, while the room swam around me. I let the wall hold me up.

"Do you need me to help you stand?"

"No." The room had righted itself.

"Eden," Dad's voice trembled. "I didn't mean to."

I didn't look at him.

"Please, baby girl. I didn't mean to."

I took hesitant steps past him toward the sliding door.

"Where are you going?" Marnie asked.

"To the bay." The door shushed open.

"Marlene," he said.

"Shit, Byron," she hissed, "have you lost your mind?"

"Doll—"

"Get out of my way." Her feet thudded on the deck behind me. "Eden, wait."

I stopped. She circled around me and scrutinized my face. After pushing away a lock of hair with gentle fingers, she gasped. "Sweetie, I'm sorry."

"You left me alone with him." The words seemed to scald my

throat. How could she have let this happen? She should've known how it would go.

"I'm sorry." Her fingers started to explore the side of my head. "How hard did you slam your head?"

I jerked away from her touch. "Hard enough."

"Do you have a lump?"

"Stop, Marnie. I need the bay." Before I fell apart.

Her hand dropped. "You're babysitting tonight."

"I won't be late."

I went to the water.

It was almost seven before I made my way back to the house. My time at the bay had calmed me, as I knew it would, but it hadn't helped me understand how I felt about what happened.

When Boone and I were little, Dad had whipped us often enough, as spanking was one of the few tools in his parental-discipline toolbox. He'd always been matter of fact. *This is going to hurt me more than it does you.*

No, it hadn't, but whatever.

Marnie hated spanking, so it stopped when she came to live with us. Boone had been paddled a few times since, but not me. Twelve years had passed with no physical punishment.

Until now. I didn't know what to do about it.

I ought to feel . . . something. But what? I wasn't sad. I wasn't scared. I wasn't mad.

I felt betrayed. By my dad, for hitting me. By my stepmom, for not protecting me.

When Mundy saw the bruise on my face, she would ask if I'd done anything about it, like march my father down to the sheriff's department.

But what would they charge him with? Being a redneck? A racist? I wasn't going to bother. Our local law enforcement didn't care if a father gave his mouthy teenaged daughter a little skin-on-skin discipline.

The Mundys of the world believed in a sunshiny legal system that would find a way to make this type of situation better, complete with suspended sentences, community service, anger-management classes, and family counseling. I knew better. The Edens of the world grew up in trailer parks, and they had different rules.

Justice changed depending on where we lived.

I would handle this myself, and it would be effective. Dad ought to be worried about what *I* would do next.

My first objective was to hide the bruise on the right side of my face. I'd have to get up an hour early tomorrow and see what the wonders of makeup and hair style could achieve.

It was time to head out for my job and do everything I could to avoid looking my boss in the eye. She might feel obligated to report this.

I fumbled in my closet for a different shirt, since I would have to wear longer sleeves to hide the bruises he'd made on my arm. As I was making a final check of my backpack, something bumped into the door to my room.

Marnie leaned against the doorframe, keys dangling from her index finger. "Ready to go?" she asked, her voice rough.

I hesitated. Of all the people in my life, Marnie was the only one I'd never fought with. Not in any real way. We'd always had an amazing relationship. Until this evening. "I don't want to say good-bye like this, Marnie."

"Yeah." She opened her arms and I fell into them, shuddering while she murmured comforting words that made no sense but that I understood. Once the shudders slowed, she tucked a finger under my chin and turned my head to the side.

"Crap," she muttered. "It's looking worse."

I said nothing.

A grim expression settled on her face. "I told your father if he hits you again, you and I are leaving. Forever."

Damn, I loved her. "Has he . . . ?" I frowned, wondering if she would tell me the truth. "Has he ever hit you?"

"Once. When we were dating."

"Then why did you marry him?"

"My first husband smoked too much, drank too much, and had another girl on the side. With Byron, it's been better. He adores me, he doesn't care that I can't give him kids, and he's great in bed."

I cringed. I would've preferred a life that didn't include knowledge of that last part.

"Mostly, though, I married your father because it was the only way I could have you and Boone." She kissed my good cheek. "Sweetie, if you want to leave anyway, I'll figure something out."

The offer surrounded me like a soothing hug. In a way, I should feel sorry for my dad. If his kids had been the main draw, what would happen to their relationship after I left? Maybe Boone and I were the glue that held them together. Did Dad worry about that? Was this why he'd been so insistent that I live at home? Was that even more important than having me work at the hardware store or go to Cape Fear?

If saving his marriage was the real explanation for all of the grief he'd been putting me through, Marnie's reaction today must terrify my father. Too bad I didn't have any sympathy to spare him. "We don't have to make any decisions."

She nodded. "Do you want to take the car?"

"Aren't you working in the morning?"

"I can drive Byron's truck."

I took the keys. "What about him?"

"He's running scared right now. He won't argue with me. A day stuck on the property will do him good."

"Okay, I'm out of here." After grabbing my backpack and a change of clothes, I headed for the front door. She turned away.

"Marnie?"

She looked over her shoulder.

"Will you please quit working at the convenience mart?"

"Yeah. Soon."

"By Thanksgiving?"

"Probably."

"Definitely. Promise?"

She gave me a half smile. "Promise. Now leave."

⋆ 24 ⋆

In Jeopardy

I made it through the evening and the next morning with head bowed, lots of makeup, and loose hair, parted to hang over my bad cheek. Mrs. Fremont would've said something if she'd noticed, but she hadn't. Maybe my plan would work.

When I got to school, I waited outside on the bench under the big oak tree, hoping to catch Ash as he walked in from the senior parking lot. His entourage stood not far from me on the sidewalk, occasionally throwing tense glances my way. Clearly, they blamed me for what was going on.

Ash wasn't with them.

They stirred as a group and turned toward the bus lane as a tired yellow school bus slowed and stopped. The doors opened and students spilled out. Ash was the last one off.

Ash rode a *bus* today? That couldn't be good.

I knew the exact moment when someone told him where I was. He stiffened, his gaze seeking mine. After speaking briefly to his friends, he headed for me.

"Hi," he said.

I held out my hand to him, careful to keep the good side of my face toward him. "Why did you ride the bus?"

He hesitated a moment before taking my hand. "I've been grounded from using my car."

"How long?"

"A couple of days. I hope."

"I'm the reason." It wasn't a question. Of course, I was.

"Lying is the reason."

"Lying about *me*."

He shrugged. "They want to meet you."

"I'll bet." I backed up, tugging him around to the far side of the tree, away from his friends and into the shadows.

A line of students streamed past on the sidewalk, laughing and talking and watching us.

I waited until no one could hear. "How pissed are your parents?"

"Pissed enough to turn on the GPS on my phone to track me." His eyes narrowed on my face. "You put on makeup today."

"A little." I looked at my shoes, allowing my hair to swing forward over my bad cheek.

"And you're wearing your hair down."

"You like it that way." I wrapped my arms around his waist and leaned into him.

"Not going to work. Something's wrong." With one hand, he placed gentle fingers under my chin and tilted my head. With the other, he tucked a loose strand behind the ear on the sore side of my face. "Eden," he gasped in shock and horror. "How did this happen?"

"Not saying."

Outrage vibrated off him. "Was it your father?"

"Not. Saying." There was a confused little girl inside me who wanted Ash to hold and kiss me until it was all better, but this wasn't the right place for that.

"Are you going to report him?"

"Marnie has it under control."

"I'm not impressed."

"She couldn't reach me in time yesterday." I shook my head, denying the issue and its hold over me. It was more important to focus on Ash and fixing our mess. "When do I meet your folks?"

"Eden." My name came out on an agonized groan. When his fingertips feathered over my bruised cheek, I flinched away.

He lowered his hand to cup my shoulder. "Your father hit you because of me."

"I can take care of myself." I nodded with confidence. Dad couldn't compete against me *and* Marnie. "Do your parents want to schedule something?"

He frowned, his breathing labored.

"I'll be okay," I said. "We'll be okay."

"I don't know if we will."

His statement sent a ripple of dread through my body. "Don't talk like that. It scares me."

"Can you come over to our house tomorrow night? I'll pick you up."

"I'll have to leave for the Fremonts' by seven, so I'll drive myself." The first bell rang. Around us, the stampede began as students hurried inside. Standing on tiptoe, I raised my lips to a millimeter below his.

"Trying to make a point?" he murmured, his warm, minty breath enticing me.

"To you."

He closed the distance. Our lips clung, lingered.

Our first public kiss felt more like a defeat than a victory.

Mundy plopped onto the desk beside me in English and leaned across the aisle. "How did last night go? Did your parents take it well?"

I shrugged, my face averted. "Not entirely."

She made a kind of grunt in her throat, stood, and walked around to my other side. Lifting my hair, she hissed, "Sonofabitch."

If I hadn't been so tense, I might have laughed. Swearing, from Mundy, almost sounded cute.

"Eden?"

"Drop it."

She slid back into her desk. "You haven't reported him. Have you?"

"I haven't told you how I got the bruise."

"I'll tell Cam."

"And you'll both be embarrassed if you press this. I'll deny everything, and the county legal system will breathe a sigh of relief."

"This isn't right—"

"Mundy. Eden," Ms. Barrie interrupted us. "Let me know when I have permission to proceed."

We nodded and faced forward. My eyes sought Ash. For a flicker of a moment, our gazes held, sweet and tormented.

As today's lecture wound through the twisty narrative of Faulkner's *As I Lay Dying*, I lost focus. When the bell rang and the classroom burst into noise, it jolted me. I clutched my backpack and headed for the teacher's desk, hoping to get in a question between classes. The Peyton application had to be turned in by next Wednesday, and I hadn't requested the teacher recommendation yet. Under normal circumstances, I would've asked Mrs. Barber, but she was the Honors Committee chair. The obvious next choice was Ms. Barrie. She might be pissed about writing one fast, but writing was her talent. I was prepared to beg.

Standing beside the desk, I turned so that my good side was toward her. While waiting for her to look up, I gave myself a mental pep rally for the coming ordeal and reflected on how odd it was that my favorite teacher could be so unapproachable.

I'd taken two classes from her: junior English in addition to this year's English Lit. Both classes had emphasized writing, and it wasn't enough for our essays to communicate. She inspired us to communicate beautifully. I loved how much she loved language.

Why, then, did talking to her intimidate me?

Maybe it was the contradictions in her appearance. She had to be six feet tall with the build of a weight lifter, yet she wore delicate sandals with toenails painted, this week in zebra stripes. She had iron-gray hair, cut in a no-nonsense style close to her head, while sparkly chandelier earrings dangled from her ears. It was hard to know which Ms. Barrie was the real one.

"Yes, Eden, how may I help you?" Her head remained bowed.

I clasped my hands to keep them from shaking. Why was this hard? She liked me. I knew she did.

She twirled a finger impatiently, as if to speed things up.

I spoke in a rush. "I'm applying for the Peyton Scholarship, and I was hoping . . . that is, it would be an honor if you would write my teacher's rec." I drew the instructions sheet out of my notebook and offered it to her.

She stared at it, her expression unreadable. With a sigh, she pulled off her glasses and rubbed the bridge of her nose. "I'm sorry, but I can't."

Disbelief arced through me like an electric shock. "All right." I returned the sheet to my backpack, my thoughts muddled.

"I've already written one for Ash Gupta." She finally looked up at me. "It wouldn't be appropriate to write one for a second student, no matter how much I admire her abilities."

"I understand." And I did, but I didn't like it. After thanking her, I left, trying not think about how pissed I was for allowing this awful week to distract me to the point that I'd put my Peyton application in jeopardy.

Dr. Holt was waiting outside the door to the art room, leaning against the wall, hands in his pockets. When I approached, he straightened and gestured me over.

"Eden," he said, his voice tight with concern.

"I asked Mundy not to say anything to you."

"I'm glad she did. May I see?"

In answer, I lifted my chin and shook my hair back. Might as well have one teacher who knew the complete truth.

He exhaled an angry breath. "Are you in pain?"

"I'm fine, Dr. Holt. This is private. I have it under control."

"There are things we can do—"

"Please. Stop. You've done your duty." I looked away, hiding behind a curtain of hair again. "If you want to help, don't let this be discussed in the teacher's lounge."

The bell rang. He pulled the door almost shut, leaving us alone in the now-empty hall.

"You're welcome to stay at our house, Eden. As much as you want. Just call, day or night. We'll pick you up."

"Thanks." I forced out the word through a throat thickened by unshed tears. He was wonderful. Mundy's whole family was wonderful.

"Art can be a tool for channeling emotion. It's yours to use." He opened the door and held it for me. "Okay, come in. And if you feel like you need to leave—to be by yourself—there will be a pass waiting for you."

I took my place at a table next to Mundy and listened as he described the assignment. When he was done, he reached for a familiar green slip of paper, scrawled something on it, and pushed it to the corner of his desk.

Around me, the other students got started. I sat quietly, thinking about that pass, so very grateful that it was there while knowing I wouldn't use it. Because this was where I wanted to be. I *needed* art today.

After school let out, I went straight to the computer lab. Mrs. Barber wasn't there, so I flopped onto a computer chair and waited.

The *thock-thock* of wooden-heeled clogs entered the lab. I looked up to see Mrs. Barber disappear into her office. She hadn't noticed me sitting here.

Anxiety whimpered in my gut as I stood. I had to have it out with her, since it was likely her fault that the Ash-Eden photo hit the Internet. I wanted answers.

I braced against the doorframe for support. "Got a moment?"

"Sure, what's up?" Her tired smile flattened when I pushed the door shut with a soft click.

"Did you upload this image?" I held out a hard copy of the photo.

She glanced at it and nodded.

"Without my permission?"

"Watch the tone, Eden," she said, her eyes narrowing. "I did have your permission. When you mailed it to me on Monday, you told me to add it to the candids page."

"I did *not* send you this photo."

Frowning, she opened the laptop and keyed in her password. "The message came from you."

My brain whirled with this bit of information. Could someone have hacked into my account? Nah. My password was too tight. "Do you still have the e-mail?"

"Maybe." Her fingers flew over the keyboard. "It's not there. Let me see if it's in Deleted Items."

She typed *Eden* into the mail application's search function and up popped a deleted message.

> From: Eden Moore
> Subject: photo of me to upload
> Attachment: topsail.jpg
> Please add this shot to the candids page.
> Thanks, Eden

"My account was spoofed," I said. "What is the actual address?"

She hovered over my name. *Totalbeach@freemail.com.*

Somebody had gone to a lot of trouble. It was disturbing. "Does the e-mail address still work?"

Mrs. Barber clicked Reply. A few seconds later, the message bounced.

Mail returned undelivered: Account Not Found.

"I apologize, Eden. I never thought to check."

Of course she didn't. The perpetrator had counted on that. "This is an elaborate fake out."

"Who would've done such a thing?"

"I'm not sure." I did, however, have a strong suspicion. It was too bad that Gina had overlooked the safety net we had in place. "If it had really been me, I would've uploaded the photo to the staging area and asked you in person to post it. You had to know that."

"I was excited to see you and Ash together. You make a cute couple. I didn't think about how strange it was to receive the image by e-mail." She paled. "I'm sorry."

I inclined my head, yet I couldn't bring myself to say it was all right because it wasn't.

"Will you report this?" Her eyes were anxious.

"No."

"Thanks." She shuddered. "Do you want me to remove the image?"

"No, ma'am. I took it down."

After retrieving my hard copy of the photo, I left her office and sat down before one of the lab computers. My discussion with Mrs. Barber might be over, but I was hardly finished with the topic. The guilty party had to be located. I logged into the web site's administrative account, and rechecked the opt-out list for my name. Yes, it was still there. Whoever had sent that e-mail must've known Mrs. Barber wouldn't upload it otherwise.

The Webmaster's Club and the Journalism Club had access to the opt-out list. The criminal was probably in one of those two groups.

Where had the photographer been standing when the photo was snapped? When Ash and I went to the beach, there had been no one near us. We'd been too careful. I remembered a few people farther down the shore, noisy and laughing. It must've been one of them. And from their distance, a normal zoom lens wouldn't have given enough clarity.

I had to organize the available data. The criminal had:

1) Artist-quality photographic talent
2) Access to expensive camera equipment, including a telephoto lens
3) Knowledge of the opt-out list
4) A grudge against me or Ash

All clues led to Tiffany.

· 25 ·

Definition of Perfect

As I walked up the sidewalk to the school on Thursday, there was a burst of familiar giggles behind me. I stopped in my tracks and spun around. Just who I wanted to see. "Tiffany."

She and her best friend froze. Around us, our classmates slowed as if they smelled a fight.

Licking her lips nervously, Tiffany took a few steps nearer to me, clutching her bag to her chest like a shield. "What do you want?"

"Drop the act. You already know."

Her gaze held mine for a moment before drifting to my bruise. "Did Byron do that to you?"

"What do you want the answer to be? Would it ease your guilt if I said *no*?" I leaned in, shaking from some emotion that I couldn't identify. "You may have thought it was just a stupid joke, but it set off a lot of bad shit."

Regret flickered in her eyes.

"Why did you do it, Tiffany?" Had a whimper of betrayal crept into my voice? Nope. Couldn't allow that.

"The photographer is anonymous."

"No, she's not." It overwhelmed me to think that she'd created such a spiteful plan. She might've fooled herself into believing she had legitimate reasons to be pissed at me, but to this level? It hardly made sense.

From a short distance away, her friend Starr watched us silently, a smug curl to her lip.

Wait. Was Starr in on it? Had this crime been an impulse that got out of hand—with Starr egging Tiffany on?

That must be it. *Mean* was contagious. "Whose idea was it to involve Gina?"

"I don't—"

"You could've gotten her into a lot of trouble. Did Starr come up with that part?"

"Do you think I'm not smart enough to come up with this on my own?" Tiffany's chin lifted. "You need to back off, Eden. It's done. It's over. You don't have proof, and you never will."

"I'll find some."

"No, you won't." She stepped around me.

"Really? You think you get to walk away, like nothing happened?"

She stopped to glare. "Yes, but go ahead. Do your best. It won't matter." She gave a spoiled-princess toss to her head and ran toward the front doors. Starr caught up in two strides.

I barely survived my first two classes, anxious that I couldn't get Ash to do more than mumble a few words to me. By lunch, I was desperate for a break. Clarissa Cruz-Holt had been sending in good food lately, including enough for me. There seemed to be a lot of raw veggies in today's lunch pack, which Mundy loved. She could have them. I'd eat the trail mix with M&Ms.

Mundy spoke between crunches. "You're meeting his folks tonight?"

"Yeah." I was glad for the conversation. Anything to divert my attention from dark thoughts. "I'm nervous."

"He adores you. You adore him. His parents are bound to notice." She made it sound easy, when I knew it wouldn't be.

"That won't make them like it."

"True. It's too bad love can't be enough." Mundy stared off into the cafeteria, people-watching, a bright smile on her face.

She was beautiful and fun. It surprised me she didn't have a steady boyfriend. In fact, there was something wrong with a universe with a dating Eden and a single Mundy. Maybe it was time for a change. "Is there any guy you like?"

"I have a terrible crush on someone."

"You've never told me that. How come I don't know something so important?"

"We don't talk about me. Your problems are much more interesting."

"Oh, yeah. That makes me feel better." What kind of friend was I? "Want to give me a name?"

"Sawyer Atkinson."

How cool. They would make an adorable couple. Especially since he felt the same way . . .

"I'm an idiot." My heart skipped a beat. He liked her. She liked him, and I was responsible for ensuring they hadn't found each other yet. What kind of friend was I? "He asked me if you ever mention him, and I said *no*."

"That's true, though. I haven't until now." Her smile grew even brighter. "What else did he say?"

"He thinks you're amazing."

"He does?" Her gaze zeroed in on where Sawyer ate several tables over. "I want him badly, but I shouldn't start something with him at this point. It wouldn't be fair."

"*Fair?*" I frowned. "Why did you use that word?"

She continued as if I hadn't spoken. "I don't care. I'm going for it anyway."

Mundy marched over to where he sat in the midst of the other popular kids. She gave a lengthy monologue in her own animated way, hands gesturing wildly. The group reacted with increasingly comical levels of shock, especially Tiffany, whose gaze bounced between Sawyer and Mundy with alarm.

Once Mundy ended her speech, Sawyer scrambled to his feet, clasped her hand, and pulled her to a corner. An intense conversation followed after which she smiled, nodded her head, kissed him on the cheek, and returned to our table. He watched her stroll away, utter worship transforming his face.

My glance slid past Tiffany and returned. She was staring at me with fury. I shrugged. This match had happened in spite of me. I hadn't set Sawyer up with Mundy, but I was glad because they would be great together.

"So?" I asked when she was seated again.

"We have a date tomorrow night."

"Did you ask him? In front of all of the popular kids?"

"Yes. He thinks I'm amazing, remember? He wasn't likely to turn me down." She made it sound as if it were only natural.

I laughed as I rummaged around inside her paper sack. There were two Godiva chocolates. She was a good friend. "Why did you say it wouldn't be fair to him?"

She went still, her smile vanishing. "I don't want to tell you yet."

Mundy had no secrets. What was she hiding? "Too late. Tell me."

"Cam is returning to his old job."

My brain broke her statement apart, processing the pieces a little at a time, hoping to make sense of it.

Cam is returning to his old job.

Cam's old job was teaching art at a community college.

In California.

Cam was returning to California. With his family.

I didn't want to think this through, but the horror flared into comprehension anyway, taking over my being, shining a light on my life before Mundy arrived and my life after.

Before Mundy, I'd sat alone, attended class alone, gone home alone. And I'd been fine because I hadn't known any differently.

Since she came, *alone* had been replaced by anticipation. I'd expected to eat lunch with her. To hang out. To know that her parents didn't mind me being around.

Friendship with Mundy was good, and I was hooked.

"Excuse me," I said, hopping to my feet, "I have to get out of here."

Mundy rose, catching my elbow in a firm grip. "You understand, don't you?"

"Got it." I jerked away from her and lifted my tray.

"I'm sorry, Eden." Her voice, muffled and sad, followed me as I walked off. "We'll be gone by January."

Somehow I held it together for the rest of the day, but barely. When I got home, I retreated to my bedroom, curled on my bed, and stared at the wall.

How could I stand to lose Mundy?

I'd always been a freak in this town—a girl with too many brains and too much history. I'd resigned myself to being on the fringes. Not missing what I didn't have. I had goals instead of relationships.

It was strange how quickly I'd become attached to Mundy. We were nothing alike. We had nothing in common except being outsiders in Heron.

Neither of us fit in, so instead we fit together.

Watching Mundy hang out with me must've confused our classmates. It changed my value. I'd always believed I could be a good friend, but they hadn't. Mundy made them wonder. Once she left, they would stop.

I felt so tired, so fractured, so . . . angry.

Yeah. Angry at *her.* Mundy must've known all along that she would return to California. She should've told me. It should've been my choice.

Maybe I should detach from our friendship today. I could pretend she was already gone.

Would that work?

Questions swirled in my brain, repeating themselves, weaving in and out of my consciousness. I huddled on the quilt and focused on my breathing. It gave me something to do. Something other than think about the news I couldn't accept.

It was time to leave for Ash's house. This day had already been one of the worst of my life and, before I could recover from it, I had to face his parents. That meeting had me so scared that I could hardly function.

I stared into the mirror, my stomach twisted in knots. Even

though I'd piled on the makeup, there was no hiding the bruise. The Guptas would see it. She was an ER doctor. She would know how it got there. I didn't want to go.

After changing into my good khakis, I agonized over what shirt to wear. There weren't many choices in the "nice" range. Another quick glance at the clock forced a decision. I slipped a silky blue shirt from its hanger and whipped it on, frowning at the way the button between my breasts strained. Was it too much?

I shouldn't second-guess myself. Grabbing my overnight things and the keys to Dad's truck, I ran for the front door.

"Eden?"

I hesitated, my hand gripping the knob. Marnie came over and studied my expression.

"What's happened, sweetie?"

"It's not a good day." A headache pounded between my eyes.

"Will you be okay?"

"I hope so." I gave her a tight smile, walked out to the truck, and drove to the Guptas' home. It took me a while to find it since I'd never been to their neighborhood before. But at last I saw their house number and pulled onto the brick driveway curving through a wooded, landscaped yard. I parked and stared at their house. Their really huge house.

Ash exploded through the door and jogged to a halt a few feet away. Frustration glittered in his eyes.

"You're late."

I glanced at the clock. Three minutes. I inhaled to calm myself. It didn't work. "I got lost."

"Fine. Come on." He led the way through the front door and veered left, into the biggest living room I'd ever seen. His parents stood side by side before the fireplace. His father wore a suit. His mother had on a turquoise silk dress and lots of gold jewelry.

Had they dressed like that for me?

I shifted closer to Ash, longing to touch him somehow, knowing that would be a bad move.

After Ash made the introductions, Dr. Gupta, the father, said, "Eden, welcome. Please sit." He gestured toward a white sofa covered with silver and violet throw pillows.

I wanted to check the back of my pants before sitting on something so white, but that wasn't cool. Instead, I perched on the edge.

Ash stepped past me and sat at the other end. All prim and proper. Whatever. I warmed my freezing hands between my thighs, gave them both a quick smile, and glanced down at the wrought-iron coffee table.

An inlaid tray of wood and mother-of-pearl slid across the glass surface of the table, stopping near me. It held a dozen small cookies, each in its own pleated paper cup.

"Please have some dessert," Dr. Gupta, the mother, said. She had a soft, musical voice. It must calm her patients.

"No, thank you."

None of them got a cookie either.

Mrs. Gupta's gaze took in my bad cheek. Her eyes narrowed, but otherwise her expression remained mild. "Ash says that you would like to go to Carolina."

"Yes."

"What other schools are you considering?"

Should I mention Cape Fear? Probably not. "Only Carolina for now. I'm still looking, though."

Ash's parents exchanged glances. Apparently it was the father's turn to talk because he gave me a beaming smile. "Have you decided on a major yet?"

"Education. I want to be a teacher." Duh. What else did education majors become? I rolled my eyes at my own stupidity.

The room grew silent.

This was incredibly awkward, and I didn't know what to do about it. His parents were the ones who were running this show. Right?

I'd tried to corner Ash at school today—to ask him about the expectations for this meeting. To let him soothe away my fears. But he'd been impossible to get alone and he hadn't responded to calls or texts.

So here I was, totally unprepared. On a good day, I wouldn't have had a clue how to behave around the Guptas. I'd never talked to a boyfriend's parents before. Hell, Clarissa and Cam were the only parents-of-friends that I'd talked to in years, and they were so amazing that it was easy to be comfortable around them.

I glanced at Ash now and found him staring at my chest. The straining button? Could he see cleavage? My gaze switched to his parents. His father was staring at his hands. His mother looked from her son to me, eyebrow arching high.

Was this yet another way I'd screwed up?

I looked at the fireplace, needing to stare at something that wouldn't judge me. Over the mantle hung an oil painting, Georgia O'Keeffe–like. Lavender peonies on a blue background. Very nice.

This house was nothing like I'd imagined. It smelled faintly of lemon, instead of Indian spices. The living room had the put-together feel of an expensive interior designer. There was nothing exotic about it. This could've been any rich doctor's showcase mansion. I tried a tentative smile with his mother. "You have a lovely home."

"Thank you." She toyed with a bracelet made of heavy gold links. "You are on your way to a job this evening?"

How much should I share? I shouldn't bring up Mrs. Fremont's childcare arrangements, in case Dr. Gupta didn't already know.

"Yes, ma'am. I have to be there by seven. I babysit two kids three nights a week."

"Do you have time to study?"

"After they go to bed, I finish my homework."

She transferred her attention to Ash. "Do you have much homework tonight?"

While he gave a brief description of what he had to do, I watched his hands. He gestured as he spoke, each movement expressive. I'd never thought about how beautiful his hands were.

"Eden?" Mrs. Gupta prompted.

I wrenched my gaze back to her. "Yes?"

"I understand that you are cousins with Tiffany Barber. She is also competing for the Peyton. I've heard that she is quite a talented girl."

My body, face, everything stiffened. Had Mrs. Gupta just complimented the despicable witch who'd caused this misery with her *talent*? "Tiffany is my stepmom's cousin. She's no relation of mine."

Mrs. Gupta's lips thinned. Ash stared at me through eyes wide with horror. What was his problem? I'd been mild, and I hadn't cursed.

A cocktail of fiercely unpleasant emotions flared in my gut. I had to get out of here, to catch my breath, to beat the feelings back. "Excuse me," I said. "Could you tell me where the bathroom is?"

Her plucked eyebrows arched into points. "In the foyer, second door on the right."

"Thanks." I slid off the silky sofa and left.

The bathroom was immense and dramatic. Black, white, and silver wallpaper and furnishings. I'd never been in a bathroom so elegant that I was afraid to use it.

Tugging at the button, it was clear that nothing could make my shirt stop gapping, but it wasn't too awful. Barely a hint of my curves was visible.

I needed to calm down, get over it, and relax.

A glass shelf held a collection of tiny thimbles. I studied them, fascinated by all of the styles, colors, and sizes.

My face felt hot. I splashed it with water, then checked out the collection of soaps. Five different scents. I settled on vanilla.

Rather than mess up the white guest towels, I dried my face and hands on my shirttail and tucked it back in.

There was a knock at the door. I opened it a crack.

"Is there anything wrong?" Ash asked, his voice hoarse.

"No. Why?"

"You've been in there over five minutes."

"Shit. Sorry." I flicked off the light and stepped into the hall. His parents waited behind him.

Great. I had just turned *bad* into *worse*.

The whole evening had been a catastrophe, and there was no way to salvage it. I ought to go. "Thanks for inviting me over, but I have to leave."

They murmured stilted good-byes.

Ash was silent as we walked out to the truck. He held the door open while I buckled in.

"Do you realize how screwed we are?" he bit out.

Today had been too much to bear. I was saturated with pain. I couldn't handle his frustration too. It seemed to hang in the air, not sinking in. "I guess so."

"We had to be perfect, and that was a disaster. What happened?"

If he'd wanted me to be perfect, why hadn't he talked to me

today? I had no clue what his parents' definition of perfect was. "I've never done this before."

"Done what?"

"Gone to someone's house and talked to their parents."

"Clearly. Otherwise you wouldn't have been late or shown up dressed like that."

I looked down. It was the nicest outfit I owned. "I don't know what to say." I had the strangest urge to cry, but my eyes felt hot and dry.

He sucked in a couple of loud breaths, like he was gasping for air. "Why didn't you try harder?"

I shook my head, so weary it felt like I might not be able to lift my hands to the steering wheel. "I'd better go."

"I don't think I can fix this, Eden."

His statement jarred me. I looked at him, shocked at the anguish etched into the lines of his face. "What do you mean?"

He gave a tiny shake of his head, slammed my door shut, and strode back to the house.

I slumped in my seat, hands folded in my lap, going over what he'd said. Frustration welled within me.

He shouldn't have let me walk in there without coaching. I knew how to please teachers and how to mock Marnie's cousins, but I knew nothing about impressing adults like the Guptas, and Mundy's news had messed me up.

My momentary flash of anger drained away. I fumbled to get the key in the ignition and crossed my fingers that I could make it to my job without crashing.

· 26 ·

Bleeding Into the Boards

Last night, Ash's behavior had been upsetting. Today, he'd terrified me.

When I waited for him at the bus lane this morning, he brushed past me, saying, "Can't talk now." His entourage had closed around him like a shield.

He'd avoided me in the hallways all day and didn't answer his phone.

I texted him to ask if he would meet me at the gazebo. I finally got back: *see you at 8.*

Until I'd experienced the gazebo alone, cold, and in the dark, I couldn't have acknowledged what a scary place it could be. My heart pounded so hard it pulsed in my ears. Yet my fear over the upcoming discussion loomed bigger than the dark.

A car purred into the parking lot. A door *ka-thunk*ed. Then nothing. A minute passed. Shoes thumped up the wooden steps.

I turned slowly, nervous about what I would see.

He stopped a few inches away from me—tall, straight, still. The moon gleamed silver behind him.

"Eden." A single word. Soft. Flat. He'd never said my name that way before.

"Ash, I'm sorry about last night." My hands were cold. I should've worn gloves. I couldn't think with cold hands. I jammed my fists into my pockets. "How can we fix it?"

"It's too late for that."

"Too late?"

His mouth opened. Closed. He looked past me into the park, as if searching for something out there in the shadows. "I'm here to break up with you."

"*No.*" When I reached for him, he backed up a step, as if I didn't have the right to touch him. "You can't mean this, Ash. We can work something out."

"They've forbidden me to see you."

He kept throwing these awful words at me. I knew what they meant, but how could he be using them with *us*? "That's crazy. And completely unenforceable. We go to school together. They can't—"

"I can only speak to you if we're assigned to the same project."

It was like he'd memorized a script, except this was real.

I watched him carefully, looking for a sign that I'd misunderstood, but I hadn't.

Forbidden.

Longing and desperation overwhelmed me. I stumbled forward and fell into him.

He tensed, his body so rigid it could've been carved from stone. I burrowed against his chest, seeking a response from this unemotional statue that I didn't recognize.

A strangled gasp hissed from his mouth. His arms whipped around me, one hand tangling in my hair, the other slipping beneath my jacket, his fingers caressing the skin of my back.

"Please, Ash. I don't want this to be true."

"It is." He spoke sadly. Hopelessly.

The silence swirled around us. I smelled wood smoke and his clean, spicy scent. He must be mistaken. We were meant to be together.

"How can this happen after one bad meeting? Don't I get a second chance?"

"That was your second chance. They already knew they didn't want you in my life. Last night confirmed it."

I shifted to look into his eyes. "Why don't they like me? Because I'm white?"

"Being white isn't really the problem."

What was he trying to tell me? Something nasty was there, on the periphery. Something I didn't wish to face but that I already knew.

"It's me specifically." I pushed away from Ash with deliberate movements. "I'm the trailer-trash girl who's corrupting their son."

His nod clawed at my soul.

Whoa. I needed a moment to take that in. White girls in general might be tolerated, but not Eden Moore. I struggled to keep my voice even. "They're both doctors. They're smart enough not to buy into the stereotype."

"It's not just that. They've heard things . . ."

"From your friends?"

"Yeah."

This scared me like holy hell, but I fought off the panic. "What have your 'friends' said?"

He looked at the dome, exposing the smooth column of his

throat. "That you're bad for me. That you distract me from my priorities. That I can't succeed with you in my life."

"We have proof otherwise. Our grades haven't suffered. We can fight this."

"My parents heard things from me, too. I'm responsible for their opinion." His gaze lowered to mine. "*I* did this to us."

"You? What things?"

He raked a hand through his hair, bitterness twisting his lips. "For years, I've complained about you. I've told them that you're rude and sarcastic. That you swear . . ."

I'd confirmed all of those flaws last night.

". . . That you don't care about your appearance."

No. Not letting that one slide past. "I dressed up last night."

He frowned. "What?"

"That's one of the nicest outfits I own." I gripped his arm. "I tried to ask you for help, but that didn't happen because you ignored me all day."

"My friends were watching."

"Why were they more important than letting me go in there unprepared?"

"I could hardly think straight. My parents and friends already believed that I'd lost my mind, that you had a strange hold over me." He swallowed hard. "My mother found the condoms."

"What? She went through your things?"

He winced.

"I see." Anger roared through me. It felt good. I knew what to do with anger. "Not only have your parents violated your privacy, they assume that I've lured you into a relationship with sex. You corrected them, right?"

His eyes widened with horror. "I don't discuss sex with my parents."

"Well, great. Letting them believe that I'm a slut is so much better." He'd covered for his ex-girlfriends at my expense. "Coward."

He jerked back as if I'd slapped him. "Nice, Eden. I think I'll go now." He spun around and stalked over to the steps.

This couldn't be happening. It was too soon. Our relationship had brought me so much joy, and it was crumbling with each step he took. "Don't leave me, Ash. Please."

He paused at the top of the steps, bracing himself against the frame.

I crossed to him, frantically hunting for something that could salvage us. "We can still see each other. We'll be careful."

"No." His tone was dull. "I can't take the risk."

"They don't have to know. We can find places to hide."

"Maybe you don't mind deceiving your parents, but I wish to honor mine."

"Great catch there, Ash. Dishonesty is totally how redneck families operate."

His head dropped to his chest, his shoulders sagging. "I'm sorry, Eden. I don't think that."

Why were we attacking each other this way? It didn't lighten the pain or delay the inevitable. We'd both been guilty of sneaking around, but it had only been because our parents had forced deception on us.

Defeat radiated from him. I watched for an agonized moment, choking on its bitter taste.

Long-buried memories flickered, of Christmases past. I'd wanted to believe in miracles so badly. I'd tried hard to be good. I would awaken early each Christmas morning and tiptoe out to the tree, hoping that this would be the year I'd get what I wanted. But it never had been there. Santa couldn't come to homes like mine.

For one short month, Ash had been my miracle, and I was losing him too.

When I pressed a hand lightly to the small of his back, he shuddered.

The answer might break my heart, but I had to ask. "Why am I not worth the risk?"

"They'll take away everything."

"Your car? Your phone?"

"So much more."

No longer denying myself the need for an embrace, I locked my arms around him and rested my forehead against his back. He straightened and placed his hands over mine. Trembling, I waited for him to pry me away, but he didn't. Instead, he linked our fingers tightly.

"Do you think I'm bad for you?" I whispered.

"*No.*" He spun around and hauled me up against him, an arm hard at my waist, a hand light against my sore cheek. "*No.* You're the best part of my life." The pad of his thumb brushed gently over my bruise. "Your father hit you. Do you know how much that tortures me?"

No, not that. I wouldn't allow my dad's actions into this. "I can take care of myself."

"Eden." His jaw clenched as something intense raced through him. "I've had to put up with a lot over the years because my parents weren't born in this country, but I've never had someone else take the blows."

"It doesn't matter. We can keep our relationship a secret. We'll only see each other after dark. We'll call at midnight. Our parents don't have to know."

"They'll take away Stanford."

"What?" Shock rippled through me. "How can they do that?"

"If I don't stay away from you, they won't pay."

I breathed in his statement. Let it fill me.

His parents were brilliant. They'd played a card that I'd never imagined they would use, and not for a second did I wonder if it was a bluff. This threat was masterfully designed to achieve its goal. They were willing to take away his dream to get rid of me.

I loved him better than that. "Okay, Ash. They win."

"What are you saying?"

"I give up. You can't lose Stanford." We both needed to escape Heron. Me, because it was too little. Ash, because it was too much. "We're done."

He scanned my face as his thumb traced the curve of my lips. Leaning closer, he angled his mouth over mine, his kiss soft, reverent. It wasn't enough. I threaded my fingers through his hair and pressed harder, needing more.

It was as if my touch unleashed something in him. He moaned, his hands roaming my body. We kissed over and over, hungry and crazy and wild, like we couldn't get enough of each other.

Like we were saying good-bye.

He wrenched his mouth away. "I love you. Always."

"I love you, Ash."

He pressed his lips to my temple as his hands slid slowly down my back to my hips. Reluctantly, he pushed me away. "I'm sorry, Eden. I've got to go."

He rushed down the steps, his footsteps fading into the dusk. There was a moment of silence, then a car roared, spitting rocks as it screeched from the parking lot.

I crumpled onto the gazebo's bench and clung to one of the wooden pillars, surrounded by the scent of decaying leaves, the click of bare branches colliding in the wind. My throat ached with tears.

The night Heather abandoned us had been like this. Cold and windy with a big moon painting the outdoors silver. Boone and I had been eating at the kitchen table and trying not to listen to an argument that she and Dad were having in the foyer. Their voices came and went in a weird, staccato rhythm. Then there was a shriek and a thump and a crash.

I had dropped my spoon and glanced at Boone. We turned in unison to gape at them. Dad seemed to be hugging the wall, crying. Our latest family portrait lay on the floor, shards of glass sparkling around his dusty boots. Heather stood by the front door, dressed in her Sunday best, suitcase in hand.

"It's no use, Byron," she said. "I'm tired of playing house." The screen door thwacked behind her.

Slipping from my chair, I squeezed past my father and onto the front porch, my feet bleeding into the boards. "Don't leave me, Mommy," I screamed. "Please."

The clip-clop of her high heels stopped, tapped twice, then returned. She emerged from the shadows. "I'm sorry, Eden. I've got to go."

With a smack, she planted a strawberry-scented kiss on my cheek. Then she hurried down the sidewalk, her footsteps fading into the dark. Two car doors slammed. A motor whined down the street, growing fainter. Then silence.

She never came back.

⋅ 27 ⋅

Gaping Wound

The sun rose at 6:37 on Saturday morning, a neon orange ball illuminating the wavy line of scrub grass on the other side of the bay. I studied it objectively, wondering how I would capture the image if Dr. Holt assigned such a project in 2-D art.

A boat puttered in the distance. The wind gusted, peeling back a corner of my blanket. I wiggled on my low deck chair, burrowed deeper into the blanket's warmth, and waited for the hours to pass.

Footsteps thudded on the dock. Marnie's voice floated past me on the breeze. "Have you been up long?"

"I never went to bed."

She crouched beside my chair, smelling of coffee and bacon. A travel mug appeared before me. "Here."

"Thanks." I took the mug and sipped. Paul Newman's Bold. A luxury.

"Do you want company?"

"I prefer to be alone."

A sympathetic grunt. "Do you want your phone?"

She knew about that? I shook my head.

"Mundy called twice last night and once already today."

Ah. I hadn't put it on silent. "Don't want to talk to her."

The footsteps receded.

I rested my chin on my knees, retreating into my blanket like a turtle into its shell. My thoughts drifted lazily.

Boots clopped on weathered boards, intruding again.

"You won't answer the phone," Mundy said, "so I came to you."

I poked my head over the edge of the blanket, up to my nose, but I didn't look at her.

She dropped next to me onto the end of the dock, her legs dangling over the edge. "I had my date with Sawyer last night. It was fabulous."

"Not. Interested." I could feel her gaze on me, but I still didn't look her way.

Her boot kicked a pillar of the dock, *thump-thump-thump*ing. "We haven't really spoken since Thursday. What's the deal?"

"Didn't Marnie tell you that I want to be alone?"

"She did. I knew I was exempt."

I finally peered at her from my blanket, marveling at her lack of perception. "You aren't exempt. *Especially* you."

"What do you mean?"

"You're leaving, Mundy. What's the point?"

"The point?" She recoiled. "We're friends. Friends talk. They listen to each other's problems."

"Can't listen if you're not around."

"I'll be in California, not Antarctica, although that wouldn't be a problem either since I suspect the Internet works there as well."

"Hanging out is a big part of friendship. Being trustworthy is too. You went after me, knowing the whole time that you'd move soon."

There was a long pause. "That's true."

"You could've let me know up front. You could've let me make the choice."

"I didn't want to. You would've turned me down."

"Yes, I would've, but you did what you wanted, without caring how it affected me." I blew out a shaky breath. "You wouldn't leave me alone, Mundy. You forced me to talk and got me used to something I'd never had before. And soon you'll be gone."

"Wow. I've never thought about it like that." Her voice softened as she worked through her thoughts. "I've never had this type of friendship either. With homeschooling, we have all of these events planned. There're a mix of ages, and we hang out however we want. But you're the first friend I've ever had where it was just the two of us. And now I'm going back to my old group. And you're . . ."

"No shit."

"Stop it." Her mouth twisted. "You've had a sucky life. I'm sorry about that. I'm sorry that Heather abandoned you, and I'm sorry you don't know where she is."

"Lovely. Can't wait to hear where this is going."

"Hush." Mundy stood and glared down at me. "Maybe I should've told you that I'd likely be here one semester, but I'm not apologizing. You know why?"

"I'd rather not."

"Stop being a jerk." She clomped a few steps away, then halted. "I'm glad that I didn't give you a chance to turn me down, because that would've been wrong. Our friendship's been the best thing about living here, Eden, only now it has to change. Like all good relationships do. As far as I'm concerned, a few months were better than none."

"Glad that worked out for you."

"Fine, then. You want to be alone. I'm giving you your wish."

I spent Saturday evening the same way I'd spent hundreds of nights, quietly studying in my room. It was the way I liked it. To escape, I had to make stellar grades. I had to stay focused on the future.

The clock ticked away the hours. The pages of my literature textbook blurred and swayed. Eventually I gave up.

I couldn't sleep or think, but I could feel.

I missed her.

I missed him.

My time with Ash flickered on the edge of my consciousness, like a beautifully framed image except the glass had shattered. I couldn't stop myself from thinking about the cracks.

I needed to lean on someone. Mundy would be willing, but she couldn't help me because I sent her away.

The best thing about living here . . .

She was right. It had been. I'd been happier in the past two months than I could ever remember being. Ash was a big part of that, but so was Mundy. With him gone, I needed a friend more than ever, and I was only an apology away from having one. I also needed to have it out with her—to let her know how much her deception hurt me—but we had to be talking first.

It took me until lunch the next day to work up my courage. I borrowed Marnie's car and drove into town.

Mundy answered the door, gazing at me blandly through the screen door.

248 + Julia Day

I shifted from foot to foot, not sure of my reception. "Hi."

"Hi."

Good. Instant rejection would've been hard to get past. "Can I come in?"

"Are you going to apologize?"

"Are you?"

She shook her head.

I shrugged. "Me neither."

She opened the door wider and got out of the way.

We sat in our normal spots on the sofa. She looked at me expectantly, but I didn't know where to start.

"Well?" she prompted.

This was awkward. It would be appropriate to get emotional and spill my guts, but I wasn't the mushy type. Which she knew. "Uh—"

Shrieks from the second floor interrupted me. Naked Destin charged down the stairs, dripping from his bath. Close behind him chased Clarissa, red towel dangling from her hands like a matador's cape. They ran giggling around the sofa until Destin dived into my lap and rubbed his soaking-wet, shampoo-laden hair into my shirt.

"I've got you," his mother said. She swaddled him with the towel and rushed up the stairs.

The whole thing lasted less than a minute. Mundy and I looked at each other, then burst out laughing. Thank God for Destin. He broke the ice.

"I need us to be friends again, Mundy."

"Yeah, me too." She scooted around to face me and crossed her legs. "Tell me everything I've missed."

I wasn't quite ready. The gaping wound where Ash used to be

was still too raw to probe. "I want to hear about Sawyer. What did you do?"

"We had batting practice."

"What?"

"Have you been to the Battleship Fun Park in Wilmington? They have a batting cage with this machine firing baseballs at you."

Unbelievable. "How'd you do?"

"Better than Sawyer." She smiled smugly. "I played short for my homeschool league's coed softball team."

"How did Sawyer handle it?"

"Well. Sawyer is impressed by excellence."

"Uh-huh." The Sawyer I knew didn't like to be beaten. The poor boy must've been impaired by hormones. "What happened next?"

"We ate hot dogs, which were disgusting, and came here. Mom fixed us popcorn, and we sat in the porch swing and talked."

"That has to be the tamest date Sawyer has had in years."

"He obviously didn't mind, since we have another date tonight." She sniffed. "What did you do this weekend?"

"Completed the work on my Peyton application. Prepared for a statistics test."

"Boring. You may not mention school again in this house. There are much better things to discuss. Like Ash. Did you see him Friday night?"

I nodded, blinking back the moisture stinging my eyes. "We broke up."

"Wow. Do you think you could've shared this, oh I don't know, two days ago?" She scooted closer, until her knees were touching my thigh. "No matter how enlightened his parents might try to be about their son dating outside their community, they couldn't get past your baggage."

Deep breath. By coming here, I'd chosen Mundy's brand of sympathy. "Yeah."

Leaning forward, she peered into my face. "Is there anything else I should know?"

Yeah. Lots. Retelling the story hurt almost as much as living it had, but I told it all.

"Ash is right about your dad, you know." She studied my bruise, her frown intense. "You never filed a police report?"

I shook my head. "Homegrown justice is taking care of this."

She made a rude sound with her lips. "I'm skeptical. Do you want to stay here tonight?"

"I'm babysitting for the Fremonts." Grief had me caught in a vise. "How can I make it through tomorrow? How can I see him?"

"Eden." Mundy dropped an arm over my shoulders. "It'll be awful, and you'll survive it anyway."

For the first time since Friday, I cried.

· 28 ·

Too Tired to Lie

I handed Kurt a plate with two pieces of toast, lightly buttered, no jelly, cut into fingers instead of triangles. He inspected them suspiciously before grunting, "Juice?"

"Right here." I set his favorite red cup within reach.

Breakfast was underway for Marta. She fixed her own cereal and milk.

The garage door whined open and the SUV pulled in. Marta looked up, chewing furiously. Kurt nibbled toast. I glanced at the clock, surprised. Mrs. Fremont was a half hour earlier than normal.

Their mother trudged in through the utility room and leaned against the kitchen counter. "How are my babies?"

Marta giggled.

Kurt scowled. "How many times do I have to tell you? Children stop being babies when they reach their second birthday."

"Thanks, I'll try to remember." She exchanged a tired smile with me. "How did everything go last night?"

"Smoothly."

When she yawned, I placed a mug of coffee in front of her with a soft click. She wrapped her fingers around it and took a sip. "Mmmm." She yawned again. "Marta, you can ride the bus this morning. Kurt, finish up. We'll leave in a few minutes."

"What's happening today?" I said, mopping crumbs into the sink.

"I'm having a parent-teacher conference before school. I hope you don't mind being dropped off early."

"With Kurt's teacher?"

"With the educational support team. They say that Kurt's misbehaving in class."

"Am not," he shouted, then jumped from his chair and stormed down the hall.

I waited until Marta left before continuing the conversation. "What exactly are they complaining about?"

"His classroom teacher says he sits by himself, refuses to do his work, and growls at the other kids." Mrs. Fremont's face sagged.

Kurt wouldn't act out without provocation, and Mrs. Fremont was tired. After a night at the hospital, she wasn't at her best. I had to help. "May I come with you?"

"Why?"

"I could babysit him in a corner." The more I thought about it, the better I liked the idea. "I want to be a special-ed teacher someday. Maybe I could listen and learn."

The glaze faded from her eyes. "You'll miss your first-period class."

"If you want me, I'd rather be with you and Kurt."

"I'd like that."

. . .

Following Kurt through the maze of hallways in his school brought back memories. The scent of yeast rolls baking in the cafeteria was overpowered by the nauseating antiseptic cleaner the janitors used to wash everything. Finger-paint paintings and Popsicle-stick sculptures had been attached to every spare stretch of open wall space.

I remembered it without a trace of fondness.

Mrs. Fremont introduced me to the school support team, although I already knew the classroom teacher. Mrs. Mannis (The Menace) and I had crossed paths in my elementary days. Ours wasn't a happy history.

For fifteen minutes, I did my best to be nice. I stayed quiet, sitting on the floor midway between the teachers and Kurt. He played in the corner, consumed by an elaborate airport model.

Mrs. Mannis droned on and on. *Blah de blah de blah.* She didn't come right out and say it, but the woman resented having to teach an unconventional child. That was the bottom line. He wasn't normal, and it was too much effort to help him.

I held my tongue. I'd promised myself to be an observer.

Then the teacher said the magic words that set me off.

"He's defiant," The Menace said. "He refuses to color because he doesn't *like* it."

I spun on my butt to face her. "Do you use crayons?"

The other people at the table went still and blinked at me.

"Naturally. What else would we use?" the teacher asked with a patronizing smile.

"Colored markers."

"We don't offer those."

"Then, *naturally*, Kurt will refuse to color. He can't stand the smell of crayons."

"The smell?" Her lip curled. "They don't really have a smell."

"Yes, they do. Kurt's nose is better than yours, and you'll only make him use crayons under duress." I leaned forward, warming to my explanation. "And never ask him to use orange. He hates that color."

"Hates orange?"

I nodded. "It offends him."

All of the school staff frowned except the special-ed teacher. Mrs. Hartford tapped a manila folder on the table. "We do have it noted that Kurt has sensory disorders."

Mrs. Fremont nodded. "Odors and textures."

"Unfortunately, the specific problem with crayons isn't in his paperwork. I'm sorry. I wish we'd known." Mrs. Hartford made a notation.

Relief energized Mrs. Fremont. "This is a simple problem to solve. I'd be happy to send in a box of markers."

The Menace sniffed. "It's not fair to the other students."

"Not fair?" I repeated, my voice rising. I took a slow breath and tried again, as calmly as I was able. "Let me tell you what isn't fair. It isn't fair that Kurt is different. It isn't fair he'll spend the rest of his life in a world that doesn't try to understand him. But what's most unfair is that his teacher acts like he's to blame.

"If you don't want him to stick out, maybe you could find color markers for everyone. It's easier for the other kids to change than it is for Kurt, and the changes will be good for everyone. Gentle colors. Soft carpets. Quiet time. The freedom to concentrate on one thing." I leapt to my feet, too agitated to sit any longer. "Other kids will learn his way. Kurt won't learn theirs."

Mrs. Mannis opened her mouth to speak, but I kept barreling on. "Look at him. He's been playing over there quietly by himself for thirty minutes. How many six-year-old boys do you know who could've done that?"

I turned to Mrs. Fremont. "I'm sorry. I tried not to jump in, but I'm tired of him being the problem when, really, it's the rest of us. Now, I'm going over there to hang out with Kurt."

I plopped my butt down on the rug next to him. "Hey, I'm here."

He didn't acknowledge me as he finished what he was doing. After a few seconds had passed, he looked up. "Do you like the scene I've created?"

"Yes."

"It is good." He stood, turned his back to me, and dropped into my lap. I kept my hands on my knees. He wouldn't want to be cuddled.

I glanced over my shoulder. The special-ed teacher and Mrs. Fremont nodded knowingly, but the other women gawked. Yeah. They'd never seen him like this before, and it was their fault.

If I was interpreting the look on Mrs. Hartford's face correctly, the crayons were doomed.

I missed my entire first-period class, and I didn't mind at all. Seeing Ash in English would've been more than I could stand.

Mrs. Fremont and I had a quick breakfast at Charlie's Diner. When she dropped me off at the high school, second period was in progress. I detoured to the media center. I couldn't have handled statistics today either.

I ran into Ash. Literally. I wasn't paying attention to where I was going, came around a corner, and slammed right into him. He caught my arm.

"Sorry," we said in unison.

He didn't let go. I didn't want him to.

We gazed at each other. Not smiling. Not frowning. The truth between us left unspoken.

A couple of junior girls walked past us, craning to see or hear what we were up to. They broke into excited whispers. The rumor mill beckoned.

We stepped apart.

I reached for his hand. "I love everything about you."

His fingers tightened around mine. "Ardently," he said, his eyes bleak. He dropped my hand and took off down the hall.

I watched him go, hurting so badly I could hardly move. How could this be? He existed, I existed, but *we* did not.

Destination forgotten, I slumped to the floor, undone by what might have been.

I was running out of time to get my teacher recommendation done. After 2-D art ended today, I approached Dr. Holt. "I have a request."

"Go ahead."

Asking for help never got easier. I clasped my hands behind my back and forced myself to relax. "I need a teacher rec for a scholarship application. I hope you'll write it."

"Have a seat."

Oh, damn. We were going to talk about it.

While I perched on the edge of a chair, he sat on his desk. "Why me?"

If I were smart, I'd make the answer up. I'd pretend that he was my favorite teacher ever, flattering him into writing me an incredible rec, except I was too tired to lie. "Ms. Barrie is already booked."

"I'm second choice."

"Yes."

He laughed lightly, picked up a pen, and spun it between his fingers. "You've known the other teachers at this school longer than me. Why am I second?"

It was an interesting question, one I hadn't considered. I'd just known he was.

Part of the reason was an element of safety. He was Mundy's dad. If he refused me, he'd have to deal with her.

But it was more than that. I would've wanted his rec without the Mundy connection because of the kind of teacher he was. "I admire Ms. Barrie because she excites me to be better for my own good. To take risks with confidence. To see beyond the grades.

"I admire that about you too. I started out the sorriest art student ever. I was scared to try. You showed me how to gain fuel from the fear. You've helped me realize that it's all about the trying."

He smiled, not only with his lips, but with his eyes and his whole body. I ached with envy for Mundy. Did she know how lucky she was to have someone like him for a father?

With a push, he slid off the desk and bent over it to tidy a stack of folders. "When is it due?"

"Wednesday."

"E-mail me the details. I'd be honored to write your recommendation."

All day Tuesday, I worried about what to do with my consent form. Tomorrow was the due date for the Peyton Scholarship. Even if I had been speaking to my dad, it would be pointless to ask him to sign. He would refuse.

There was a solution. I could forge his signature and hope he never found out. If I got the endorsement, I'd find a way to change his mind. It would bother me to cheat, but that signed form was going in.

Distress drove me out to the dock. I sat at its end and watched the moon climbing the horizon. It was beautiful here at twilight. And peaceful.

Behind me, I could hear the faint crunch of shoes on dry grass. It was a familiar gait. My father's. As if my thoughts had drawn him to me.

His shoes thumped softly on wooden planks. When he was a few feet behind me, he stopped. "Can I join you, Eden?"

"That wouldn't be my choice."

"I've said I'm sorry."

"Words are easy, Dad."

He huffed in frustration. "What do I have to do to make it up to you?"

"Never hit me again."

"I won't. I've promised." His voice shook. "Mr. Cooper wants you to work a few hours at the store. On the inventory. The holiday season is coming up."

No need to react. I didn't care.

"Okay?"

"Okay, what?" I looked at him. Was he crazy? "I'm not helping with that. You have to find someone else."

"He trusts you. He'd rather not take a chance on someone else."

"Not my problem, Dad." I faced the bay.

His breath whistled out between his teeth. Then silence. It stretched, intensified, like storm clouds on the horizon. I focused on the water.

"Marlene says the boy dumped you."

"Shut. Up." Dad managed to say the one thing I couldn't ignore. He'd better let this go.

"It's for the best."

"Shut the hell up." My voice had risen, echoing across the bay. I scrambled to my feet and turned. "I love him, Dad."

"His folks will never let you—"

"Stop." My hands fisted at my sides. "We get it. His parents can't stand the idea of me any more than you can stand the idea of him, and now we're apart." When I tried to walk around my father, he held up his hand, blocking my path on the narrow dock, halting me in my tracks. No way would I touch him, even to move his arm.

"Listen to me, Eden. Don't be acting surprised about how this turned out. You're poor, you're white, and you're Christian. They don't want none of that for their son."

"Got it, Dad. Hate won this round. Bet that makes you proud." I pushed past him and ran before I could say something we would both regret.

✦ 29 ✦

More Natural Consequences

Mrs. Fremont got me to school early Wednesday morning, so I headed straight to the computer lab. It was eerily silent. All the machines had been powered down this past weekend, the furniture scrubbed, the carpets steamed. It was as if no one had been in here since.

The lights were on in Mrs. Barber's office, but she was nowhere around.

The Peyton application was due. Most documents had been submitted online. The essay. The resume and transcript and recommendations. I'd played their games and bragged until I was sick of thinking about myself. It was out of my hands.

"Mornin', Eden." Mrs. Barber burst into the lab. "I checked your Peyton entry. Everything's there but the consent form."

"Yes, ma'am."

"Do you have it with you? I have to fax it in by noon."

"Yes, ma'am."

She continued into her office.

I opened my backpack and pulled out the form. The signature line was bare. I stared at it, my chest growing tighter. Fumbling around in the bottom of my backpack, I found a black pen. With my left hand, I scribbled *Byron F. Moore* on the form.

Trembling with reaction, I walked into her office and handed her the sheet.

"Thanks, Eden. You're all set."

I glanced at the clock. Still a few minutes until school started. With the Peyton paperwork behind me and no boyfriend as a distraction, I was ready to investigate the photo of me and Ash at North Topsail.

The weird thing about this vile mess was how unnecessary it had been to involve the school web site. Tiffany could've posted that photo anywhere online. It would have been all over the place in a heartbeat. My relationship with Ash would've been destroyed either way. But no. She used the school's web site against me. She went to major lengths to taint the one thing I did at school besides academics, and she'd involved her aunt as an unwitting accomplice. Why had Tiffany wanted to hurt me so badly that she was willing to sacrifice her journalistic ethics over it?

Dropping onto a chair, I logged into a computer and went to my personal account. The image appeared on the screen, bringing with it the ache of loss. It really was a beautiful shot. A sweet memory of a happy, private moment. Clicking on the properties sheet for *topsail.jpg*, I checked the Details, only to discover they had been wiped clean. No information on the camera model or how the photo was taken. No data on the type of editing software used.

I wasn't surprised. Any criminal who'd gone to as much trouble as she had would've been too smart to leave obvious details.

What could I do next? If I couldn't track the image back to a specific camera, I couldn't track it back to her. I had to prove Tiffany was in North Topsail on October 26. But how?

Witnesses would work. Electronic would be better than human. Did the pier have a security camera? Could I see its footage simply by asking?

A brief search on the Internet revealed both answers. *No* and *no.*

Okay, human witnesses it would be.

I might go after Desiree Barber. She would know, but she wouldn't tell me anything, which meant I'd have to involve Marnie. I wasn't willing to bring my stepmom in. Yet.

But there had to be other witnesses. Tiffany hadn't gone to the beach alone. Her two best friends probably went with her. Starr was a lost cause, so I'd have to corner Tatum.

It helped that she was naïve.

I got an opportunity as I was leaving school the next afternoon. Tatum was standing by herself at the carpool lane. I headed for her.

"Excuse me." I smiled in genuine delight. "Hey."

She backed up a couple of steps and eyed me warily. "Hi."

"How are things?"

"Fine." When she tried to walk around me, I fell into step beside her.

"So—"

"Shut up, Eden. I'm not saying anything." She pivoted toward a blue Mercedes that was pulling up to the curb.

Crap. My informant was escaping before sharing secrets. "But I haven't asked you anything yet."

She halted, her hand on the car-door handle. "Do you think I'm stupid? Because I'm not. I won't answer any questions about North Topsail or the photo." Tatum yanked the door open and slipped inside.

Not as much as I'd hoped for, but I did learn one critical piece of data. Tatum knew where that photo had been taken.

The two newest members of the Webmaster's Club needed extra help this afternoon. After getting them started with image-editing tasks, I returned to my computer to continue with updates to Heron High's web site. I became so engrossed that it took the smell of raspberries to break my concentration.

After saving the file, I twisted in my seat. Tiffany stood out of arm's reach, with a chair between us as if to ensure that I couldn't resort to physical violence. The possibility had crossed my mind, but I would stick with the more natural consequences of ending her career in tabloid journalism.

"May I help you?" I said in my least helpful tone.

"You could stop stalking me and my friends."

"I could accuse you of the same thing."

"Stalking isn't necessary when you have karma on your side."

"I hope you reap what you sow." Anger drained out of me, replaced by sad regret. "I could've ignored this if it had only been about me, but you burned Ash and deceived Gina. Bitch move."

"Whatever. You really should give up."

"Thanks for the advice, but no."

"You're just pissed because you didn't know I was smart enough to pull this off."

"Wrong. I didn't think you were sleazy enough to want to. But that's okay, Tiffany. I'll find a way to track it back to you."

"Sorry, but you won't." Her lips curved into a falsely apologetic smile. "The image is scrubbed. The e-mail address is gone. The witnesses will never say a word. I'm safe."

I watched her saunter out of the lab, leaving me on fire to

find the proof. Every cop show emphasized three elements to a crime: motive, weapon, opportunity. I would just have to work my way through them.

Tiffany's motive couldn't be proven, though it was the most ironclad part of the equation.

Her weapon? A camera. The journalism club had three incredibly expensive models. If she'd borrowed one with a telephoto lens, I could place a weapon of the right caliber in her hands. I would check the sign-out logs, if I could get to them.

Opportunity had to be established. Where was Tiffany on October 26?

It was time to involve Marnie.

I took a high-quality copy of the photo home. Marnie stood before the stove, stirring a pot full of something heavy on the garlic and oregano.

I peeked in. Homemade marinara sauce. Yum. "I need your help."

She tapped her wooden spoon on the side of the pot and set it on a ceramic spoon rest. "How?"

"Have you seen this?" I handed over the photo.

"You two were so happy." She looked at me with sad eyes. "I wish you had let me in on that. I would've loved seeing the two of you together."

"Sorry," I said around the lump in my throat. I'd hurt us both with that decision. "Tiffany took the photo, but she won't claim responsibility."

"Why not?"

"She broke a lot of rules to post it."

"Why would she do that?"

"I think it's because I humiliated her in front of Sawyer and put Mundy on his radar." When it was said out loud, the reason sounded so petty. "Tiffany saw an opportunity to pay me back and took it."

Marnie shook her head in disbelief. "Seems extreme."

"It is. I'd bet that she thought it was a big joke, until it went out of control."

"What are we going to do about it?"

Marnie used *we*. Like it was her problem, too. I was so lucky to have her. "Ash and I were at North Topsail Beach on October twenty-sixth. Can you help me find out if Tiffany was there too?"

Marnie turned off the heat under the spaghetti sauce. "Where's the laptop? I want to do some searching."

"We don't have Internet."

"The neighbors do. If you sit in the backyard, you can get it."

"Whoa."

With a laugh, she grabbed our ancient laptop, went outside, and sat on the deck steps. Nothing moved but the mouse.

"Damn." Her eyes blazed.

"What?"

"Tiffany's blocked me."

"Not surprising."

More clicks interspersed with more *damn*s. Then a crafty smile.

"What are you looking at?"

Her gaze flicked to me, then back to the screen. "Desiree has blocked me everywhere except her blog, which has a huge photo gallery. She uses it to show off the best shots that Tiffany's taken. The gallery has some recent additions."

I leaned over her shoulder. There were five shots altogether.

One showed Starr and Tatum, arms intertwined, walking backwards on a beach. "Can you zoom in on this?" I said, pointing at the dark line jutting into the ocean at the upper edge of one of the images.

She homed in on the object and tapped the magnifying glass twice.

"Ash and I were at that pier. What's the date on the image?"

"October twenty-sixth." She shook her head. "Here's proof."

"Not enough. She'll deny it. Her friends and Desiree will back her up." I nudged Marnie over. "Let me check something."

After saving a screenshot of Desiree's web page, I copied the image of Tatum and Starr to my flash drive. "Now, if we check the properties . . ." I released an excited breath. "The details are still there."

"Why is that important?"

I pointed to some text in the properties sheet. "A Nikon camera was used. A very expensive Nikon. Not many of those around. I think the Journalism Club has the same model. If Tiffany had it checked out that weekend, there's our proof."

"How hard will it be to get that information?"

"It'll be easy to make sure it's the identical model of camera, but who had it checked out will be hard. The club sponsor keeps the sign-out logs put away in the Journalism Club storage closet."

"Can't you just ask?"

"Not Mr. Applewood." The guy had no sense of humor, and he was anal about rules. He would want to know why I needed the logs. If I couldn't find enough proof, it would be bad for me, and he was on the Honors Committee. "I'll think of something."

Actually, I already had. I knew where the master key was, and I wasn't afraid to use it. But it would have to wait until after my Peyton interview. I wasn't risking that at all.

· 30 ·

The Future I Needed

A muffled ringing interrupted my sleep Saturday morning. I peered at my alarm clock. 6:15. Must be a wrong number. It was too early to be awake. Today I met with the Honors Committee, and I could use the beauty sleep. I snuggled deeper into the covers.

Moments later, my father's voice boomed in the den, drawing closer. My bedroom door whooshed open. I peered at him through half-closed lids. Thankfully, he'd put on pajama bottoms.

"She's here," he said. "She can be at your house in half an hour. I'll drop her off. Don't worry."

Totally awake now. I rocketed into a sitting position. "What? Dad?"

He shook his head at me. "Sure, Heidi," he said into his cellphone, "it'll be fine. You go on."

Heidi? As in Mrs. Fremont? "Dad, no," I said, shaking my head frantically. "I can't babysit today."

He held his palm up. I clamped my lips together.

"Right. She has your number if she needs anything. Bye." He clicked the phone off. "There's been a four-car pileup on I-40. The emergency room staff has been called in. Heidi's expected at the hospital."

"I can't babysit."

He kept talking as if I hadn't said anything. "The kids are still asleep, but I figure you'll be there before they wake up."

He didn't know about the Honors Committee, and I couldn't tell him. "I have plans today, Dad."

"With who?"

"Gina Barber." Which was true.

"She won't mind if you pick up extra money instead." He scratched the stubble on his chin.

What should I do? There weren't many people who could control Kurt. Once I showed up, he wouldn't let me out of his sight. I flopped backwards onto my bed. It was catastrophic.

"What's happened?" This from Marnie.

I turned my head toward her. She was leaning against my father, clad only in his pajama top, mouth rounded in a yawn. Gross. I couldn't take anymore.

"Dad booked me a babysitting job this morning."

She pinched his side. "Eden isn't available."

"She'll have to be, doll. Those kids need watching."

Couldn't argue, but I wouldn't miss the interview either, even if I had to hold Kurt on my lap the whole time. I swung my legs over the side of my bed. "Marnie, can you come with me?"

My dad grunted. "We have plans."

"Not now, we don't," his wife said. "I'll be ready in ten minutes."

. . .

Marnie's car sputtered to a stop in front of the high school auditorium. I gritted my teeth to keep them from chattering. We were forty-five minutes late. I'd texted Gina, but would that be enough?

After unbuckling the seat belt, I kicked open the car door. Outside, I smoothed my black skirt and my best blue shirt into place, checked the side mirrors for any last-minute repairs, and combed loose strands of hair back with my fingers. I was ready. Now if they would just be nice about how late I was.

"You look beautiful, Eden," Marta said from the backseat.

"Thanks. I believe you." With a heave, I pushed the door shut.

Kurt yelled, "No."

I had to walk away. Marnie said she would handle it, no matter how bad he got. She would drive around, bribe him with food, whatever it took.

I turned from the car and hurried toward the glass doors.

"Don't leave me, Eden. *Please.*"

My footsteps faltered. I looked with longing into the lobby. I looked back at the car. Marta scowled at her lap, Marnie was frowning out the windshield, and Kurt could barely catch his breath for his sobs.

I couldn't leave him.

Returning to the car, I wrenched open the door. "Marta, unhook your brother."

Marnie leaned across the empty passenger seat. "Eden, I got this."

I shook my head and held out my hand. "Come on, Kurt."

He stumbled out of the back and crawled up my body until his arms locked about my neck.

"Hey, buddy, you can stay with me, but you have to follow the rules. Promise?"

He mumbled against my shoulder. "Promise."

"Are you paying attention to me?" At his nod, I said, "Here are the rules. You must wait until your turn to talk. You may not touch anything. And you must be able to see me from wherever you are. Okay?"

"Okay."

"I'm putting you down now."

When I set him on his feet, he gripped the waistband of my skirt and waited.

I gestured at his sister. "Why don't you climb into the front with Marnie and keep her company until I'm done?"

Marta nodded solemnly. "You can count on me."

I walked to the front of the auditorium, much more slowly this time since a kid was hanging on to me. The door was ajar. We bumped through it and skidded to a stop on the newly waxed tiles of the lobby floor.

Ash and Mr. Applewood stood framed in the entrance to the stage, talking. They turned as our footsteps clicked across the floor.

"What are *you* doing here?" Kurt demanded, his eyes focused on Ash.

"The same thing as Eden." Ash's gaze drank me in.

I looked back just as hungrily. He was my main rival for the Peyton. I adored him, and I wanted to win.

Kurt stomped over to him and frowned, head tilted up and arms crossed. "You haven't come to see us. Why?"

Ash knelt to Kurt's level. "I've been busy."

"I like Raj."

"I'll let him know."

Mr. Applewood watched us with keen interest. I needed to

take control of this conversation. "I apologize for being late, but a friend had an emergency. I sent a text to Mrs. Barber."

Mr. Applewood smiled faintly. "She let us know."

"Am I last to interview?" I asked. *Please, please.*

"You are. You go on ahead of me, Miss Moore. I'd like to finish my chat with Mr. Gupta."

Kurt and I waited in the wings of the stage, discussing the purpose of various objects, until Mrs. Barber called to me.

All four members of the Honors Committee sat on one side of a long table. Their heads were bent over legal pads.

On the opposite side of the table waited a lone chair. I sank onto it.

"What am I supposed to do?" Kurt had followed me.

"You can investigate the stage," I said in a low voice. At his eager smile, I raised a warning finger. "But remember the rules."

"I already promised."

I held out my fist. He bumped it with his and took off. I watched him until I knew he was safe. When I turned back to the Honors Committee, they were staring at me politely.

"Hi, Eden," Mrs. Barber said. "As you know, I've recused myself from voting on the recipient of our endorsement. My role is primarily to moderate."

"Yes, ma'am."

"Good. We'll get started." She nodded at Mrs. Parsons.

"Hello, Eden," my former track coach said. "As a freshman, you had solid extracurriculars, but they dropped off dramatically the next year and never recovered. Explain."

I sucked in a nervous breath. "I've held down a job since my sophomore year. I spend all of my free time either studying or working."

"So you've held a job steadily since you were fifteen?"

"Yes, ma'am."

"Without a break?"

"No breaks."

"Why have you chosen to be employed instead of being involved at school?"

I frowned at her, unblinking. Mrs. Parsons knew the answer. Even though I could see the purpose of the question, I felt betrayed. But she'd asked it, and if this helped me to win the endorsement, I couldn't afford to ignore the opening. "When my father was laid off, we lost his income and all of his benefits. My family needed money. I had to pitch in."

"Thank you." Mrs. Parsons gestured at the next teacher.

Ms. Lee smiled, her teeth big and white. "You've had no fine arts on your transcript until this semester. Now you are taking 2-D art. Why?"

This was an easy question. "I can't sing, dance, or paint. I'm awful at anything remotely artistic. When I originally planned out my high school courses, I decided to avoid electives I wasn't likely to do well, especially when there were so many others that I could enjoy." I darted a quick glance at Kurt. "Then I started babysitting for the Fremonts, and I fell in love with the kids. It didn't take me long to figure out that I wanted to be a teacher. I might have to ask students to draw, and they might not be good at it. I ought to know how that feels." I smiled. "I love my art class, and I'm not any good."

"Thank you."

She seemed nice, although I'd never had her for a class. I nodded at her before checking again on Kurt. He was studying a broken chair with complete absorption.

"Miss Moore?"

I looked at Mr. Applewood. I'd taken a sociology class from him. He rarely smiled. "Yes, sir?"

"Which candidate is most deserving of the endorsement?"

Whoa. I'd often tried to imagine what I'd be asked, but this was a question I'd never thought of. I knew why I was the *right* candidate. I knew why I needed the money, but the phrase *most deserving* tripped me up.

If I'd learned anything from Mundy over the past few weeks, it was that truth, even when it was brutal, was something I liked. The honest answer might completely kill off my chance at the endorsement, but I had to say it anyway. "I'm not the most deserving candidate, not when you look at our high-school resumes. Ash is."

Mr. Applewood's brow scrunched. "Are you suggesting that we choose Mr. Gupta?"

"No, I'm being realistic. If you're judging based on academics, extracurriculars, and leadership, I won't be your choice. I'm hoping you'll decide based on other reasons." I paused and looked at my hands. I wouldn't mention that a full scholarship was my only chance for a bachelor's degree or that Carolina was my dream school. I wouldn't say that neither was true for Ash. If they didn't already know those things, they wouldn't hear them from me.

Nor would I drop in what I knew about Tiffany. Until I had solid proof, I wasn't saying anything.

There was laughter from the wings of the stage. Kurt knelt on the floor, studying the pulleys and ropes operating the curtain. In that instant, I knew what I would say.

"My friend Kurt is why I'm the right candidate for the endorsement." I scanned the panel, my confidence swelling. "Kurt has special needs. He's loud, grumpy, and easily frustrated. But he's also charming, eager, and smart. He deserves to be surrounded by people who care enough about him to push past the obvious."

I hitched forward on my chair, anxious for them to understand. "Kurt's on the autism spectrum. I'm committed to teaching kids like him. Carolina is the place to be if I want to learn from the best."

Mr. Applewood sniffed, as if insulted. "There are many excellent colleges where you can learn to teach."

"Eden," Kurt shouted. He ran to my side. "Is that man talking about you? Marta says that you're going to college to be a teacher."

I gave him a stern look.

"Sorry." He frowned. "It wasn't my turn to talk."

"No."

"Can I ask anyway?"

I threw the panel an apologetic look. "Sure."

"Marta says that we won't see you anymore. Is she right?"

Oh my god. I blinked back tears. How could I leave him? Or Marta? Or Marnie?

No, I had to shake off the doubts. It would hurt, but this was what I had to do. I had to fight for what was best for me. Whether it was the Peyton or something else, college was more than escape. It was the future I needed.

"You and Marta will see me less, but I'll visit. We're friends forever."

"Promise?"

"Promise."

"Good." He ran back to the wings.

I looked at the panel again. "Mr. Applewood, you're correct.

Plenty of colleges have good education programs, but Carolina will give me experiences that I can't get anywhere else. That's why I want the Peyton. All four of your candidates have what it takes to excel at UNC. If you don't give the endorsement to me, I'll still find a way to work with kids on the spectrum, but there is no way you could endorse someone who wants it more than I do."

· 31 ·

The Missing Link

With the interview behind me, I had a crime to wrap up.
I arrived at school early on Monday morning and went
to the Journalism Club's storage closet. It was unlocked, no one
lurked about, and the logbook sat on a table by the door.

Oh, yeah. I didn't have to use the key, and there were no witnesses. Very un–Mr. Applewood–like.

First, I rummaged through the equipment locker, and there
she was. The Nikon. A beautiful camera with the same model and
specs used by our perpetrator. It even had a shiny new telephoto
lens.

Next, the logbook. I flipped through the pages. November,
September, August.

Um . . . Let me recheck that.

November, yes. September, yes. August, yes.

The October page was missing, which could be no coincidence.

I'd be impressed if I weren't so pissed. Tiffany was a natural
at crime. I stormed out, letting the door slam behind me.

Mrs. Barber walked out of the computer lab as I was leaving the storeroom.

"What were you doing in there?"

I pasted on my innocent look. "The door was unlocked."

"I wonder if one of the custodians forgot."

She'd taken the bait. "That's probably it." I hurried past her, glad to have dodged that problem.

"Eden." Her voice vibrated with suppressed excitement. "I have a secret."

I halted. "Does the secret have to do with me?"

"It does."

"Will you tell me anyway?"

"I'm not supposed to." She pumped her fists and wiggled around in a bad imitation of a football player's touchdown dance. "I won't tell you directly, but if you guessed, my face would give it away."

Something alive and dense swirled deep inside me. There was only one thing that I wanted desperately enough to warrant a bad dance from her. "Heron High will endorse me for the Peyton Scholarship."

"Woo hoo." She threw her arms around me, laughing and jiggling.

I could hardly believe it. Ash didn't get the endorsement. In what sane universe could that be true? "Really?"

"Yes."

"Thank you, Mrs. Barber."

Her arms tightened. "You earned this, Eden. No need to thank me."

The first bell rang. I backed away, embarrassed by our show of emotion. She was usually professional at school, and on the rare occasions we attended the same family function, she was quiet.

On the fringe. Maybe she felt the same way about them that I did. Maybe we were more alike than I realized. "What happens next?"

"You'll interview in Chapel Hill next month, and we'll know about finalists by February." She rocked on her feet, her smile wide. "I don't think you have anything to worry about, though. The Peyton Foundation is biased toward strong candidates from rural schools, and you're spectacular in an interview."

"Thanks."

"I'll go with you to Chapel Hill, of course, to represent the school. And bring Marlene or Byron, if you can. The foundation's board likes to meet with your parents."

"Great" came out on a squeak. The smile froze on my face.

The forged signature. What would I do about that?

Ash and I reached our English classroom at the same time. He stopped to let me enter first.

"Hi," I said. Had someone told him?

"Hi." He headed for his seat.

I made my way slowly to the back. He'd been too calm, too neutral. Ash didn't know about the Peyton yet, which made sense. I wasn't supposed to know either.

Mundy leaned across the aisle before I'd had a chance to settle in. "You look happy."

Freak. "I had a good weekend."

"Are you upset that he spoke to you?"

"Not at all."

"Right." She glanced around and lowered her voice. "What's the farthest west you've ever been?"

From anyone else, this would be a random question but not from her. I gave her a speculative look. "Tennessee."

"You've never been west of the Mississippi River?"

"I've never been west of the Blue Ridge Mountains."

She rolled her eyes. "If that were my truth, I'd lie."

I laughed. "Is there a point in here somewhere?"

"Yes. Drive with me to California."

Whoa. A map of the US surfaced in my brain. There were many states along the route. So many things I'd never seen. "Are you serious?"

"Yeah. Mom and Destin are flying home to California over Thanksgiving. Cam and I will stay here until the end of the semester. Since my mom needs a car, I'll drive the SUV and some of our stuff out there. I want you to go with me."

I fixed my gaze on the top of my desk, thinking furiously. I would love to do that. Driving across America with Mundy? Holy crap, that sounded like fun. "How long will it take?"

"Five days of driving, a day or two to rest, then we'll fly back."

Seven days? Disappointment hit like a punch to the gut. I would love to go, but it was impossible. "I can't miss that much school."

"Sure you can. It's Thanksgiving week. We can skip Monday and Tuesday. Teachers won't assign anything." Her smile was confident. "Cam will take care of anyone who might give us grief."

I'd miss the holiday with Marnie's family, which would be awesome. "Maybe . . ."

"Please say yes. You know you want to."

Of course, I wanted to, but what would my parents say? If I had to, I'd beg. Would Marnie agree? Dad would crumble if I had her on my side. "I can't afford a plane ticket."

"This is an employment opportunity. All expenses paid, plus wages."

Whoa. A significant detail that had been left out until now—a detail I loved. However, a token protest was in order. "I don't want to take money from your parents."

"It's an employment opportunity for me too. When they offer you money, take it." She wrinkled her nose. "What about the Fremonts?"

"Kurt and Marta are spending Thanksgiving with their father. They won't need me." I tried to stay calm, but it was hard. "This would be great. Please let Marnie say yes."

The loss of the October logbook page bugged me the rest of the day. I was running out of ideas. I didn't want Tiffany to be right, but maybe she was. Maybe the photo would be anonymous forever.

When I arrived home, instead of starting on my homework, I cranked up the laptop, put in the flash drive, and looked at the images from Desiree Barber's photo gallery.

Had I overlooked anything?

I clicked on the photo of Tiffany's friends in all their giggling glory at the beach. Opening its properties, I looked at the details tab again. Nothing new to glean.

Back to the Main Properties tab.

The date stamp of the image was October 26. Same day as the Ash-Eden photo. Of course.

The time stamp was . . . weird.

Goose bumps tickled my arms. Something was out of whack.

According to the time stamp, the image had been captured around nine p.m., which couldn't be right. The scene in the photograph happened in daylight, not long before Ash and I left around five. The camera had set the time several hours too late.

Four hours difference?

Excitement curled in my gut. Had the photo been taken at nine o'clock *Greenwich Mean Time?*

I brought up the high school web site and switched to the dance-team page. Tiffany was their self-appointed photojournalist, making the dance team one of the best documented organizations on campus.

After browsing past hundreds of images, I selected a candid from the pep rally on October 24, and checked the time stamp.

Six p.m.

Pep rallies began at two.

Four hours difference.

The same Nikon, with its fancy telephoto lens and GMT setting, had taken the dance-team photos and the photos of Tiffany's friends at the beach.

I had the missing link.

My stepmom came in later than normal this afternoon, dropped her purse on the love seat, and grabbed the laptop. After booting it up, she crossed to the sliding glass door and pushed it open.

"What are you doing?" I asked, following her out onto the deck.

"Looking for a job."

"Why?"

"I quit the convenience mart."

"Way to go, Marnie." I gave her a hug.

She laughed. "Yeah, but I still can't pay you back everything."

"Don't care."

"I do." She flopped down onto the wooden steps.

I sat beside her and watched as she logged into the Internet. In seconds, she was on a web site looking at want ads in the local area.

She frowned. "Look at all of these ads for cleaning staff. I could do that."

"Have you considered anything else?"

"I don't have other skills."

"You're pretty good on the computer. Not everyone figures out how to log onto the Internet when their house isn't wired."

Her eyes crinkled. "Nobody would hire me for things that I've taught myself."

"Not true. Dad could talk to Mr. Cooper. He might give you a job."

"At the hardware store?"

"Yeah. You type fast, you understand the terminology, and you learn things on your own."

"He wouldn't trust me. *I* wouldn't trust me."

"If it's data entry, I could teach you. I wouldn't say you were good if I didn't believe it."

Her eyes brightened. "I'll give that some thought."

"Good." I closed the laptop and set it aside. "I have two more things to ask."

"Shoot."

"Mundy wants me to drive to California with her this month. Can I go?"

"Yes."

That was easier than I anticipated. "Don't you have any questions?"

"Maybe." She scrunched her face sternly. "How long will you be gone?"

"A week."

"Any issues with your schoolwork?"

"None."

"You can go."

I laughed. "What about Dad?"

"I'll handle him."

Marnie should quit awful jobs more often. "What about our plans for Thanksgiving?"

"It'll give me an excuse to get out of the dinner at Granny's. I'll tell them Byron misses you too much to be good company. They'll be relieved."

"So will he." I gave her a disbelieving smile. "I'm shocked that you caved this fast."

"Clarissa Cruz-Holt called. We've already worked it out."

The next issue would be harder. I took a deep breath and splat it out there. "I won the Peyton endorsement."

She leapt to her feet and pumped her fists. "Oh, sweetie, what wonderful news."

"Yeah. Wonderful." I stood more slowly.

"Why do I hear a *but*? What's the catch?"

"The Peyton board likes for a parent to come to the interview."

"I'd love to come with you."

"And I want you, too. But when Dad finds out, it could get ugly. He's opposed. Loudly." My head ached with the implications if he got too belligerent. I might lose my endorsement and any other award that might come my way. I should've thought this through, although it wasn't as if I'd had choices. "I forged Dad's signature on the consent form."

"Dammit, Eden." She turned her back on me, fumed a moment, and spun back around. "Why did you do something so stupid?"

"He refused to sign. I was desperate."

"Why didn't you ask me?"

"You?" I shook my head. "It had to be a parent or legal guardian."

"Which I am."

"Wait." I clutched the railing for support. "You're my legal guardian? Nobody ever told me that."

"I'm your legal *mother*."

My lungs started heaving, like I'd run a 10K at top speed and could hardly catch my breath. She was my mother? My legal mother? "How?"

"I adopted you."

How could something that huge and amazing have slipped past me without my notice? "When?" The single word came out in a rough whisper.

"A couple of years after I married Byron. It was supposed to be a surprise for your eighth birthday."

"I didn't know." My eighth birthday? My awful eighth birthday. On the Saturday of that weekend, I'd waited patiently in the clubhouse of our apartment complex, postponing games and cake and presents, giving the fifteen "late" kids from my second-grade class time to show up. And they never had. And I'd cried all Sunday.

"Oh, sweetie. Maybe you were too young to understand."

Maybe I'd been too distraught to pay attention.

Marnie was my mother. For a moment, I felt stalled, not moving in any direction, hollow and expanding. "Did I talk to a judge or anything?" I would've remembered that. Wouldn't I?

"Not necessary. We filled in some forms and filed it at the courthouse."

"You don't use the word *adopted* when you introduce me."

"I'm your mom. You're my daughter. No other explanation is needed."

"That's true." My head pounded, as if someone was trying to

hammer the truth in but it wouldn't fit. "Dad signs all of my paperwork."

"He likes to be the one who signs stuff."

This didn't change anything, did it? "Was it hard to get Heather to give up legal rights?"

"Didn't even have to ask." Distaste colored Marnie's tone. "She signed them over to me as soon as I married your father."

I'd always assumed that Heather was worthless. Now it was confirmed. "Do you know where she is now?"

"In Hawaii with her fourth husband."

I should be relieved to learn this news. When I hadn't known where Heather was, it could've been possible she was dead, or kidnapped, or holed up in an institution with amnesia. There could've been a "good" explanation for why we never heard from her, and I would've felt guilty for my contempt, but she was none of those things. She lived in an expensive place, and she'd given away her children as if we had never been.

My mouth trembled, trying to smile. Not quite ready to believe yet. "You've been my mom the whole time I've known you. I just didn't realize the law believed it too." I locked my arms around her and hugged as tightly as I could. I didn't love her more in this moment than I had a minute before, but the world had changed for me.

"As much as I hate what Heather did to you, I thank God for it every day." Marnie dabbed at her eyes and sniffed. "Okay, my daughter did something totally stupid, and it's my job to fix it. I don't like lying to your father, but it's necessary in this case. So here's our story. I signed the paperwork, and I'll go with you to Chapel Hill."

"Gina Barber could tell him the truth."

"He won't ask."

"He'll be mad if you do this."

"Yeah, well, he shouldn't press his luck at the moment. You focus on winning that scholarship, and I'll take care of the rest."

By Thursday, I was ready to show my proof to Tiffany. Before school started, I went to the computer lab, logged into my account, and texted her.

You're wanted in the computer lab

The door creaked open minutes later, and Tiffany wandered into the room. She peered into Mrs. Barber's empty office and then frowned at me.

"Have you seen Aunt Gina?"

"I have."

"Where is she?"

"I think she's in the teacher's lounge."

Tiffany sauntered to a table out of my reach and perched on the edge. "Do you know why she wanted me to come to the lab?"

"I'm the one who wants you here. She doesn't know about it."

Tiffany straightened and turned to go. "I don't have anything to say to you."

"That's okay. I can do the talking." I held up my notes. "I found proof that you made the photo."

Eyes narrowing, she stared at the stapled sheets as if they were poison. Curiosity must have won over reluctance, though, because she took them from me and flipped the pages. Seconds passed. "It's just a bunch of photos." There was a quiver to her voice.

"Yeah, all taken by you with the Journalism Club's new camera. Notice that the Nikon put a timestamp in GMT on all of these images."

She shivered but said nothing.

"There are a couple of photos you took at the pep rally. Then later that weekend, you snapped shots of Tatum and Starr at North Topsail Beach, at the exact same pier where Ash and I were, at the exact same time."

As I spoke, she was flicking through the pages again and again, her neck and face reddening. "It's circumstantial."

"Agreed."

"Have you shown this to anyone else?"

"No."

"Are you going to?"

Tiffany watched me with anxious eyes. No, it went deeper than that. She was scared. I'd never had anyone look at me with fear before. It was an uncomfortable sensation. "Tell me why I shouldn't."

She studied me, as if seeking signs that I was joking. She must have accepted that I was serious, because she sucked in a shaky breath. "I'm sorry that so many people got hurt. That wasn't my intention. Really. It's too late to take it back, but please don't show it to Mr. Applewood. If you do, he'll kick me out of the Journalism Club."

"Possibly."

She shook her head. "Definitely, and I need that club on my resume, Eden. It could help me get into Carolina and I want to go so badly. I can't be stuck here."

And there they were. The magic words. Like me, Tiffany wanted to escape.

Any last traces of outrage deflated. She had to live with what she'd done, just as I would have to live with what came next. I pulled a DVD from my computer and handed it over. "This is yours."

She gaped at the DVD. "That's it?"

"Yes. Enough damage has been done." I stood, grabbed my backpack, and headed for the door. But I paused with my hand on the knob. I wasn't quite finished. "Tiffany, just a warning. This whole incident was a total sleaze. You can't be a serious photo-journalist and do this tabloid crap to hurt people whenever you hold a grudge."

"I didn't think . . ."

"What? That you'd get caught? It wasn't that hard to dredge up proof." I shook my head at her. "There will always be someone smarter than you, and they will figure it out. It'll be safer if you stick to using your talent for the right reasons." Yanking open the door, I took off down the hallway, relieved to finally have the ordeal behind me.

· 32 ·

Burst of Glory

Mundy and I were on day four of the Great Trip West.
She'd driven most of the way. I only helped for an hour
or two each day while she snoozed or ate or talked on the phone
with her California friends to make plans for when we were
there.

This morning, she let me take the wheel from Winslow, Arizona, to Flagstaff. Then we traded seats. Mundy turned the car
north.

I'd made A's in geography. I knew that Grand Canyon National
Park lay ahead.

There had been a dozen times over the past four days where
she'd pulled off at an overlook or taken a detour into a nearby
town. At first, I'd protested. We were on a mission. We had to
make good time and get to our planned city for that day.

Mundy shrugged away my concerns, drove exactly where she
wanted, and arrived at the correct lodging each night before
midnight.

I'd learned to keep my mouth shut, because I'd loved every place we visited.

As we approached the entrance to the park, I asked, "How long will we be here?"

"If we're this close to the Grand Canyon, we have to see the sunset."

I looked out the side window. *If we're this close* was one of her favorite phrases.

She parked in a visitors' lot, hopped out, and charged down a path as if she knew where she was going. I hurried to keep up, a little intimidated by this place.

"Come on," she called over her shoulder.

"It's three o'clock, Mundy. We're not likely to miss the sunset."

The closer we got to the rim, the slower I walked. It was already possible to see into the canyon with its miles and miles of hazy color, jagged rock, and layered cliffs.

Then we were standing near the edge, looking down, across, up—tiny humans gaping at an immense expanse that was harshly beautiful in a way that could never be described.

"There are no words," I said.

"Absolutely none."

We took a break long enough to visit the bathrooms and get a snack. Then it was back to the rim.

Hundreds of people had the same idea we did. They scattered about, cameras in hand, reverently quiet, all staring hard to the west.

The sun sank low, hovered on the horizon in a final burst of glory, then vanished. Darkness followed swiftly. People began to drift away. I sat silently, not wanting this moment to end.

"Ready?" she asked.

I nodded.

We didn't speak again until we were on the highway, heading south toward our final hotel of the trip.

"What do you think?"

"I think . . ." I bit my lip. There were so many things I'd discovered with Mundy. This trip had merely lengthened the list. "I think I'm going to miss you."

She gave my hand a squeeze. "Yeah. I'll miss you too."

The rest of Thanksgiving week roared by. At its end, I'd traveled through more states in eight days than in the previous seventeen years.

The plane trip would be a memory I would try hard to lose. Air travel would never be one of my favorites.

The Monday morning after Thanksgiving, I was still jet-lagged but glad to be back at school. By midday, things were still a little fuzzy but getting better.

"Eden, wait."

I froze. A completely motionless Eden. Unable to move or breathe. A statue outside the cafeteria doors.

Ash had called my name.

It wasn't as if I never saw him in the two classes we shared. We were in the same room every day for three hours but rarely spoke. Our statistics teacher had changed the project teams. Ms. Barrie hadn't put us together on an assignment since the MIM. They'd heard the rumors and were being kind.

I still ached for any sight of him. Still hoped too much for our paths to cross or our gazes to collide. To have him actually seek me out was sweet torment.

When he came even with me in the hall, he smiled. Okay, it wasn't exactly a smile, more of a crease at the corners of his lips. But it was beautiful just the same—and it was mine.

"Congratulations on the Peyton endorsement."

"Thanks." How should I respond? *I'm glad I won and you didn't* was the truth, but it wasn't something I would ever say.

"When do you go to the interview in Chapel Hill?"

"In a couple of weeks."

"Good luck."

"Thanks." An unoriginal response but the only thing I could think of.

He didn't walk away. Classmates flowed around us, like we were two boulders in a stream. The despair that had plagued me since our breakup had fled. In its place, I recognized a sad yearning.

"Have you heard from Stanford?"

"Not yet." He glanced back toward his friends. They were staring at us with an intensity that bordered on the creepy.

I strained to think of something else to say. It was awkward, the distance between *we are* and *we were*. "How is Raj?"

"Great. He still asks about you."

"Tell him I said hi." I backed up a couple of steps. My ability to stand here and act normal had run out. "See you."

"Yeah."

I could feel his eyes on me as I joined the flow heading to art class. I steeled myself not to look back.

The rush toward Christmas surged into overdrive. Marnie loved this season the most of any holiday, and so the festivities began. Dad hung lights from every straight surface, three Christmas trees appeared in various locations on our lot, and a baking frenzy ensued. Marnie had a profitable side business going, selling cookie samplers to the staff at the nursing home.

She said nothing about the traditional whirlwind of parties this year. We made it well into December with no events on the calendar. I had to assume it was my fault.

"Marnie," I said one evening as I squeezed black-frosting buttons onto gingerbread people, "Christmas is two weeks away. Where are all the Barber parties?"

"None this year." She moved gooey bars from a pan to a cooling rack.

"Are we being ignored over the Tiffany thing?"

"I don't know what their problem is." Marnie sniffed. "If you aren't welcome, then neither am I. We're a matched set."

I put down the tube of frosting. "I don't mind staying home. You don't have to give up your family because of me."

"You are my family." She licked melted chocolate from her finger. "I don't miss their parties."

I walked into the kitchen, wrapped her in my arms, and kissed her cheek. "Thank you, Mom."

"Always, sweetie." She gave me a hard hug and pushed me away. "Back to work."

Yeah. Always.

Mundy sat at our lunch table the next day, eagerly awaiting my contribution to the potluck. She started her meal with a lemon bar. "If Sawyer sees all of these cookies, he'll be over here."

"He's welcome to as many as he wants," I said, frowning in distraction at the document that Mrs. Barber had handed me earlier today.

"What's wrong?"

"Nothing." Liar. I was nervous. The Peyton Scholarship might be decided this weekend. "Mrs. Barber received my schedule for this coming Saturday. I interview in Chapel Hill at nine o'clock."

"Who's going with you?"

"Mrs. Barber, Marnie, and Dad. We'll drive up Friday night."

"Your dad?"

I nodded. "He's not exactly happy about it, but he is interested. Marnie says he'll be on his best behavior. I believe her."

"It's a sign. You'll get one of the scholarships." She unwrapped a tuna sandwich, heavy on the fish, and offered me half. "I'm confident."

"Glad to know someone is." I crammed the sheet into my pocket with one hand as I reached for my half of the sandwich with the other. Yum. I immediately perked up. Mundy used the best mayonnaise. "I wish Mrs. Barber could tell me why they selected me. I could focus on that part of my presentation and not be as nervous." I broke off a bit of molasses cookie and chewed it, reflecting on the interview in November and my Kurt speech. "I'd still like to know what their reasons were for picking me over Ash."

"Ash knows at least one."

"What?"

She studied me with pursed lips. "He threw his interview."

Her response zapped me like a lightning bolt. He screwed up his chance at a prestigious honor? It didn't seem possible. "How?"

"He told them that you were the most deserving candidate, and nobody else came close."

I shut my eyes and concentrated on my breathing while her explanation ricocheted inside my skull. "I'm stunned. That's amazing."

Mundy's hand patted mine. "I'd call it romantic."

Ash, why? I did deserve the endorsement, but his action was generous. Even . . . hopeful. "I can't believe he did that for me."

"It makes sense, though. He'll get into Stanford."

When I first started dating Ash, I'd thought that too. He was a shoo-in. But I knew better now. I believed, like everybody believed, that Ash would be accepted to Stanford. Everybody except Ash.

He had sacrificed for me.

I snapped to attention, my body throbbing with purpose. I had to know if it had been simple honesty or something more. "I have to thank him in person."

"Not today you won't." She waved a celery stick at me. "Or even this year."

"Why?"

"He's spending Christmas break in India." She glanced at the clock on the cafeteria wall. "He's on his way to the Wilmington airport now."

I gazed at her in awe. "I don't suppose you know when their flight leaves."

"Two o'clock, but his parents like to arrive extra early to make sure there're no problems with their luggage."

I choked back a laugh. "How do you know all this stuff?"

"I stay informed."

"Sounds like shameless eavesdropping."

"I prefer compassionate spying."

Seriously, I would miss Mundy like crazy, but no use thinking about it now. I had to thank Ash today, even if it meant going to him. "Do you have a car?"

"Yep. In the teachers' parking lot." She wrinkled her nose. "Texting him would be good enough."

"Not for me." Three weeks was too long to *not* know. I held out my hand.

She dug the keys out of her pocket and tossed them to me.

I caught them midair. "Later."

⋆ 33 ⋆

Joined Hands

The tires screeched as I roared into an airport parking space. I got here in record time.

The Guptas wouldn't leave for another two hours. Had they gone through security yet? It was the Wilmington airport, after all. Not likely to have a big rush around noon.

I ran from the parking lot, my sides aching, feet pounding the pavement. People stared as I raced past. I didn't care. I had to thank him before he hit the friendly skies.

The automatic glass doors whooshed open and then hummed shut behind me. Mundy didn't know which airline the Guptas were using. I'd have to scan ticket lines at all of them.

They weren't at any ticket counters. I jogged along until I reached security. There was no one around except TSA, a half-dozen men in suits, and a couple with a stroller.

My breathing slowed. I'd missed them. I was too late.

"Eden," a little boy shrieked.

I looked to my left. Raj charged toward me. His family—parents, grandparents, and uncle—stood nearby, silent and watching.

Raj tackled me full speed, his arms flinging about my thighs. Lightheaded with relief, I nearly fell backwards, staggering under his weight.

"Hey, there," I said, placing a careful hand on his shoulder.

"Whatcha doing here? Did you come to see Uncle Ash?"

"I did."

"He's flying to India."

"I heard." I held my arms open, and Raj practically jumped into them.

"I'm happy to see you," he said against my neck. "Where have you been?"

"Busy." I rubbed his back, relishing the appealing, little-kid smell of him. "I'm happy to see you too."

"Are you going anywhere for Christmas?"

"I'm staying home."

"Yay." He nodded for emphasis.

"Raj," his uncle said, "you're strangling Eden."

Ash's voice showered over me like warm rain. I loved the sound of my name on his lips. My gaze sought his.

"Hi." His expression was curious.

"Hi." I tried a smile and nearly succeeded.

He detached his nephew from me, swung him in a high arc, and set him firmly on the ground. "Go to your mom."

"Okay." Raj ran a few steps backwards. "Will you see me soon, Eden?"

I didn't know how to answer. Didn't know how this visit would end. "I would like to." That, at least, was the truth.

Ash had moved closer to me. "Why are you here?"

I kept my gaze on Raj's retreating form until it merged with the rest of the Gupta family, then I looked up at Ash. It would've made things easier if he were smiling. Was coming here a mistake? Would it have been better to leave it alone?

No. I had to be here, no matter what he did in the next few minutes. If I hadn't come, I would always wonder. "You sacrificed the Peyton for me."

He shook his head. "They would've endorsed you anyway. You deserved it."

"Do your parents know?"

"Yes, and they understand." His smile was sweet. "I'm glad you won, Eden."

Longing flooded through me. I raised my hands to touch him, remembered where I was, and shoved them into the pockets of my shabby jeans. "Thank you."

"You didn't drive all the way down here to say that. You could've texted."

He was right. I had come here to say more, and I had to get it out. "I miss you."

The only sign that he'd heard was a slight catch in his breathing.

"Ash," his mother called, her voice stern.

He glanced over his shoulder. "Be right there." He shifted even closer to me. "What else, Eden?"

"I love you. I wish things were different."

I could feel the warmth of his body. Smell his cologne. I ached to put my hands on him and have his on me. Why didn't he react? Was he trying to think of a polite way to reject me?

"You're brave, Eden." A delicious hunger shimmered in his eyes. "You skipped school to come to the airport. You couldn't know whether I'd push you away while my family and strangers watched." Deliberately, his hands reached for my waist and drew me to him. "I'm going to be brave too."

Dizziness washed over me. Was he really touching me? Or had I wanted it so much that this was my imagination?

Carefully, as if afraid someone might take him away, I laid my hands and cheek against his chest, savoring the solid security of Ash. His arms tightened around me. I wanted to be like this forever.

"Ash," his mother called. "We are leaving."

"Eden, look at me."

I did what he wanted, of course, since it was what I wanted too.

"I love you." He kissed me, a light, sweet brush of the lips.

When he pulled back, I gasped. "That'll cost you."

"Oh, yeah. I'll hear about it nonstop for the next eighteen hours." He dropped another light kiss on my hair. "I've missed you too. So much."

I licked my lips nervously. This whole scene had gone way better than I dreamed. I was going for the gold. "Are we back together?"

He laughed. "I hope so. That was wasted PDA if we aren't."

Was it possible to be so happy that I might shatter? "Can you work things out?" *Please, please . . .*

"I'll negotiate something. I don't know how, but I will."

I believed him. Almost. "When do you get back?"

"January third."

"Ash." This time it was his dad who called.

"I'd better go. I need my father on my side." His arms fell away. "See you in three weeks."

I nodded, not trusting myself to speak.

He walked away from me, but it didn't hurt, at least not much.

When he reached his family, he hugged his sister. Shook hands with his brother-in-law and Raj. All the while, his mother spewed a rapid-fire monologue. He listened politely, nodding at intervals.

His parents walked to the security line. He trailed after them, then stopped at the entrance and spun around. "Eden? E-mail me and let me know when you're online."

"Okay."

"I'll be nine and a half hours ahead."

I nodded. He waved and then followed his parents through security. I watched until he disappeared.

A small hand slipped into mine. I looked down and smiled at Raj. "Hello, there," I said, giving his hand a friendly shake.

"Mommy and Daddy want to meet you." As he spoke, a couple stopped before me.

"I'm Priya, and this is my husband, Sanjay." Ash's sister was tall and beautiful. "And you are Eden, the world's best babysitter."

"I told them that," Raj said, swinging our joined hands.

"Thank you very much," I said to him, then looked at his parents. "You have an adorable young man."

Raj mouthed *young man* at his parents and smiled up at me. "Can we play again sometime?"

I glanced at his parents for guidance.

Priya said, "I think that's a great idea."

Relief was sweet. Raj liked me. Ash's sister was friendly to me. This was a promising start. "Should we invite Kurt?"

"Yes," Raj said. "Can we go to the park? Will we have a picnic?"

His parents laughed. I exchanged a grateful smile with Priya as we exited the airport terminal, while a little boy danced between us.

· 34 ·

Sweet Promise

Heron High School's salutatorian and valedictorian were required to sit on stage for most of the graduation ceremony, which meant Ash and I sat together, secretly holding hands, only letting go when I gave the opening remarks and when he gave the commencement address.

After the principal made her closing remarks, the choir sang something inspirational, and the sixty-five seniors who made it this far screamed and threw their mortarboards into the air.

In the chaos that followed, Ash pulled me into a dark spot backstage and kissed me until I couldn't think straight.

"Our families will be looking for us soon," he said.

"That was hot."

"Focus, Eden."

"I am focused." I wrapped my fingers around his neck and brought his mouth back to mine.

"Eden, Ash, really." Mrs. Barber laughed as she walked by us.

He pushed away, caught my hand, and drew me with him to

the stage. His family stood on the other side, craning to see where he'd gone.

I tugged my hand from his. "You go on. I'll find my guests." Marnie, Boone, the Fremonts, and Heidi Fremont's fiancé were probably looking for me. Not my father, though. He'd come to the graduation ceremony but would've left by now, to head back to the hardware store. Dad had reached a place where he could take Ash in small doses, but he couldn't be polite to the Guptas. Not yet.

Ash placed a gentle but firm hand at my back. "You must meet my aunt," he said, urging me forward.

"I don't know." I got along well with Ash's sisters, but his parents remained somewhere in the vicinity of barely tolerant. In my opinion, the only reason we stayed civil was because his parents expected our relationship to die once we lived on opposite sides of the country.

"It'll be fine. Come on. They've spotted us now." As we approached, Ash nodded respectfully at the adults in his family and turned to an older woman standing beside his dad. "Aunt Ria, this is Eden Moore."

I gave her a nervous smile. Aunt Ria had a strong resemblance to Mr. Dr. Gupta. "Hello," I said.

"It is nice to meet you," she said. "My brother tells me of your wonderful scholarship to the University of North Carolina."

"Yes, ma'am." I glanced at Dr. Gupta, surprised and pleased that he'd mentioned it. "Being a Peyton Scholar is a great honor."

"I know it is." She looked from me to Ash. "You will be far apart from each other. It will be hard to stay friends."

Everyone in the Gupta family stilled. Aunt Ria had broached the topic that all of them must be curious about. With Ash in California and me here, would our relationship die? I gave him a *go ahead* look, as interested in his response as they were.

"I don't think it'll be hard, Aunt Ria. When you want something badly enough, you make it happen." He gazed down at me with sweet promise. "I want to stay in touch with Eden."

This was as close as he could get to claiming me. For months, to keep the peace, we'd all pretended politely that Ash and I were only friends. No PDA. Extra effort on keeping grades in the A-plus range. He'd finally hinted that what he felt went beyond friendship. It was huge for us.

"Hey," Ash said with a smile. "Your mom's headed this way."

"Okay." It was time to go. Ash and I had plans for much later tonight, but he had obligations for now that didn't include me. I understood. Sending a vague smile toward his family, I said, "It was nice to see you."

"Eden?" his father said. "Would you introduce your mother to us?"

I exchanged a hopeful glance with Ash. "Yes, sir. I'll go and get her."

"Who is that young lady walking beside your mother?" Mrs. Gupta asked, her face studiously calm.

I spun around. "Mundy?"

She waved with one hand, her other hand clutched in Sawyer's.

Ash touched my back. When I looked at him, he was smiling widely.

"Did you know she was coming?"

He nodded. "It's been hard to keep the surprise."

I gave his arm a light squeeze and took off to see my best friend.

This day had just gone from great to amazing.

. . .

It was a gorgeous autumn day on the campus of Stanford University. I sat next to Ash on the grass, feeling a bit overwhelmed, particularly from the people-watching. "There seems to be an unusually high percentage of hot girls in California."

"Uh-huh."

I glanced sideways. He was bent over his iPad. "Come on, Ash. Don't you find it distracting?"

"No."

"Not even their long blond hair or their dark tans or their big breasts?"

He grunted without looking up. "I'm being distracted all right, although I can hardly blame it on the girls from California."

I snatched the tablet away and tossed it into his backpack.

He raised his head. "What?"

"I didn't fly all the way across the country to be ignored." I smiled with satisfaction at the succinctness of my argument.

"The assignment is due Monday."

"I leave Sunday morning."

"Good point." He shifted toward me. "What did you have in mind?"

Excellent. I had his undivided attention, which had been my goal. "Lots of physical contact."

His eyes lit up happily. "Works for me."

"But conversation first."

"If we must." He got to his feet, slung his backpack over a shoulder, hauled me up, and started out across the lawn, our hands firmly clasped. "How is Mundy?"

"She had her friend Manny with her." Manny and Mundy had picked me up from the San Jose airport and brought me to Stanford. In the usual circumstances surrounding my friend, she did most of the talking while Manny worshiped in silence.

"Are they dating?"

"No, he might be interested, but she's not ready."

"Sawyer?"

"Yeah." Mundy and Sawyer had hung in there long-distance for a while, but they'd finally broken it off this summer.

Sawyer was at Carolina too, on a baseball scholarship. I tutored him every now and then. He wasn't over Mundy yet. Maybe soon.

Ash and I walked in silence, wandering in and out of the fading sunshine. He moved his arm to my shoulders while I hung on to one of his belt loops. He matched his strides to mine, our hips bumping with each step. This was more PDA than we would've ever attempted back home and less than what I was seeing around us.

"Ash?"

"Yeah?"

"Is what we have enough?"

He changed directions without warning and headed for a low wall. In one smooth movement, he dropped the backpack, grasped me by the waist, and lifted me onto the top of the wall.

"Eden." He threaded the fingers of both hands through my loose hair, cradling my head. "No matter how I answer your question, I lose. *Yes*, Skype makes a long-distance relationship tolerable enough that I can barely stand our separation. And *no*, there will never be enough e-mail or texts or phone calls to fill my need for you."

"Actually, you're scoring major points." I pressed my mouth to his and discovered that kissing from a superior height was fun. And completely delicious. "Ash?"

He sighed. "More talking?"

"I said physical contact *and* conversation."

"Can we negotiate the percentages?"

"When you're visiting me, you may take the lead."

"Uh-huh." He leaned back. "Talk then. I'm listening."

"Peyton Scholars spend a semester at a sister college during their sophomore years. Cal State Monterey Bay has an autism program that's worth checking out." I watched him closely to gauge his reaction. "Would it bother you if I was nearby?"

"Is this a trick question?" He grinned in what I had to admit looked like genuine delight. "I would love it if you came to school out here. Why would I mind?"

All right. I was shameless. "You could be interested in sampling what California has to offer and not know how to tell me."

"You could too."

"Please, Ash. Your options are endless. Mine are not."

"I would love it if you came to school out here."

I wasn't ready to be convinced. "My friends at Carolina think it's crazy to keep a high school relationship going during college."

"I've heard something similar."

"We have an existing relationship. Maybe you want some space." I understood such things about people getting on with their lives. It would be better for him to figure it out now than a year or two down the road.

He wrapped his arms more snugly about me and studied my face, but he didn't say a word. Just watched me. His expression was seriously sexy and patient.

We stayed in the embrace for a long moment. His confidence seeped into me, and I began to relax. "You would love it if I came to school out here," I repeated.

He nodded as if he were proud of me. "I'm not like your bio

mom, Eden. I left a forwarding address. I want you to know where I am."

It was the perfect thing to say. The worries fled, replaced with the need to be alone with him. "Has your roommate left for the weekend?"

"He should have."

"I think the time has come for privacy."

"Will it involve lots of physical contact?"

I kissed him. "Damn straight."

He laughed with anticipation. "Works for me."

About the Author

✦

Julia Day lives in North Carolina (midway between the beaches and the mountains) along with two twentysomething daughters, one husband, and too many computers. When she's not writing software or stories, Julia loves to travel to faraway places, watch dance reality shows on TV, and dream about which restaurant gets her business next. *The Possibility of Somewhere* is Julia's first YA contemporary romance.